ALWAYS
the BRIDESMAID

Always
the Bridesmaid

Whitney Lyles

BERKLEY BOOKS, NEW YORK

A Berkley Book
Published by The Berkley Publishing Group
A division of Penguin Group (USA) Inc.
375 Hudson Street
New York, New York 10014

This book is an original publication of The Berkley Publishing Group.

Copyright © 2004 by Whitney Lyles.
Cover illustration by Masaki Ryo/CWC International.
Cover design by Pamela Jaber.
Text design by Julie Rogers.

PRINTING HISTORY
Berkley trade paperback edition / February 2004

Library of Congress Cataloging-in-Publication Data

Lyles, Whitney.
    Always the bridesmaid / Whitney Lyles.— Berkley trade paperback ed.
      p. cm.
    ISBN 0-425-19513-9 (pbk.)
    1. Single women—Fiction. 2. Bridesmaids—Fiction. 3. Weddings—Fiction. I. Title.

PS3612.Y45A79 2004
813'.6—dc22

2003060875

PRINTED IN THE UNITED STATES OF AMERICA

10 9 8 7 6 5 4 3 2

For my parents, Martha and Dick Lyles

Acknowledgments

Words will never be able to express the amount of gratitude I have toward my parents for all of their endless support and encouragement. Dad, thanks so much for believing in me from day one, for your never-ending enthusiasm, and also for being a persistent and sometimes rather annoying writer's conscience! Mom, thanks for your ongoing faith, hope, and optimism. I am so fortunate to have such great parents. Thanks also to my sister, Jen, for cheering me on from the beginning and for providing good feedback during the early drafts of this novel.

Countless thanks to the best writing teacher I know, Mike Sirota, for all of his invaluable guidance, editorial expertise, and for never sugar coating *anything*!

I am forever grateful to Sandy Dijkstra and everyone at the Sandra Dijkstra Literary Agency, especially the champion of champions Julie Burton for picking up the project, fine-tuning the book, and sealing the deal.

I am also grateful for the opportunity to work with Leona Nevler, one of the best editors in the business.

I would also like to thank Robbie Dodds for his genuine enthusiasm, for commiserating with me as artists sometimes do, and especially for giving me inspiration.

Many thanks to the following friends and family members who have provided encouragement, or who have put up with my penniless, flaky ways for the past few years: Liz and Mary Lou Carr, Amirah Clow, Betsy Peters, my wonderful grandparents (Dorothy and Dick Lyles and Dorothy Williams), Kelly Towne, Cynthia Vega, Sharon Burnes, Susan Fowler, Drea Zigarmi, Sangeeta Mehta, Bill Endemann, Carol Dodds, Vanessa Perego, Agatha Miller, Tara Geier, Liz Banks, Steve Delorenzo, Trevor Ellingson, The Levy family (Lauren, Margot, Drake, Julian, and especially Jenn and Don, who are without a doubt the coolest bosses I've ever had), all the girls in my book club (Danielle Royster, Erica Rood, Ariella Kantor, and Courtney Brickner), the boys of Convoy; my three critics from the Jackson Hole Writer's Conference (Carolyn Lampman, Deborah Bedford, and Tim Sandlin), Fr. James Williams, Linda Dollins (who taught me a trick or two about writing early on in life), Sheldon Bowles, Chip and Liz Lyles, Barrie and Dorothy Cropper, and finally Lindsay Cropper, a dear friend and great writer who is deeply missed.

ALWAYS
the BRIDESMAID

Sarah's Wedding ·

1 • The Bride's Bouncer

It was during the first round of photos galore when Cate Padgett decided that her fake smile hurt as badly as the tight underwear she'd been wearing all day. Hours of photographs in front of Founders Chapel made her face feel frozen and tight, her jaws permanently clenched, her cheekbones forever lifted.

Furthermore, an unyielding wedge had been tormenting her for what seemed like days. She stole a look over her shoulder just to make sure her gown wasn't sandwiched between her cheeks. It was only her granny-style underwear that was causing such discomfort. She would've sacrificed two cocktails at the reception for a moment of privacy to alleviate the problem.

Just when she thought she had a shot at freedom, the photographer called her name again. "Catie, we need you again, dear." She'd been hollering it all afternoon.

At moments she'd been tempted to grumble, "It's Cate, Vicky," but decided that might ruin the atmosphere.

Nerves were already on edge. It was ninety degrees in San Diego. Besides being hot and stuffed in very uncomfortable clothing, the whole bridal party was hungry and anxious.

This was her third time as a bridesmaid. Being a veteran, she expected discomfort and stress throughout the wedding preparations and knew how important it was not to be an accessory to conflict.

"Catie," she called again. "We need one with you—"

"She goes by Cate," Sarah said.

"Oh! Ha! My bad," Vicky said in between squeals.

Cate squeezed Sarah's shoulder as she moved close to her for the hundredth time. She was careful not to incite catastrophe by snagging her veil or accidentally smearing makeup on her white gown.

"Okay, Cate. Good. I need you to leave your arm around Sarah. . . . Oh yeah. Perfect! Beautiful just like that. Tilt your chin a tad to the left. A little more. Now scoot your front forward. Lift your forehead and think of parties."

There was something very unnatural about all this.

"Yeah, perfect!" Vicky called. "Right like that! Smile! Beautiful." The camera snapped. "Now, don't go too far," Vicky called as Cate stalked across the sidewalk. "We'll be needing you again for the group shots. Oh! And bridesmaids: *Don't lose your bouquets!*"

She had just managed to squeeze into a small, private section of shade when her name was called again. She looked at Vicky and her assistant, but it wasn't either of them. They were shooting Sarah with the flower girl.

"Cate." There it was again, faint and male. "Psst. Cate. Over here."

She spun to the left.

"No. Behind you," the voice said.

She turned around and faced a bougainvillea bush. B. J. Nichols, a groomsman she recalled drinking heavily with in college, weaseled in between the red-flowered branches.

"What are you doing?" she asked. She could feel her satin gown sticking to her damp back—and that wedge. If she ever wanted to torture someone, she knew how.

"Cate, we have a problem."

"What?"

"Claude is here."

"What!"

"I'm not kidding. He's here, and I think he's drunk. He's sitting in the church, right now, as we speak."

"You *have* to tell him to leave."

"He won't leave," B. J. said between gritted teeth.

"Can't you get another groomsman to help you?"

"We've all tried. He won't listen to anyone. Besides, we're supposed to be seating people right now." He adjusted his bow tie. "He's turned hostile, Cate. And you know him better than any of us. You've gotta help."

"Does Miles know?"

"No! Are you kidding? He'll kick his ass!"

"You can't just throw him out?"

"He's telling the organist to play 'Friends in Low Places,' Cate. He *won't* leave."

"Catie! Yoohoo! It's group picture time."

Cate pretended not to hear her.

"Give me two minutes," she whispered to B. J. Straightening her dress, she headed back to the fountain.

Why did wedding predicaments always gravitate toward her? Two years ago, crisis struck at her sister's wedding when a fellow bridesmaid had spilled a glass of red wine down the front of her peach gown. Cate had remembered that white wine neutralized red wine, so she immediately sent an usher for Pinot Grigio. She poured the wine on her dress, blotted it, and hung the gown under the hand dryer in the ladies' room for a solid ten minutes. Then they made sure that the girl held her bouquet in precisely the right place to cover the faint traces of red wine.

However, she never imagined she'd have to remove the bride's ex-boyfriend from the chapel only minutes before they were supposed to walk down the aisle.

As she stood in front of the camera, she became uncomfortably aware of the look of alarm that had replaced her fake smile. She tried to think of parties instead of that dipshit Claude Mitchum singing Garth Brooks in front of all of Sarah's friends and family. How was she going to get him out of Founders Chapel? She debated telling Sarah's dad, Mr. Cross. But he was having a moment, teary-eyed, choked up, and totally emotional about giving his youngest daughter away.

"Good Lord," she muttered between her teeth as the last picture was snapped.

Founders Chapel was full of familiar faces when she entered. Old friends from college and relatives of Miles's and Sarah's filled the wooden pews, thumbing through their wedding programs.

The Spanish Renaissance church was a landmark at the University of San Diego. It had been one of her favorite places to seek solitude when she'd attended USD. But she didn't have time to admire its serene beauty now.

B. J. was escorting an elderly couple down the aisle and shot her a nervous look. She scanned the chapel but didn't see Claude anywhere. Maybe he had left. That's when she noticed B. J. aggressively nodding his head in the direction of the organ.

There he was. Sitting in the *Reserved for the Family* row, just inches away from the organist. He was arguing with her.

She took a deep breath and headed toward the front row, trying to blend in with the other guests. The pew felt hard as she slid in next to him.

"Cate! Wow. This is really going to be a college reunion. You look . . . great!"

The alcohol on his breath would've burned her nose hairs if she had been any closer. He was dressed for the occasion in a suit. A pant leg was ripped at the knee, and he had buttoned his shirt in the wrong order.

"Claude. What are you doing?" she whispered.

"Praying," he said nonchalantly as he glanced at the gold altar.

"Claude, you know you weren't invited. You can't stay here."

His jaw grew tight. "Excuse me. But this church is a public place."

"Claude." She gave him a look her mother would've used when discussing credit card debt. "You're not here to pray."

"I want to talk to Sarah. I have to tell her something."

"What do you need to tell her?"

"It's private."

"Do you really think anything you say now is going to change her mind?" she said, aware that her voice had risen.

"I know it will."

"How? What do you think is so important that it will stop Sarah from marrying Miles?"

"I have to tell her that I'm different now. I've changed and I never— not for one day—stopped loving her." A ripple of agony tore over his face. His mouth became contorted, as if he were going to scream or cry. She couldn't tell which and prayed it wasn't either one. "Oh God, Cate. I love her more than anything. If she needed a kidney, I would give it to her. I never meant to hurt her."

Cate wanted to remind him that he wasn't offering his internal organs when he slept with Dina Samley behind Sarah's back. "She's about to walk down the aisle and marry someone else. She doesn't care about what happened anymore. I *know* she's forgiven you. You have to move on, too."

"I can't let her do this," he said. "I love her. She's the best thing that ever happened to me, and I blew it. I was young and stupid."

She *almost* felt sorry for him. Nothing looked worse than regret on anyone's face. Four years ago, at twenty-two, he'd been one of the most desirable bachelors she knew. However, the bulge that hung over his belt had since altered his sex appeal. Dried blood covered his knee where his pants were ripped, and she noticed that the back of his hand was bleeding as well. He needed a Band-Aid.

"Claude, please don't do this to her. You're only hurting her more by doing this."

"You know, Cate? I like you and all, but I really think you should mind your own business."

The nerve of the little prick. "You are making a huge mistake and a fool out of yourself. You've had too much to drink. You will regret this tomorrow."

He shrugged. "I don't care. It's something I have to do, and *nothing* is going to stop me."

She glanced at the clock, her mind grasping for a strategy. Ten more minutes until the wedding. What could she do? Call the police and have him removed from the wedding? It would cause an unforgettable scene and ruin Sarah's wedding day.

At the moment, she just needed to get him out of the church. If she could relocate him to another area of the campus and stall him, she'd figure out what to do from there.

"All right, Claude. I think I can arrange for you to talk to her. She *might* be interested in what you have to say." She was lying in church.

"Really?"

"Yes. But it has to be in private. Not here." God, what was she doing? She felt like the middleman in a Mafia drug ring. "Listen. We have to hurry before the wedding starts. It might be hard to get Sarah to talk to you if we wait too long. Do you know where the men's room is on the east side of Camino Hall?"

He nodded.

"Go over there and wait inside. I'll send Sarah."

He left the pew before she did.

She waited a few minutes, so it would seem like she was *actually* going to get Sarah. It would take a few minutes to walk to Camino Hall anyway. She had deliberately sent him to a bathroom in a different building, so he wouldn't attract attention to himself or run into a guest he knew from the wedding.

She turned to the organist. "Excuse me. Do you have a Band-Aid by any chance? It's an emergency." The only way she could think to stall Claude was to get him to clean his wounds.

The organist looked irked and told Cate she would look in her purse when she was finished playing the current song.

She looked up at the high ceiling and the stained glass miracles of the Bible and tried to devise a plan. Maybe now that Claude was in the bathroom, she could have B. J. physically remove him from the premises. Since they wouldn't be in the church, it probably wouldn't create a scene. But what if he came back in the middle of the ceremony? It would be a wedding to remember.

Finally, the organist produced a Band-Aid that looked as if she had been toting it around in her purse for twenty years. Cate thanked her before she scooted out of the pew.

She could hear her crisp satin dress swishing as she headed toward the men's room in Camino Hall. What in the hell was she going to do? Tie him up?

She knocked on the bathroom door. "Claude, are you in there?"

No response. She pounded. "Claude?"

Abruptly, the door flew open. His fly was down.

"Where's Sarah?" He yanked her by the arm into the men's room.

"Sarah's coming. It's just going to take her a little while." She caught a glimpse of herself in the mirror and nearly jumped back from the reflection that stared back at her. She wasn't used to the bridesmaid look yet. Sarah had wanted all the bridesmaids to look their best for the wedding. But Cate just thought they all looked like strangers. She had always considered her blonde bob too short to wear up, but it had been sprayed and pinned into a tight French twist. She couldn't get used to seeing her blue eyes clouded with kohl eyeliner and shadow, or her narrow cheeks dusted with cherry rouge.

She noticed that her celery-green strapless dress had begun to creep down her chest again. She hadn't been blessed with the bust needed to hold up anything strapless and had been readjusting it all day. She set her bouquet on the sink before firmly pulling the dress up to cover the top of her chest.

"Why don't you clean your knee and put this on?" She offered him the Band-Aid.

"Thanks," he grumbled. "But where's Sarah?"

Footsteps approached the men's room. Her heart pounded so heavily that her nerves shook. She thought she was experiencing stage one of a heart attack.

Claude seemed disappointed when the footsteps passed. "I thought that would be her."

"I'm going to get her right now." She could always just leave him waiting for Sarah and hope that the ceremony was speedy. Then she remembered it was a long Catholic wedding. He'd be wrecking the whole event before Sarah and Miles even said their vows. She had to come up with a better plan.

Claude had broken Sarah's heart and sent her into the kind of depression that entailed drastic weight loss and excessive sleep. It had taken her months to get over him. After she had met her future husband, Miles, Cate had never seen her happier. Now Claude was about to destroy her happiness again. This was the most important day of Sarah's life, and Cate couldn't let him ruin it.

"You wait here," she said.

Outside the bathroom, her eyes caught on something shiny. It rested like a little treasure on the tiled floor. She leaned over the object. Perhaps someone had lost an earring or a key. It was a quarter. An idea popped into her head. It was evil, and she was disturbed that her mind was capable of producing such a scheme, but she was desperate.

Skillfully, she positioned the coin between the door and the door-frame. She inserted the quarter into the little gap like a coin going into a gumball machine, only this quarter stayed tightly wedged in the slot. The door was deadlocked.

It was a trick she had learned in high school when a little boy she baby-sat locked her in the bathroom for five hours. His parents had spent two hours trying to pry the quarters out of the door before they gave up and helped her escape through the window.

There was one window in the men's bathroom, and Claude would never fit through it. He was trapped. It was early summer, so the campus halls were like a ghost town. No one would hear him banging or yelling. He was virtually stranded. Guilt consumed her as she left him. She'd have to figure out a way to get him out after the wedding. That was going to be a whole other obstacle. She'd have to secretly slip him out of the bathroom before the wedding party left for the reception at the Mission Bay Hilton. It was all too much for her to think about now. She still had a toast to prepare for, and she'd been missing for God only knew how long.

She ran the rest of the way back to the bridal room. Both of her small boobs nearly popped from her dress by the time she arrived.

"Cate!" Sarah exclaimed. "Where have you been?"

Sarah's parents, the wedding coordinator, and four other bridesmaids waited for an explanation.

"The bathroom," she said, pulling her dress up.

"Well, are you . . . all right?" Sarah asked.

"Just some last-minute anxiety."

"I have some antacid in my first aid kit," the coordinator said, already rummaging through her supplies.

"It's okay. I'm fine."

"All right," the coordinator said before she began giving last-minute instructions. "Since you're the maid of honor, you're going to walk down right before Sarah, so get in line behind the other girls."

Cate stood behind one of her closest friends, Leslie, who was also getting married this summer.

The romantic notes of "Canon in D" filled the chapel.

"Bridesmaids, grab your bouquets," the coordinator said.

Bouquets? Bouquets! The men's bathroom! Shit! A striking memory of leaving her bouquet on the sink when she'd adjusted her dress struck her like a bowling ball. The other girls were moving. Frantically, she searched for something. Anything! Any bunch of flowers resembling the bouquet would do. Fake flowers, live flowers, grass. It didn't matter.

She ripped a handful of red bougainvillea from a bush just outside the chapel, a thorn scratching the side of her index finger. The sharp pain made her wince, and for a moment she considered this to be a bridesmaid battle wound.

The last thing she saw before heading toward the altar was the wedding coordinator's confused face when she looked at her bouquet.

Completely Candid

Immediately following the ceremony, Cate was thrust into another relentless series of photos, this time with the groom and groomsmen.

After plastering a dozen more fake smiles to her face, she hurried off to the bathroom, where she helped Sarah go pee. Stuffing Sarah and her giant hoop skirt into a stall was only half the battle. Two bridesmaids had to hold up her mountain of tulle to prevent any urine from spraying on the gown.

Crunched in a stall, Cate and Leslie each held up a side of the dress while Sarah took care of business. The three girls had been roommates in college. As Sarah hovered over the bowl, Cate couldn't recall ever feeling closer to them.

"Thanks," Sarah said. "I'll try to hold it for as long as I can next time."

"No worries." Cate prayed Sarah wasn't urinating all over her section of the dress.

"Get used to this, girls," Leslie said. "Because you'll both be holding up my dress in just a few short months."

It occurred to Cate that she was the only one in the stall who wouldn't be having her dress held up anytime soon. In many ways this was a relief. She didn't want anyone helping her use the bathroom, and she made a mental note that if her day as a bride ever did come, she would wear a formfitting dress. However, she felt a pang of sadness that two of her closest friends were moving into another realm of life. She was happy for them, but she knew the late nights of barhopping were over. No more crashing on each other's couches and recapping the events of their crazy evenings over breakfast burritos in the morning. Over the past year their fun times together had been numbered anyway. Leslie and Sarah had devoted most of their time to their fiancés. But now their girls' nights had really ended—for good.

While Cate cooked dinner for one or planned an evening at a new bar, Leslie and Sarah would be planning their pregnancies and trying to figure out which side of the family they were going to spend the holidays with. They wouldn't be able to relate to Cate anymore, and it made her feel a little lonely. Their futures were laid out for them, planned and stable.

"We're on a tight schedule," Sarah reminded them. "We still have to do my back." Cate noticed that a stray ringlet from Sarah's curly hair had fallen loose from her French twist. They'd have to fix her hair later, too.

They were barely finished readjusting Sarah's dress when they had to race back to the bridal room to touch up her makeup.

In the bridal room, Cate reapplied a thick layer of foundation on Sarah's left shoulder blade, covering all traces of her sunflower tattoo. She wondered why Sarah would permanently mark her body with something that she was too ashamed to show Miles's parents and the elderly. Outside the door, Leslie stood guard for future in-laws and grandparents.

"Did you think of what you're going to say in your toast?" Sarah asked as Cate brushed powder over her back.

"I'll figure it out in the limo," she said. A blanket of nervy pain spread over her stomach.

Cate desperately needed a gin and tonic—or five. That freaking toast.

Cate had been inside the reception hall at the Mission Bay Hilton for less than fifteen minutes when Sarah's Aunt Sue cornered her. She was a rotund woman wearing a long dress with a loud floral print. She threw an arm around Cate's shoulder. She could see Aunt Sue's fuchsia acrylic nails from the corner of her eye. "I can't believe how much you girls have grown up over the years. Sarah getting married. Leslie in August. It really makes me feel like an old fart. *Ha!*" Aunt Sue's laughter always came out in one giant croak. "So, hey. You're twenty-six now, Cate. When are you going to tie the knot?"

She wanted to say, *Since I discovered my psychic ability, I've been able to predict things such as these.* She shrugged and released a nervous laugh. "I don't know."

"Well, a little mouse told me you have a cute boyfriend. Don't you?" Red lipstick covered her front teeth.

"Yes. He's on a business trip in Nashville right now. He couldn't make it." She missed him deeply, but didn't add that.

"What does he do?"

She always wanted to tell people he was something exciting like a spy or a rock star. He was young, stunningly handsome, traveled all the time, and drove a hot luxury car.

"His company sells software for resorts and theme parks. He sells the software, then teaches the employees how to use it. Some of his trips end up being pretty long."

"Well, what's the problem? It sounds like he can definitely afford a ring for ya!"

"We're not quite there yet," she said, praying this conversation would soon come to a close. "But he's definitely a keeper."

Paul had all the qualities that Cate wanted in a husband. He was focused, sophisticated, and ambitious. He loved children and had even visited her kindergarten class when school was in session. He voted and had insightful opinions about current events. These were all qualities that she rarely found in men her age. Most of the guys she met were too busy surfing and getting drunk to register to vote or read stories to kindergartners.

Deep down she wondered if they would have their day at the altar. But they had never discussed marriage. In fact, neither of them had even come close to mentioning it. This was partly because their relationship had progressed at such a slow rate. His demanding job and constant traveling had put more than miles between them. It had presented a roadblock that had prevented them from bonding the way Sarah and Miles had. It wasn't as if Cate was in a hurry to get married, but with all of her friends settling down, she couldn't help but consider where her relationship with Paul was headed.

Aunt Sue's elbow jabbed her ribs. "Anyway, honey, it's very important to find the right man," she said. "*Belieeeeeeve me*. You don't want to go through a divorce. Mine was a nightmare," she advised before heading off to the bar.

There were two things that Cate could always count on at any wedding reception: a wedding drunk and a freaky relative. Occasionally, these two were combined. Usually they were two entirely different entities.

The wedding drunk was usually a middle-aged woman, going through some kind of midlife crisis, typically a sticky divorce. They usually surfaced after the meal, making a scene to remember on the dance floor. Videographers lived for these types. Cate suspected it might be Aunt Sue.

As for the bizarre relative, that was easy. Uncle Dan, Sarah's uncle who had been Catholic up until ten years ago when he moved into the Pacific Beach Hare Krishna temple. He was wearing his full regalia, ponytail and all.

"So, any marriage plans?" he asked while sipping on water.

"Not yet," Cate said. She wished Paul was standing next to her.

"Good. That's good. One should devote him or herself spiritually." He tapped her arm. "Since you live in Pacific Beach, you should stop by the temple sometime. I have some books and literature that might interest you. You should just see if you like them." Uncle Dan's attempts to recruit her into his cult were slightly insulting. Cultists had a profile for people they tried to lure. Self-conscious loners looking for some kind of acceptance. Her feelings were a little stung.

Thankfully, they were interrupted. "Cate? Cate Padgett? Wow!"

"Ethan! Ethan Blakely! Oh my God! What are you doing here?"

"I'm catering this wedding." A wide smile covered his face, and his round eyes were still the bluest she had ever seen. He opened his arms wide, and she slipped into his embrace, catching a whiff of something clean and fresh.

"It's so good to see you, Cate," he said after they pulled out of the embrace. "How long has it been?"

"Well, since gosh . . . my freshman year of college? Six? Seven years maybe."

"You look great," he said.

"You do, too." She looked at his baggy white chef's clothes. He had always been on the shorter side but had grown a few inches since she had last seen him. He looked older, too, but maybe that was because of the five o'clock shadow that darkened his chin and upper lip. She didn't remember him ever having facial hair or sideburns. However, he still had the kind of hair that made Cate want to rub her fingers through it. His uneven crop was thick and soft and stood on end like a dark, cozy shag carpet.

"What have you been up to?" he asked.

"I teach kindergarten, and I live in Pacific Beach. What about you?"

"I live in Pacific Beach, too. I run a catering business with a friend of mine."

"I had no idea that you moved back from San Francisco."

"Yeah, a couple years ago. I was thinking about calling you, actually, but wasn't sure how to get in touch with you. My mom mentioned that your parents moved."

"Yeah. They're still in La Jolla, but they don't live across the street from your parents anymore."

"Listen, I've gotta get back to the kitchen, but I'll catch up with you later. For sure."

Running into Ethan was unexpected. As children they had been like brother and sister, sharing their Big Wheels and pulling each other's hair when one wouldn't share a pack of bubble gum or access to Super Mario Brothers. Then in high school, before they had their driver's licenses, they spent lazy summer days prank-calling every pizza place in La Jolla, ordering pizzas with everything on them that they never intended to pick up.

They used to go joyriding in his mother's Oldsmobile and put rocks in Mr. Kramer's mailbox. Ethan was the first person she ever got stoned with. He had been almost as close to her as her best friend, Beth. After high school, Ethan had moved to San Francisco, and Cate had moved into the dorms at USD. They kept in touch for nearly a year, sending each other letters and sharing late-night long distance phone calls.

He had been the closest thing she had ever had to a brother. They would spend hours talking about what kind of major Cate should pick and the fact that Ethan's parents were disappointed that he had chosen culinary school over college. She would send him pictures of her new friends and her minute dorm room. But as soon as Cate met her first real college boyfriend, Ethan's letters and phone calls became less frequent. Their lapse in communication had been mostly Cate's fault though. When she became serious with her boyfriend, her record of returning Ethan's calls wasn't exactly stellar. Eventually they had lost touch. Over the years Cate had wondered about him. She never drove past the Pizza Cove without thinking about their prank calls. Whenever she heard Guns n' Roses or The Cure, she was reminded of Ethan and how they used to play those CDs to death.

She noticed everyone taking their seats and unfolding their linen napkins. It was time to eat.

At dinner Cate barely touched her portobello-stuffed chicken. Thoughts of her toast had stolen her appetite. She envied the rest of the bridal party, sipping their drinks, laughing, and relaxing, while she was on the verge of a nervous breakdown.

Toasts were the things that people talked about on the car ride home. They would comment on Sarah's dress and discuss the wedding drunk and Uncle Dan at great length, and then it would be the toast. They would say, "And can you believe the maid of honor's toast?"

The Tijuana border was just a cab ride away. There was still time to flee. She imagined what everyone would say later, the scandal she would create if she vanished.

All plans to escape were aborted when Sarah's dad approached the microphone. The toast process reminded her of the first day of school when teachers made everyone go around the room and say their name, what they did over the summer, and what their favorite hobby was. Sarah's dad and the best man had to go before it was her turn.

Mr. Cross's toast had been quick. "I'm very proud of Sarah and Miles. I have three beautiful daughters, and now . . ." Tears sprang to his eyes. "I have a great son, too." Then he'd gotten too choked up to continue.

Mark was next. When he took the mike from Mr. Cross's hand, some of his cocktail spilled over the side of the glass and onto Mr. Cross's tux.

"Hellooo, Wedding Party!" Mark was an aspiring musician, and the way he greeted the wedding reception sounded as if he were greeting a sold-out stadium. He may as well have yelled, *Hello, San Diego!* "I decided to do my toast a little bit differently than the typical toast. I did what I'm best at, and I wrote Sarah and Miles a song." Oohs and ahhhs filled the room as the audience eagerly awaited the entertainment. Cate wondered how she would ever live up to this.

"It's called 'Whipped,' and it goes a little something like this."

" 'Whipped'?" Leslie whispered gruffly in Cate's ear.

B. J. handed Mark his guitar. Soft, lilting melodies flowed from the acoustic instrument. *"It starts with one kiss and it leads to pure bliss. The next thing you know you're in love and it shows."* He continued strumming away, holding the audience captive. The strumming grew faster. Mark's voice turned rough. *"It leads to more. It's ownership and the next thing you knooooow. The next thing you know is that you are whipped!"*

Leslie and Cate glanced at one another.

"You're whiiiiiiiiipped!" He did a little jump in the air, missing the cake by inches. Cate could actually hear Sarah's mom gasp. When he landed, the melody grew soft again. *"And it's love,"* he bellowed calmly before concluding the song.

A moment of dead silence followed. Slowly, people began to clap. Mark took a bow before leaving the spotlight.

Leslie squeezed Cate's arm. "Anything you say at this point will be better than 'Whipped.' What the hell was he thinking?"

The coordinator was holding the mike and beckoning for Cate.

She pulled the top of her dress up again and prayed that she wasn't exposing herself to everyone at the wedding as she walked to the microphone.

The spotlight was rudely bright on her face. She could feel the heat from its beams on her skin. She looked out at the faces watching her, waiting. She cleared her throat. "Well. I have to admit I'm very nervous. And I don't have a guitar." Light laughter filled the banquet hall.

"I've been trying to think about what to say for weeks now. I could tell a story about the newlyweds, I guess. After all, I lived with Sarah for three years. So I really know what went on behind the scenes." She looked at Sarah and Miles. They were smiling at her. "Um . . . I'd rather talk about who they are, instead of what they have done. So I am not going to tell any stories." Her eyes wandered over the sea of faces, most of them strangers. "Sarah is one of the best people I know. And I am proud to call her my friend. She is an extraordinary, genuine, solid, and car-ur-ring—"

Her voice had cracked. For a moment she felt flustered, rattled by the nervous squeak. What was she saying? She couldn't remember. Oh yeah. She cleared her throat and continued. "She is a caring woman of character. Miles is also one of the greatest people I've ever met. He is an extraordinary, solid, and caring man of character." She paused. "Together they have created an extraordinary, solid, and caring relationship. They are a wonderful pair. One we can all admire and aspire to emulate." She raised her glass. "So let's raise our glasses to two extraordinary people and the life they will create with one another."

"Hear! Hear!" someone yelled as champagne glasses began to clink together.

Sarah and Miles stood and hugged Cate.

Leslie was waiting for her with a gin martini. "You earned this," she said.

Cate welcomed the cocktail.

The conclusion of the toast had been a release. Her shoulders relaxed, and her smile finally felt natural. Now she could get her camera and take candid pictures of her friends dancing.

Photography was one her favorite hobbies, and capturing people in their most natural and unassuming moments was her favorite thing to photograph. A wall in her apartment was devoted to black-and-white eight-by-tens of her friends and family merely being themselves.

On her way to the dance floor, the videographer went racing past like a lifeguard rushing to save a drowning child. He offered no apologies for gruffly bumping her shoulder or hitting her hip with his equipment.

Ignoring the smart of pain in her hipbone, she followed the videographer into the crowd that had formed on the dance floor. She inched her way through the path he had created. A space had cleared in the center of the crowd, forming a circle. From the middle of the circle sprang Aunt Sue, thrusting her pelvis in ways a woman her age shouldn't do. Hooting and smiling, she kicked up her feet, missing Cate's shins by an inch. Suggestively, she licked her lips and sashayed around the circle. Her eyes were glazed over and transfixed on nothing in particular. *God, she's going to be hurting tomorrow.*

Cate remembered when Aunt Sue used to bake them Rice Krispies wreaths at Christmastime and give out her salsa Mexican casserole recipe. She shot half a roll of film on Aunt Sue.

Applause broke loose when the song ended.

Everyone lined up in rows on the dance floor when "Electric Slide" began. The fact that she loved doing the electric slide was a secret she kept to herself. In fact, she thought she was pretty good, too. She even threw in extra little kicks and stuff when she did the turns. B. J. danced next to her on the right and Leslie did the grapevine on her left. She was thoroughly enjoying herself when B. J. glanced over his shoulder and smiled.

"This is a great wedding!" he yelled over the music.

"I know!" She said as she did the grapevine. She held her camera in her right hand.

He lowered his voice a notch. "Hey, thanks for taking care of, uh— Claude. How'd you get rid of him anyway?" He turned with the rest of the dance floor, snapping his fingers.

Cate froze. Leslie danced into her, her pointed heel crushing Cate's toes. Pain shot up her foot. *Claude! How could she have forgotten him?*

"Cate! Keep moving!" Leslie yelled as she danced with the rest of the group.

She could feel the color draining from her face, the hair on her arms standing on end.

B. J. grabbed her shoulder. "Cate? Are you all right?"

"Oh my God! Oh shit. I have to leave," she muttered before fleeing from the dance floor.

The air was crisp outside. Her car was parked at USD, and she didn't have a dime to spend on cab fare. She looked for the limo that had taken them to the reception. She spotted the vehicle in a far corner of the parking lot, several teenage guests decorating it with whipped cream and toilet paper. Even if she did talk the chauffeur into driving her to USD, there was a remote chance that Sarah and Miles would decide to make their exit. Cate pictured this nightmare all too vividly. "The blonde bridesmaid with no boobs and a big nose took the limo," the teenagers would say. It would be another disaster.

She attempted to run her hands through her hair as she often did when she was stressed but found she couldn't. Her hair was as hard as the bathroom tiles Claude was probably sitting on. It had been hair-sprayed into a rock earlier that morning at the salon.

"Damn!" she muttered. If she asked someone to drive her to USD, she would be ruining his or her time at the reception. She could walk. It would probably take her about an hour, and besides, her left foot was throbbing from where Leslie had stepped on it.

This was all her fault. How could she have forgotten about Claude? She could always make an anonymous phone call to the police, tipping them that someone was locked in a bathroom on the University of San Diego campus. But then what if Claude blamed her, and she was arrested? She wondered what she'd be charged with.

"Aren't you supposed to be inside?" It was Ethan. Smoke billowed from his mouth as he puffed on a cigarette. "They're doing the bouquet toss now. Shouldn't you be in there?"

"No. I mean, yeah, I should . . . but something has come up. I really need to leave."

He held out a pack of Marlboro Reds. "Cigarette?"

She didn't smoke but took one anyway. He lit it for her.

"Are you all right?" he asked.

"I really need to get back to USD." She took a violent drag from the cigarette.

"Well, I'll tell you what. I have to finish packing up, but I can give you a lift. You'll have to ride in the catering van though."

"You have no idea how much you are helping me right now."

"Not a problem. Can you wait a few minutes?"

"Sure."

Instead of waiting outside, she returned to the reception hall for her purse. She debated telling someone where she was going. However, her abrupt departure might raise suspicions. There was no time for questions. Besides, no one would miss her. She'd see them later, when she returned with her car. Or maybe she'd be asking them to post bail for her.

A huge white van resembling a UPS vehicle pulled up in front of the hotel. *Good Time Catering* and a phone number was written in red across the van. She could see his dark hair through the windshield.

"Sorry, we have to ride in this," he said as she climbed into the passenger side of the van.

"That's okay. If you towed me on a skateboard I'd be grateful at this point."

She expected the van to smell like food, but instead it smelled like pine air freshener.

He had changed from his white chef's uniform and was dressed in a pair of jeans and a T-shirt. She still couldn't get over the fact that he had facial hair. All she could envision was his scrawny shoulders beneath an oversized Guns n' Roses T-shirt.

"USD, right?" he asked as they pulled out of the circular driveway in front of the hotel.

"Yeah."

"Good toast," he said.

"You heard it?"

"Yeah. It was good. Seriously, I've heard millions, and yours was pretty good."

"You cater a lot of weddings?"

"Tons."

"What's the worst one you've ever heard?"

He let out a sharp chuckle. "I have heard some pretty bad speeches. Lemme think about it."

Visions of Claude pounding on the bathroom door, fists raw and bloody, throat sore from screaming, plagued her mind.

"I think the worst speech I've ever heard was when the groom's father slipped and called the bride the groom's ex-girlfriend's name. Then to make it worse, he tried to rectify the situation by saying that he got confused because the two women were so much alike. The old man was three sheets to the breeze." He paused. "However, I think the new worst one that I've heard was the song that guy sang tonight. What was up with that?"

She laughed. "Mark. He thinks he's a rock star."

It felt strange sitting next to Ethan Blakely, chatting about toasts as if no time had passed between them. His throaty chuckles still sounded so familiar. She remembered the way he used to laugh when they would look at the candid pictures Cate would take of their science teacher Mrs. Prissard when she wasn't looking. Cate had managed to snap a few of that old goat picking her nose. But her thoughts of Mrs. Prissard and Ethan were interrupted by another vision of Claude, sweating, dying of heat exhaustion. His last words: "Cate. You bitch."

She tried to think of something else. "So, you live in Pacific Beach now?"

"Yeah. I live with a couple of friends. You should come over sometime. We always have barbecues and stuff."

"That sounds good."

"You still hang out with Beth?"

"Yeah, in fact I'm in her wedding in October—Halloween."

"She's getting married on Halloween?"

"Yes. And we all have to dress up."

"That is *so* Beth. What are you going to dress up as?"

She shook her head. "I have no idea."

He looked at the camera on her lap. "You're still into photography?"

"Yeah. I have a lot of free time right now because it's summer break, so I'm not teaching." Another vision of Claude crying, begging for mercy, being taken from the bathroom in a straitjacket and repeating Cate's name over and over again. Her stomach turned sour.

"Well, here we are," he said as they pulled into USD. "Where to?"

"Right here is fine," she said, even though they were three buildings away.

"Well, where is your car? I'll drive you to your car."

"Uh . . . that's okay. I actually have to go inside first." She released an uneasy chuckle.

"It's dark. Are you going to be all right? I mean, I can drop you off wherever you need to go."

It *was* dark and the looming shadows across the campus were scaring her. However, what would he think if he learned that she'd accidentally locked someone in a public rest room for five hours? "Really. I'll be fine," she said. "Thanks so much for the ride."

"Lemme give you my card real quick. We should hang out sometime."

"Yeah, I'd love to." She wanted to tell him that she was responsible for someone else's mental health at the moment and that she'd look him up in the phone book but didn't want to seem ungrateful.

He pulled a business card from his wallet.

"Great," she said as she snatched the card. "I'll give you a call."

She put his card in her handbag as she headed toward Camino Hall.

There were no squad cars in sight. That was a good sign. A layer of coastal fog had already begun to roll in, and dewdrops had settled on the lawn. The campus grounds were eerily empty. Wet grass rubbed her toes as she stalked across the lawn. She knew her gown was dragging, but she was beyond the point of caring. Lights filled the windows in the girls' dorms above Founders Hall. She remembered that there were usually teen summer camps that used the USD dorms at night to lodge their tenants.

Luckily, the whole building was open. She walked past the church, her heels clicking on the tiled floor, and rounded the corner toward the men's bathroom in Camino Hall. Her heart beat with each step, pumping dread through her veins.

The door was closed. She set her purse and camera on the floor before she knocked. "Claude? Are you in there?"

No response.

She knocked again. "Claude!"

Nothing.

She pounded. Then she faintly heard someone shuffling around. "Hello." His voice sounded groggy and weak.

"Claude. It's Cate. Are you all right?"

"What time is it?" He sounded as if he'd been thrust from a dream.

"I don't know. Six maybe." A blatant lie. It was almost ten.

"What happened?"

"Uh. There was a slight misunderstanding. But I'm going to get you out now."

"All right. I don't feel good."

She tried the handle. It turned, but the door wouldn't budge. She pushed hard. Still, no budging. "Hold on, Claude!"

She pulled a bobby pin from her hair. God knew she had enough of them implanted in her coiffure to break into the White House. She pried the pin open, suddenly thankful that Sarah had insisted they all wear up-dos.

She shoved it in the crevice of the doorjamb where the quarter had been inserted. Feeling like a criminal, she picked at the coin, prodding and pulling at it with the hairpin. It was a cruel tease when the quarter shifted but failed to dislodge from the crack. She decided to shove the door again. This time she threw herself into the barricade. The door flung open. She toppled onto all fours in the bathroom, the quarter landing with a light ping next to her hand. The tiles felt freezing on her palms, and her knees throbbed with pain from the spill.

"Thank God," she mumbled as she stood up. The room smelled strongly of bleach, and she felt a headache coming on.

Claude looked confused. "What happened?" he asked. "I just remember that damn door wouldn't budge. I eventually got tired and fell asleep."

"You don't remember crashing the wedding?"

He suddenly seemed wide-awake. "I did what?"

"Claude, you showed up at the church. You wanted to talk to Sarah."

"Oh God." He rubbed his hands over his face. "I didn't. Please tell me I didn't make a scene."

"She doesn't even know you were here."

"I'm such an ass." He leaned against the wall and slid to the floor, burying his face inside his hands.

Cate stepped outside for her camera and purse. When she returned, he was still hunched over.

She didn't want to instigate further conversation because then he might start asking how he ended up locked in the bathroom. For a moment she thought he was breathing heavily. Then she realized that he was crying.

"Oh Claude." She sat down next to him on the floor. His shoulders felt limp and weak when she put her arm around him. "I know today wasn't easy for you."

He nodded. "I never wanted to hurt her."

"She doesn't care anymore. She's happy now. And I think she'd be very flattered to know that you still care."

"It doesn't matter, Cate."

There were two kinds of people she could not fathom crying. Grown men and old people. Tears made men seem so vulnerable, and old people seemed so helpless. Watching Claude's contorted face, his flaring nostrils, and the hot tears that were streaming down his cheeks made her want to cry, too.

"Cate?"

"Yeah."

"What's he like?"

"Who? Miles?"

"Yeah. I mean . . . is he a good guy?"

Cate wanted to think of something bad to say about Miles. She wanted to make Claude feel better, and wished she could tell him that Sarah's husband was a worthless, fat shithead who couldn't control his rage and had bad breath. Truth: Miles was great. He had his priorities in order, and Sarah had always been at the top of his list. He called her three times a day just to hear her voice, and he shared exciting news with her before telling anyone else. He brought her lunch when she couldn't leave her office, and replaced her windshield wipers when they broke. He loved her family. He was funny and sincere, and he had his head screwed on straight. There was one thing though. Sarah had mentioned that he sometimes farted during sex. She decided not to share that detail with Claude.

Instead, she chose her words carefully. "He's . . . good for Sarah."

"It's okay. I shouldn't have asked you that. I don't even want to know."

"I know how hard this must be for you, Claude."

"I let her go." He shook his head. "I was such an idiot, and now I'm going to end up alone. I've never had that kind of chemistry with anyone else. I've never had another girl call me a nickname or leave me a burrito and a nice note on my counter when I had a bad day. I've never felt that way again. I don't want to be alone."

They sat together for a long time on the tiled floor, not saying much. He rested his head on her shoulder. In all the wedding chaos—the photos, the toasts, the hairdos and electric slides—she never really thought of those who were left behind. She'd never considered that while she was eating her wedding cake or watching the wedding drunk that someone's heart had broken. She picked up her camera. She held it at arm's length in front of them, aimed toward their faces. The last picture on her roll: she and Claude leaning against the tiled wall of the bathroom floor.

3 • Leftovers

Cate awoke to a light yet demanding tap on her eyelid. She released a *leave me alone* groan and rolled to the opposite side of the bed. Seconds later, Grease stepped on her rib cage, oblivious to the pain his paws shot up her chest and traveled to the other side as well. He sat there for a moment, watching her.

Again, he pressed on her eyelid. This time she felt the tips of his claws. Patiently, he stood vigil, waiting for her eyes to open. Another tap.

Before he had the chance to touch her again, she surrendered and woke up. His blue eyes were fixed on her face.

"Happy now?" she muttered.

Triumphant, he let out a high-pitched meow and stood up, stretching his back and tail. He jumped from the bed and immediately pranced toward his food dish in the kitchen.

He wasn't officially Cate's cat, and his name wasn't exactly Grease, either. He belonged to the losers that lived on the first floor. For several months Cate had noticed him hanging out in the parking garage, his white coat saturated in heavy grease and oil as thick and dark as tar. After petting him, her hand always smelled like freshly laid asphalt. She'd always worried that a car would hit him, or that he would die of starvation, or be abducted and tortured to death by devil worshipers. Two winters ago she had started leaving him leftovers.

Then he began following her home. Now he pretty much lived there. There'd never been any inquiries or "missing cat" signs featuring his handsome face. No one seemed to notice his absence.

At first Cate understood why he might have been abandoned. He had been borderline terrorist in his younger days, hiding beneath her bed, then attacking her leg when she walked unassumingly past the dust ruffle.

"What happened to your legs, Miss Padgett?" her kindergartners would ask, pointing to the red welts and scratches that covered her calves.

For three months she'd taken to wearing two layers of sweatpants around the house, just to protect herself.

The worst Grease event occurred one night when Paul slept over. They were both sound asleep when, for no reason, Grease jumped on the bed and bit Paul's right nostril, two fangs puncturing each side of the hole. To this day Paul's scream still resonated in her ears.

Eventually, Grease had mellowed out, and now he was a persistently affectionate cat.

As she entered the kitchen, he aggressively rubbed the side of his face against her calf. His food sounded like a hailstorm as she dumped it into his dish.

After she put the food away, she looked for her cordless phone. She had phoned Paul yesterday before the wedding, and he hadn't returned her call yet. This had happened three times on his last trip. Each time he had provided mundane excuses for his behavior. Busy.

Tired. Dead battery on cell phone. But it was weird. In the past he'd always been prompt and considerate when returning calls.

At first Cate hadn't thought much of his flakiness. She had believed his excuses and forgotten about his disappearances. But she was starting to feel anxious when he didn't call. She found herself creating frightening scenarios that often involved Paul in a party hat, dancing sandwiched between two Brazilian Victoria's Secret models that actually had boobs. She knew that he met people on his trips. Part of his job as a salesman was to schmooze with his clients. He took them to lunch, happy hour, dinner. He always returned from his trips full of stories about all the interesting people he had met. She just hoped he wasn't taking busty blondes out for dinner. Fortunately, her worries were interrupted when someone knocked on her door.

Jill. She must've heard the hailstorm, too. When Cate opened the door, her downstairs neighbor stood in the doorway, holding a box of Krispy Kremes. "Breakfast is served!" she announced, her blue hair standing on end. Patches of leftover eye makeup were smeared beneath her eyes. She wore a terrycloth bathrobe and slippers.

"My God." Jill laughed as she touched Cate's hair. "Look at your hair. It's bigger than you."

Cate turned to the mirror next to the front door. "Weddings," she said. "They always hair-spray the hell out your hair for these things." She'd been so drained when she returned from USD the night before that she hadn't bothered to wash the twenty gallons of aerosol hair spray that had cemented her hairdo at the wedding. Now she wore a giant blonde hard hat. Her bouffant was bigger than her head and made her skinny neck look like a toothpick. She stepped aside from the doorway. "C'mon in."

Jill went straight to the kitchen cupboard, pulled out two plates, and placed a donut on each. Cate filled two glasses with milk before heading to the couch.

"Are you having a party?" Jill asked.

"No. Why?"

Jill reached for Ethan's card. It had fallen from Cate's purse when she tossed it on the coffee table the night before. "I just saw this catering card."

"He's a friend of mine from high school. I ran into him last night." Cate picked up the card and returned to the kitchen. She placed the card on the refrigerator under a magnet that was shaped like an apple and read # *1 Teacher!*—a gift from one of her students. "You'll never believe what happened," she said as she returned to the living room.

She spilled the whole story about Claude and Ethan over donuts and milk, still feeling colossal relief that Claude had been okay.

"I think you should call Ethan," Jill said.

"I will. He lives in Pacific Beach now."

"He sounds cool. Did you ever date him?"

"No. Not really."

"Not really? You hooked up with him. Didn't you?"

"We just kissed. Senior year of high school. I've pretty much erased the incident from my memory. It was one of those drunken, fun things to do at the time. Really, it was nothing."

She remembered Beth's graduation party. They had all gotten smashed off a case of Keystone that Ethan's older brother had generously bought for them. Later they went swimming in Beth's parents' pool, wearing their underwear. In the Jacuzzi Ethan had planted sloppy kisses on her mouth and neck while their friends did back flips off the diving board. The pink tip of his erection had poked through the hole of his boxer shorts. His had been the first penis she'd ever seen. To her recollection, it had been rather large next to his skinny legs.

"What happened after you kissed him?" Jill wanted to know.

"Nothing. We went on like nothing had ever happened. Probably because I made it clear that I only wanted to be friends. He's really sweet, but I've just never liked him that way."

"Why not?"

"I don't know. I just . . . he's Ethan." She shook her head. "It would just be too weird."

"Is he cute?"

Cate thought for a moment. "He's not tall, dark, and handsome or drop-dead gorgeous. He's cute the same way a puppy is cute. He's really sweet-looking."

"Hmmmm. I see. So he's not the type of guy you could imagine kicking someone's ass for you?"

"Uh . . . well. I hadn't exactly thought of it that way. But I guess now that you mention it, no. He isn't that type."

"I still think you should definitely call him," Jill said. "I want to meet this guy."

"Well, I probably will. But just to hang out. Besides, I have Paul."

"Oh yeah. Paul. When does he get back?"

"Next week I think."

"You should see what he is doing this weekend."

"Paul?"

"No. Ethan."

"I can't. I have to go to Vegas for my cousin Val's bachelorette party."

"I forgot about that. You're like the professional bridesmaid."

"I know. After this summer I'll know so much about being a bridesmaid you could put me up for rent. Bridesmaid for hire, anyone?" She sighed. "Always the bridesmaid. Never the bride." With the exception of Jill, it seemed as if all her friends were joining the permanent world of couplehood. She was suddenly stricken with a frightening thought. What if Jill suddenly met someone and got married? And what if Paul dumped her? She'd be totally alone. Where was she going to find anyone? She certainly wasn't going to meet a guy teaching kindergarten, and she wouldn't even have a single buddy to go out with. She'd just have Grease. God help her.

"I'm really starting to wonder where things are going with Paul,"

Cate said, hiding her panic. "I mean, I'm not asking for a ring. But don't you think it would nice to at least know who you were going to spend the rest of your life with? To never have to wonder?"

"No." Jill said it as if she had been offered ketchup at a drive-through window. "Waking up to the same face every morning, the same stinky feet—no thanks. It just doesn't appeal to me. What a boring life. You'd both get fat. Sex would go down the shitter, and you'd find yourself trapped and fantasizing about running away with the hot, young carpet cleaner who came by a few times a year. I think I'd just end up cheating on whoever I married."

Well, she didn't have to worry about Jill getting married anytime soon. "Don't you want kids though?"

"Fuck no. I hate kids." Jill truly was another species. "No offense. I know you love kids, but you have to remember all the little stepsiblings I had when I was growing up. My high school career was spent baby-sitting. It was probably the best birth control I've ever had."

She was the only girl Cate knew of who had no desire for a husband or children. Something about Jill's attitude toward settling down seemed powerful. She was free from desire. Free from wondering. Free from worrying about her biological clock. She was independent, happy with being alone. Sometimes Cate wished she could feel as free.

They each ate another donut before Jill declared that she was going to puke if she touched any more food. They wrapped up the remaining donuts and decided to go for a walk by the beach.

Before leaving, Cate put on a baseball cap and lathered her arms, legs, and face with sunscreen. She tanned the same way a Swede would. If she didn't wear sunscreen, she'd fry. For a native Californian, this was a challenge.

Jill wore her usual cropped jeans and bikini top, and if Cate could've borrowed some of her boobs, she would've considered wearing the same thing. It seemed like everything Jill ate went to her chest. She was curvy, voluptuous. Walking down the boardwalk with Jill typically entailed forty-five minutes of listening to catcalls, which Jill always seemed oblivious to.

They walked to the end of Loring Street, then headed down the trail that led to the boardwalk. It was a warm day, but the ocean breeze kept the air comfortable. Seagulls cawed above, occasionally swooping down to steal a fallen potato chip or the crumbs of a deli sandwich. From the boardwalk she could see people cooking their bodies in the sun, children building sand castles, and surfers perched on their boards, the sun glistening over their wet heads as they waited for the next wave.

A child's stubborn scream drowned out the seagulls as she resisted her mother's attempt to lather her face with sunblock.

Sometimes Cate missed the carefree days of being a little girl at the beach. The days when she didn't care about wrinkles and thought that applying sunscreen was actually a method of torture inflicted by her mother. The days when it didn't matter if she looked bad in a bathing suit, and the sand caked inside every crevice of her body didn't seem totally loathsome.

The sound of skateboard wheels racing over the concrete came up close behind her, and she moved closer to the wall so the skater could pass.

"I say we stop at La Haina's for a pitcher," Jill said.

"All right."

Hard rock blasted from the open patio at La Haina's. It was crowded, and they ended up standing against the wooden railing on the deck, sharing a pitcher of Bud Light. They spent the afternoon gazing at the boardwalk, people-watching, and debating which color Jill should color her hair next. She was finishing up beauty school and often experimented with all kinds of different shades and bleaches. She'd been dying to get her hands on Cate, but Cate wouldn't let her.

They were interrupted when two guys visiting from Italy closed in on them. One of them was wearing a Speedo and penny loafers. He may as well have run up and down the beach with a banner across his chest reading, "European!" Poor guy. His swimsuit branded him a tourist. Cate kind of felt sorry for him and managed to participate in a few minutes of conversation, even though she couldn't understand three-fourths of what he said. The other one had a more reasonable fashion sense and sported trunks. Jill, apparently feeling the effects of the pitcher they shared, took their hotel phone number before they headed back home.

"You have two new messages," the Sprint lady said when Cate checked.

The first message was from her mother. "Cate. I'm calling from Palm Springs. Just wanted to know how Sarah's wedding went. Don't forget it's Sunday. You should go to Mass."

Delete.

Next message: "*Hola,* Cate. *Esta* Paul." He had a unique habit of mixing Spanish in with his English. He came from a Scottish and Welsh background with no traces of Latin blood whatsoever. "Just wanted to see how your night went. Sorry I didn't call you back the other day. I've been swamped. I have good news though, so call me on my cell. I recharged it. Adios."

She dialed his cell phone.

After the third ring, his voice mail picked up. She'd heard the greeting so many times lately that she practically knew the message by heart. "Hi. You have reached Paul Strobel with Software Solutions. Please leave me a detailed message, and I will get back to you as soon as possible. Thank you, and have a great day."

"Hey. It's Cate. I just got your message. I have some good stories for you, so call me when you get in. Miss you. Talk to you soon."

She checked her E-mail. No word from Paul, but she had one E-mail from Leslie Lyons.

DATE: July 8
SUBJECT: Fitting at The Bridal Chateau

Hello Bridesmaids!

We're just a month away now. As you all know, I've already ordered the pieces you'll be wearing. I just need you all to go to The Bridal Chateau July 19th promptly at noon. For most of you this will be your lunch brake so it's probably best that we're all on time. Anyway, I just wanted you to mark your calendars now, but I'll give you more details as soon as we're closer. I am so thrilled to have each one of your share this special time with me.

Love,
Leslie

Brake was right. She wanted to put on the brakes. She hadn't even hung up her dress from Sarah's wedding, which was still strewn across her wicker chair in her bedroom, along with all the other things she didn't know what to do with. Grease was curled up on top of the pile of things she hadn't sorted through in over a month.

By the end of the summer, she'd have a gallery of bridesmaid's gowns. Hell, she could even teach classes on how to be a bridesmaid. Bridesmaid 101. She thought of some of her class titles. *Reasoning with Drunk Wedding Crashers. Making the Last-Minute Bouquet.* Or, *Speeches for Idiots: No Singing Allowed.*

She disconnected from the Internet, and her phone rang.

"*Hola!*"

"Hey," Cate said. "We finally get to talk."

"I'm sorry I haven't gotten back to you sooner. I've just been swamped with work."

They talked about his job and Nashville. Then Cate proceeded to tell him about locking Claude in the bathroom. Claude had been one of his friends in college, so he found the story to be quite interesting.

"That's too bad," he said as she concluded the story. "Well, I hope you're not busy Thursday, because I'm coming back early."

"Good." She was pleased to hear that he was returning early. She was leaving for Vegas and wouldn't see him until the following week if he had returned as planned on Friday. "What time does your flight get in?"

"Hold on. Let me check." She could hear papers shuffling around in the background. "Five-forty-one. Delta."

"All right. I'll pick you up then."

"Sounds good. It's right in time for dinner, so think about where you'd like to go."

Mi Casa Es Su Casa

Paul's flight was late. She was tempted to park her '82 Volvo station wagon and go track him down somewhere between his gate and baggage claim. But by the time she found a spot and hiked back over to the airport, he'd probably be waiting for her on the curb. She was forced to drive around in circles, wasting gas and listening to the ticking noise the Volvo made every time she went around a corner.

She'd just found a spot at the curb, right in front of baggage claim, when her cell phone rang.

"*Hola!* I'm grabbing my luggage and I'll be out in two minutes max."

"Okay. I'm parked right outside behind a giant orange bus. You can't miss me."

Nervousness stretched a tight vice over her stomach, and her palms felt sweaty. She was always seized with anxious excitement every time he returned from a trip. It had been two weeks since they had seen each other.

When she looked up, an airport security man was heading for the wagon. She pretended not to notice him, or the gigantic stick he was vigorously brandishing. Instead, she applied her lipstick in the rearview mirror.

"You must circle around, ma'am. No parking at the curb." He waved his stick at her.

She pretended not to hear. His stick sounded loud when he tapped it on the window. "You need to circle around," he said. "No parking at the curb."

She put on her most sincere smile and rolled down the window. "My friend will be out in just one minute. I literally *just* talked to him on my cell phone. He's on his way out *right now.*"

He shook his head, and his neck looked like a thick slab of ham above his buttoned shirt. She suspected he was wearing a bulletproof vest and could understand why he might need one. "You need to move, ma'am."

"But he's on his way out. He'll be here in one minute."

"It takes me one minute to write you a ticket." He began to reach for his ticket pad in his back pocket.

"All right! I'll move!" She looked around as she began to pull away from the curb. Most of the traffic had dissipated and, aside from a giant orange bus, there weren't many other cars.

Anger replaced her anxiety. She fumed as she began to make her twenty millionth circle around terminal two. She'd been driving for no more than five seconds when her cell phone rang again.

"Where are you? I thought you said you were next to the orange bus."

"Sorry, the curb jerk made me move. I'll be right over."

As she approached the terminal again, she saw the stupid jerk threatening others with his stick. When she drove past him, she pretended to scratch the side of her face with her middle finger.

Paul was easy to spot because he stood a head taller than most of the people at the curb. No matter how long Paul's trips were, he never seemed to lose the suntan he got from surfing the Pacific Beach waves. Cate marveled at how he always looked healthy and fresh after long flights, his sandy blond hair neatly combed, jeans unwrinkled. *God, he's cute.* He practically glowed next to the rumpled and exhausted-looking crowd of people on the sidewalk. He exposed his even teeth to her, held up a sinewy arm, and began to wheel his suitcase closer to the street.

She pulled to a halt in front of him. His body felt warm when she hugged him. He kissed her on the cheek, then handed her a small bouquet of sunflowers.

"Oh that's so sweet," she said as she took the flowers. "They're beautiful."

"I just bought them in the airport."

"That was so sweet of you."

"Are you hungry?" he asked as Cate popped the trunk.

"Starving."

"Good. I'm really in the mood for sushi. How do you feel about Zao's?"

She agreed.

While Cate drove them to the restaurant, they talked about Paul's trip. He told her about being humiliated when his luggage was thoroughly disemboweled at the airport security checkpoint.

"They held up my travel candles, and one of the agents started laughing," he said, still pissed.

Cate had forgotten about the travel candles. His sister had given them to him for Christmas. The square candles came in a portable case and were meant to make frequent travelers feel comfortable in unfamiliar hotel rooms. It was a nice gesture, considering how often he traveled, but Cate hadn't expected him to actually pack them on his trips. Every time he mentioned the candles, she imagined him drawing a bath in his hotel room, soaking in warm sudsy water, while his candles, burned nearby. Something about that image didn't seem right. If she had been given travel candles, they probably would've ended up on the wicker chair in her bedroom.

"Then they made me take off my shoes and hold each one up. I'm one of the most conservative people in the whole airport, and they search me. As if I was smuggling a bomb or drugs in my shoe."

"Well, you don't look like a terrorist to me," she said, squeezing his hand. "I think those searches are random. They do it by every tenth or twentieth person that goes through the line. I'm sure it had nothing to do with you."

He smiled at her affectionately before he began to flip back and forth between radio stations.

Finding a parking place on Prospect Street was like finding a hundred-dollar bill next to a public trashcan. Impossible. The busiest street in La Jolla was lined with the finest restaurants, art galleries, and boutiques. She didn't waste a second looking for a parking spot and went straight to the valet.

As they walked to Zao's, she could feel her hair becoming softer from the ocean's moisture. Her bob would be wavy by the time they ordered their food. They rode the escalator up to the sushi restaurant.

"Shit," Paul muttered when they saw the crowd of people waiting outside. "I hope it's not a long wait."

"It's an hour for a table," the hostess said over the swanky music that played from the restaurant speakers. "But you're welcome to sit at the bar if you can find a spot."

After weaseling their way through the crowd, they found two stools at the bar. "What do you want to drink?" Paul asked as they sat down.

"I think I'm just going to stick with water since I'm driving."

He shrugged. "All right." He ordered himself a Stoli Vodka martini.

"So what are you doing this weekend?" He scanned over the menu. "Do you want to go to the beach on Saturday?"

"I wish I could. I'm going to Vegas for Val's bachelorette party." She closed her menu, feeling a little annoyed that the one weekend when Paul was in town she had to attend a bridesmaid obligation. "Do you think you'll be able to take me to the airport on Saturday morning?"

He nodded. "How many more weddings are you in this year?"

"Three. My cousin Val's, Leslie's, and Beth's."

"That's kind of crazy. All those people getting married."

"Why?" *Does he have something against marriage?*

"Well, I don't know. That's just a huge step. It's scary. I'm not saying that I don't ever want to get married. I'm sure that *someday* it would be great. I just think that *right now*, marriage seems kind of freaky."

She debated taking this conversation even further. How far away was someday? Was she a part of someday? She wanted to ask. However, if he considered marriage to be *scary*, she would send him running from the restaurant and out of her life forever if she started questioning him about the future. She wanted to talk about these things, but she sensed that she was going to have to wait.

"That reminds me," she said. "Are you going to be in town for Halloween?"

"Halloween?" Paul reached for a piece of bread.

She knew it was pointless to ask. His trips were almost always planned a month in advance—no earlier but often later. "Yes. I know it's crazy. But Beth is getting married on Halloween. She's making us all dress up, too."

He shrugged. "I don't know. October's usually a little slow. I might be here."

He plucked the olive from his martini, then popped it into his mouth. Cate hated those olives.

"Anyway," he said after polishing off the condiment. "What shall we order?"

"Yellowtail, of course," she said. "And a holy moly roll."

"Yum. That sounds good." He checked her orders off on the tab as well as three other rolls that he liked. "And I'm really in the mood for shrimp, so we may as well just get an order of those, too." He made a big check next to shrimp before handing their order to the bartender.

Going to sushi with Paul was the best. He loved to try everything, so they always ended up ordering an array of different rolls and sashimi.

He looked at Cate as if she had said something that amused him.

"What?" she asked. "Why are you looking at me that way?"

He laughed. "What way?"

"I don't know. You're just looking at me kind of weird."

"I just missed you on my last trip, Cate. That's all." He reached for her hand.

"I missed you, too," she said and squeezed his palm.

"I want you to start coming with me on some of my trips."

"You are saying all the right things tonight."

"I mean it," he said. "I missed you a lot."

Again, why no consistent phone calls? She forgot about his flaky streak when their food arrived.

She took a piece of the holy moly roll and dipped it in garlic ponzo sauce. God, she loved sushi. They feasted on the food, leaving only a couple of pieces on the plate. Paul ordered another martini, and they talked about his trip until the bartender brought their check.

Paul picked up the tab, then reached into his back pocket. "Dammit!" he yelled, causing people to look over their shoulders.

"What?"

"I left my wallet in my backpack. It's in the car. Shit!"

"It's okay. I'll take care of it."

She took the bill from his hands, gave it a once-over, then slipped her credit card into the leather folder.

"I'm sorry. I'll get you next time," he said.

"No worries."

She signed the sixty-dollar tab, twenty-one of which were Paul's martinis, and left the bartender a ten-dollar tip.

The breeze outside was crisp when they left the restaurant. Paul pulled her into a snug embrace while they waited for the valet to bring the Volvo. She pressed her cheek against his chest and enjoyed the warm blanket his arms created around her body.

"It's good to be back," he whispered before he kissed the top of her head.

She could feel his erection against her leg. Laughing, they ignored the other people who waited for their cars, not caring if anyone was watching. She suddenly felt eager to get home.

Sex with Paul was mind-blowing, to say the least. This was partly because he had made her feel completely comfortable when they were in the bedroom, showering her with compliments and taking each step slowly. He loved her body and made her feel relaxed and proud to share herself with him. He was also the only guy she had ever known who understood that foreplay actually involved more than a few sloppy kisses and a couple seconds of heavy petting. Her previous boyfriends had always raced to the finish line, making Cate feel panicked as if she were in a race, too, and if she didn't climax quickly, it would be over before she knew it. Paul could last forever in the bedroom.

She breathed in the scent of his Armani cologne mixed with everything else that was Paul. There was nothing like the way he smelled. When he was away, she missed his scent the most. It wasn't just his cologne. It was his hair and his breath. Even his bad breath didn't smell bad.

"Ben is working tonight. We could rent a movie . . . watch it naked on the couch," he said playfully.

"That sounds like fun."

The Volvo was making its rattling noise when the valet pulled up behind a Jaguar at the curb. Cate paid and tipped the valet before she sat down behind the wheel.

"You should really get that noise checked out," Paul said as he slid into the passenger seat.

"I know. It's summer, though, and I'm not making much money, so I might have to wait a little while."

He flipped on the radio, stifling the ticking sound.

At Blockbuster they browsed around the video-covered shelves.

"*Amélie!* I have always wanted to see this!" Cate exclaimed.

Paul picked up the case, looking to see if the movie met his standards. "It's in subtitles?"

"Yes. It's French. It's supposed to be sooooo good. I've heard nothing but great things about it."

He shook his head. "From who? Beth. No thanks." He placed it back on the shelf. She'd actually heard it was good from Sarah and Miles—two of his friends also—but didn't get a chance to mention that. "I am not going to *reeead* a movie," he said. "You can rent that one with Jill. How 'bout this?" He held up *Domestic Disturbance*.

Cate shrugged. "All right." Vince Vaughn was in it, so it had to be pretty good.

Paul had taken his wallet from his backpack when they had driven to the video store, and he paid for the movie.

His house was dark when they arrived. His roommate was a fireman, so he spent half of his week living at the firehouse. They rarely saw him. This living situation allowed them to spend careless nights cuddled up, naked, beneath blankets on Paul's fluffy ivory couch. In the middle of the night they also had the freedom to walk to the bathroom or the kitchen without dressing.

Paul dropped his suitcase by the front door. As he walked through the living room, he began flipping on light switches. He stopped to shuffle through a stack of mail that had accumulated since he had been away. "Mostly garbage," he said before tossing half the pile into a nearby wastebasket.

Cate liked his place more than she liked her own apartment. She loved the sound their shoes made when they walked across the hardwood floors and the cool breezes that drifted from the bay in the morning.

He and Ben had nice things, too. Comfortable couches that they had purchased at Pottery Barn, instead of taking them from their grandmothers' garages. He had art books on his coffee table and original framed and matted prints that he had purchased from artists on all of his travels.

"Well, you can tell I've been out of town," Paul said irritably as he pointed to the pile of dirty dishes that had accumulated in the kitchen sink.

Ben had a habit of leaving his dishes in the sink, or worse, on the coffee table. Instinctively, Cate began to line up the dirty bowls and glasses in the dishwasher.

Paul pulled her away. "Don't do those. Go sit down. I'm going to open a bottle of wine."

He gave her butt a playful pat before she left him in the kitchen.

Nights like these were usually Cate's favorite. She loved the simple things with Paul, the cozy routine they shared when he was home. They would watch a movie, drink a bottle of wine, and fall asleep spooned against each other's warm bodies. In the morning they would lie in bed, watching an episode of *Trading Spaces,* still curled together in each other's arms. Then they would eat brunch at the Brockton Villa, ordering an extra side of potatoes and tasting each other's entrées. It was the little things that made her happy, and she never wanted these weekends to end. But tonight she felt strange, as if some unknown worry were gnawing away at her nerves.

Maybe it was because of their conversation at dinner. Was he afraid of marriage? Or was he afraid of marrying her? She felt as if they had started watching a movie and had left the theater before it ended. Now she wished she had drawn the marriage conversation out a little further. However, she didn't feel like they were at a level where she could openly discuss these things with him.

She knew she was going to have to be patient if she wanted answers. Things had always moved slowly in their relationship. They'd been friends for three years before he even made the first move. She had always considered his traveling to be the main reason as to why their relationship had progressed so slowly. They didn't spend every free second together, the way Sarah and Miles did, because he was gone half the time, and when he was home, he had a million things he needed to do to catch up. She often felt stumped when people asked about him.

"What's Paul doing today?" Leslie or Beth would ask. "He's back from his trip, right?"

She'd feel chagrined when she stammered for a response. "Yeah, he's back, but well . . . I . . . uh . . . well . . . I haven't talked to him since yesterday morning." Then she'd find herself fighting off annoyance until he called. Her engaged friends always knew the exact whereabouts of their boyfriends.

She'd been so lost in thought that she hadn't even heard him approach.

"You look like you're waiting for something," he said.

She turned from the window. He was holding two glasses of wine. "Waiting? What do you mean?" She took one of the glasses.

"You just looked like you were waiting for something, or someone— standing by the window like that."

For a second she felt tempted to tell him she was waiting for something, only she wasn't sure exactly what she should say. *Will you please quit your job and tell me that you see a solid future for us?*

She shook her head. "No. I wasn't waiting for anything."

He pulled her into his arms and laughed. "My little Cate. It's good to see you again."

"You, too," she whispered, all the while trying to figure out exactly what she was waiting for.

Cousin Val's Wedding •

5 • Tips—Vegas Style

Las Vegas, the City of Thirst. That's what Cate thought as she rode in the airport shuttle toward Mandalay Bay. After only ten minutes in Vegas, the dry heat had sucked the moisture right out of her hair. Her bob had fallen flat and thin and hung like a limp rag around her face.

The desert, lacking all that was vital, seemed to take things from people. It made them *need*. They needed to win. They needed to party. They needed deodorant.

"The locals say this is the nicest hotel on the strip," the driver said as they pulled into a driveway that looked as if it covered twenty acres. "Nicest restaurants. Nicest bars. Best pool. You'll have a great time."

A blast of heat covered her as she left the air-conditioned van. It reminded her of going swimming when she was little. It felt like stepping out of a cold pool and into a sun-soaked towel that her mother held open for her, wrapping her tiny body inside its oven.

She handed two crisp one-dollar bills to the shuttle driver.

A piercing squeal shot in her direction, causing her ears to ring. "Ahhhhh! Caaaaate!" A squad of blondes surrounded her.

Although there were *only* ten bridesmaids in the wedding, Val had invited half of her sorority to Vegas. They were all waiting in front of the hotel when Cate arrived. Fruity cocktails in hand, they wore swim-suits and skimpy poolside cover-ups.

Val threw her arms around Cate's shoulders. "I'm soooo glad you're here! We need to get you in your bathing suit, and you need a cocktail pronto. Can someone please get this girl a Long Island? Now." Promptly, one of her friends scouted out a cocktail waitress.

The only thing Cate and cousin Val had in common was that their mothers were sisters. They were worlds apart, but had always been friends. At twenty-two, Val was four years younger than Cate. Her parents were loaded. She was an only child, and her father had sprung for the entire bachelorette weekend.

She pinched the side of Cate's arm, sending a smart sting up her bicep. "It's soooo good to see youuuuu."

"I've been looking forward to this weekend for a while," Cate said.

She glanced at Cate's hands. "What are you holding? Your lug-gage?" She spun around. "Excuse me! Sir!"

A bellman, out of breath, approached them. "What can I do for you, miss?" Sweat soaked his Mandalay Bay–issued shirt. Cate thought his glasses were going to slide off the tip of his nose because his face was so slick from perspiration.

Val pointed to Cate's bags. "Room 3103. We'll be up in a minute. Thank you." She handed him a five before she turned to Cate. "You're sharing a room with me. We have a suite."

The lobby felt like the Artic Circle. Nearly frigid air-conditioning filled the hotel. Two women wearing loud tropical print dresses held parrots near the front desk. They looked as if they had just come from the Playboy mansion. A small crowd of men gathered around them. Admiring the birds?

Cate could hear the sound of coins jingling, slot machines buzzing, and the beeping sounds of victory from the casino around the corner.

"We have lots planned," Val said as she led Cate through the busy hotel. "Cocktails . . . tanning poolside all day. Then we're off to strip clubs!"

Cate had never been to a strip club before. She knew that women took it all off. She wondered if men wore their birthday suits, too. Did they dance around with their wangs swinging and dangling in all directions?

When they reached the hotel room, one of Val's friends was waiting with a Long Island for Cate.

"Why don't you sip on that while you change into your swimsuit?" Val said. "We'll meet you by the pool." She left a key on the nightstand.

Cate admired the room before changing into her bathing suit. The bathroom was approximately the size of her kitchen in Pacific Beach. Everything was polished and new. The marble floors and counters shined. The towels were neatly folded and stacked. She picked up a bar of glycerin soap and inhaled its sweet rainwater scent.

She opened the curtains to a sprawling view of the Mandalay Bay water park below. The pool was practically a small ocean. Eager to get in the water, she left the view to change into her bathing suit.

When she arrived at the pool, the girls had already staked out an entire corner of the wave park. Val had saved Cate a lounge chair.

Feeling self-conscious, Cate removed her shorts and tank top. She'd never tanned well. Her fair skin didn't tolerate a lot of exposure. She felt like a glowing albino next to all of Val's friends, who looked as if they had grown up along the French Riviera and had never experienced a bad sunburn in their bronzed lives.

Val handed her a bottle of fifteen-proof sunblock. "You're going to fry," she said, letting her eyes wander over Cate's body. "You'll need this."

Cate lathered the front of her body in sunblock, especially her face and chest.

"Val, would you mind putting this on my back?" She handed Val the bottle. "I'll put it on your back, too, if you want."

Val smiled. "Oh. That's okay. I don't wear sunscreen. But I'll do yours." She took the bottle from Cate, squirted a generous portion of lotion into her hands, and spread it all over Cate's back. When she was finished, she patted her on the shoulders. "You're all set, sweetie."

A cocktail waitress wearing butt-tight shorts and high pumps came around the corner. "How are you guys doin'?" she asked.

"We'll need another round of Long Islands. Thanks," Val said.

Cate could already feel beads of sweat forming around her hairline, and decided to take a dip in the pool. She waded into the cold water. Waves splashed over her shoulders. It was just like the beach. There was even sand. She cooled off in the water until her hands became pruned and a teenager trying to body surf nearly plowed into her.

A cocktail waitress was passing out a fresh round of Long Islands when she returned to her lounge chair.

"Thanks." Cate took a cocktail. Her hair was dripping, and a few droplets of water plopped into her drink when she took a sip.

"Just charge everything to the room," Val signed a receipt for drinks. "I want everyone to have a good time this weekend."

A blonde wearing pink-tinted pilot's sunglasses and a shimmery bikini sat down on an empty lounge chair next to Cate. "Hi. I'm Loni." She had a Southern drawl.

Cate introduced herself as they shook hands.

"That's a cute suit," Val said.

Loni turned to Val. "Thanks. But I shaved my bikini line this mornin', and now I've got razor burn that looks like herpes."

"Oh! Me, too!" another girl said. "It looks like I have an STD."

"That's why I don't shave anymore," Val said. "I get waxed. The Playboy wax, actually."

"Waxing gives me ingrown hairs," Loni remarked. "I could spend hours pickin' out those hairs with a needle."

"Doesn't that hurt?" Cate asked. The thought of hair being ripped or picked from any part of her body was unbearable.

Val shook her head. "Are you kidding? I love it. Jim loves it, too. My esthetician waxes everything off. I tip her ten bucks every time."

"How is Jim?" Cate asked.

"Great! He's having his bachelor party this weekend, too."

"He's such a wonderful guy," Loni added. "A real catch. Val is one lucky gal."

"He'll make a great *first* husband," Val said.

The other girls burst into laughter.

"I'm just kidding," Val said. "I swear. I'm kidding. I love him. We did just sign a very rewarding prenup though! Let's just say that I won't ever have to worry, but he will! Ha!"

More laughter.

Cate sipped on her cocktail, listening to the girls suggest remedies for razor burn and ingrown hairs.

"Rub exfoliating scrub over all the ingrown hairs. It makes them pop out," one girl suggested.

"Don't use dull razors if you don't want razor burn. If you use a dull razor, you may as well scrape a pair of scissors over your coochie," another said.

"I'd like to go to a good sex shop while I'm here," Nikki said, looking up from the latest issue of *Cosmo*. "I just read an article on vibrators, and I think I want one."

"I love mine," Loni added. "It's waterproof. I can take it the tub with me if I want."

"That's what we'll do!" Val announced. "We'll all buy vibrators while we're here. As a party favor."

Cate had never considered purchasing a vibrator. Even if she ever did think of buying one, she'd be scared shitless that someone would find it. A stark vision of herself dying in a car wreck, her parents stumbling across the thing while they cleaned out her apartment flashed through her mind.

The combination of heat and liquor was draining. Instead of feeling buzzed, she felt fatigued. The sun smothered all her energy. Two Long Islands later, she began to feel tired. They were still talking about vibrators when she drifted into a deep sleep.

It was quiet when she awoke, and afternoon clouds had cast a shadow over the pool.

She sat up. Most of the girls were gone.

"You've been sleeping for a long time," Loni said. "Some of the other girls went upstairs to get ready."

Cate felt as if she'd just rolled off a barbecue. She pulled back the side of her triangle top and suddenly felt wide-awake. The striking contrast of her red chest next to her white boob was frightening. "I'm fried."

"Yeah. You are pretty red." Loni noticed, too.

When she returned to the suite, Val was blow-drying her hair. "Hello sleepy hea . . ." her voice trailed off. "Wow. You got some color today."

Cate looked at herself in the mirror. "Oh my God," she mumbled. She was as bright as an explosion. Her face was beet red, and her chest was so flaming that it scared her to look at herself.

"Didn't you put on more sunscreen, you dingbat?" Val asked.

"I fell asleep." Cate glanced at Val. She didn't have a red mark on her body, and she hadn't even worn sunscreen. She was the type of girl that soaked up countless hours of sun during the summer and hit tanning beds on a daily basis during the winter. Her deeply tanned skin could withstand hours of harsh sun exposure.

After Cate showered, it only became worse. Her skin was crimson.

When Nikki came in to borrow the blow dryer, she looked startled. "You've got it bad, girl. That is the worst sunburn I have ever seen in my entire life. That looks painful. And, what . . . oh my God. Who the hell put lotion on your back?"

Cate turned around to examine herself in the mirror. At first she couldn't figure out what was all over her back. It looked like white blotches and patches. Then she noticed the distinct shape of handprints and random little finger streaks. The places where Val had successfully applied lotion were white and formed the shape of her hands. The rest of her back was flaming red.

"Cate! I am so sorry. I had no idea. I thought I was doing a good job." Val looked as if she were going to cry.

"Don't worry about it," Cate said. *I'll just die of skin cancer by the time I'm thirty, but no worries.* "It's no big deal. No one will see my back anyway."

"Remind me to never let Val put lotion on my back," Nikki said.

It hurt when Cate lifted her arms. It hurt when she put clothes on her body. And, worst of all, when she had rolled over while sleeping on the lounge chair her bikini had hiked up her butt. Her ass was burned beyond recognition. It hurt to sit down.

Before they left for the strip club, Val's friends came over with a huge bag of goodies for the night. Among the party favors was a crown for Val. It was adorned with small, plastic penises that protruded from the headband. The girls draped a blazing, hot pink Bachelorette banner over Val's chest.

"I am not wearing a bra or underwear, and I am ready to go!" Val announced in her red tube top and black miniskirt.

Cate noticed that every single one of Val's friends sported nice golden tans. Cate looked like she was from Wisconsin.

"And while everyone was getting ready," Loni said, "Nikki and I went to a sex shop and purchased lipstick vibrators for everyone!" They passed out the treats. The vibrators really did look exactly like a tube of lipstick. The sound of little motors filled the room as each girl turned hers on.

"You can carry it in your purse and no one will ever know the difference," Nikki said.

Cate thought of her unsuspecting mother borrowing lipstick.

The first thing Cate saw when she entered Olympic Gardens was a vagina, shaved to complete baldness. Startled, she turned her head in the opposite direction and faced a pair of huge, bare boobs, their pink nipples coming at her like blaring headlights. They were everywhere, inescapable.

"What are we doing here?" Cate yelled over Britney Spear's "Slave 4 U." "I thought we were going to a male strip club."

Val grabbed her arm. "C'mon. We have to go upstairs!" Her penis crown was crooked.

They weaved in and out of naked dancers until they approached a staircase. Two men wearing Speedos and lace-up boots of the military variety met them at the top. One of the men hooked his arm around Val's elbow. "You must be the bachelorette."

"Yes!" she squealed, dreamy eyed.

The other linked arms with Cate. "You got some sun today," he said in a way that didn't offend her when she looked at his biceps. "Allow me to escort you to a table."

Cate could only recall seeing a similar physique when Brad Pitt starred in *Thelma and Louise*. Bare-chested men, toned, muscular, tan—everywhere. Tight buns and sinewy thighs, hairless chests and backs as smooth and firm as glass greeted her at every corner. Was it rude to stare at someone's butt?

She felt slightly self-conscious, being that she'd never received attention from men who probably posed for the covers of romance novels. However, their personable smiles cast away any discomfort she felt and instead made her feel as if she had just walked into a room full of long-lost friends, all of them hot.

"Would you like to buy the bachelorette a lap dance?" he asked as he led her toward a table. She had an urge to reach out and press his pecs.

"Uh . . . a lap dance?" She hadn't thought about it and wasn't even sure what a lap dance entailed. "Sure."

"They're twenty dollars, and we can bring her onstage if you'd like."

"Okay." Cate bought Val two lap dances, picking the strippers as if she were ordering two tank tops in her favorite colors from the J. Crew catalog. She wondered what Paul would think if he could see her right now, or what her mother would say about all this. For a moment she thought of herself as Miss Padgett the kindergarten teacher, buying lap dances in the summer and singing nursery rhymes in the fall.

A waiter wearing nothing but a bow tie and G-string took their drink orders.

The strip club wasn't as raunchy as Cate had imagined. There were no runaway wangs flying around. The dancers kept their Speedos on. An announcer introduced each stripper before he performed. It was like a play, a stage production, with half-naked men skipping all over the place.

Except for a few, most of the men were gorgeous. There were a couple that looked as if they had done too many steroids and there was one that was plain cheesy. Cate was willing to bet that he was the tackiest male performer in the state of Nevada. And that was saying a lot. One, she was too poor to be making bets. Two, Nevada was the reigning palace of tacky.

His dyed platinum hair hung over his shoulders like dried-out hay. When he spun around beneath the spotlights, his mane was almost as green as his fluorescent G-string. He was fake tanned to the point of appearing orange. To complete his entire image, he wore a pair of cowboy boots, his calves sticking out from the shoes like a pair of Popsicle sticks. He reminded Cate of someone out of a bad eighties metal band who hadn't realized that the eighties as well as the nineties had passed. Val called him Cheesedick.

"I dare someone to get a dance from Cheesedick!" She said. All of her friends laughed.

Looking at Val, one would think she had just broken up with someone rather than had recently been engaged. She acted hungry, and devoured every minute of the attention she received from the dancers, practically licking her lips with pleasure. She could hardly sit still, squirming in her seat as she anticipated each lap dance.

Her first lap dance was given by a Spanish man with biceps bigger than her thighs and deep-set eyes crowned with bushy eyebrows. He hovered over Val, his washboard stomach coming within inches of her chest. When he moved his hands up her thighs, Val tossed her head back and giggled. Her penis crown fell to the floor. Nikki was about to retrieve it when a stripper wearing a camouflage Speedo skipped over and swiped it from the ground. The military man ran his fingers through Val's hair, massaging her scalp, before returning the crown to her head.

Cate noticed that Val's bare butt was exposed for all of Olympic Gardens to see. For a moment she debated hopping on stage and pulling Val's skirt back down. She changed her mind when Val took the strippers' hands into her own and placed them on her bare ass.

Cate couldn't help but wonder what kind of damage a camera could cause for Val. What if someone took pictures, and they accidentally ended up in Jim's hands?

Val had barely taken a seat when the announcer said, "Next up is Billy dancing for the bachelorette, Valerie." Val cheered when she heard her name for the fourth time. Billy, a well-endowed cowboy, wearing chaps and a G-string, took Val by the hand and led her on stage.

He spent a minute or two twirling around her. Then he took her knees, moved them apart, and began to dance inside her legs. Val looked as if she were in heaven when he began to rub her inner thighs. Cate watched as Val's fingers latched on to each of Billy's tight butt cheeks.

It was hard to keep from wondering what Jim would think if he witnessed his bride exchanging pelvic thrusts with a male stripper. What came next made Cate's hair stand on end.

"And next up," the announcer beamed, "is a dance for one of Valerie's bridesmaids, Cate Padgett."

Gin and tonic sprayed from between her teeth when she heard her name. Hoots and squeals came from the other bridesmaids. "Get up here, Caaaaate!" Val cheered as she wrapped her legs around Billy's waist.

Her body became immobile, and she could feel her cheeks growing hot. Chrissy and Nikki grabbed each of her arms. Then Kimberly and Loni hoisted her up to stage level before Michelle gave her a swift kick in the ass, sending Cate sprawling onto the stage. She was saved from falling flat on her face by her private dancer, a yummy blond with a fire-engine red Speedo. Okay, maybe it wasn't so bad.

He placed her in a chair facing Val, who gave her a mischievous wink. Cate sat upright, back straight, legs closed, and ankles crossed. When the next song began, she expected to see the fire-red pelvis thrusting within inches of her nose. Instead, a fluorescent green G-string came spinning toward her like an out-of-control Frisbee. The last thing she saw before Cheesedick began attempting to work his magic was the horrified expression on Val's face.

She thought she heard Val scream, "That's not the one we ordered!" over the music.

"Hi, cutie," he whispered in her hair. "I'm Brett. What's your name?"

"Uh . . . er . . . ummm . . . Cate?"

"Relax, Cate," he said as he ran his fingers through her hair. He looked at her playfully. His teeth were bleached.

She glanced at the other girls out of the corner of her eye. Nikki was shaking her head, furiously mouthing, "We didn't order *Cheesedick*! There's been a *mistake!*"

Chrissy was screaming at the man who took orders for lap dances, waving her arms around like a madwoman, and Loni was on her cell phone, pacing around the stage.

Brett lightly touched Cate's chin and turned her to face him. "You look preoccupied," he said in a playful, boudoir type of way.

He moved his pelvis in circles like a belly dancer, occasionally giving his head a kinky little toss, sending his chlorine-colored hair over his shoulders. Cate noticed that his whole body was shaved—legs, chest, and arms—and she sensed that . . . his area was bald as well. He parted her thighs, and she wanted to clench them shut but she also didn't want to be a poor sport.

He hovered over her, his bare chest coming within inches of her nose. She inhaled musky cologne. His chest felt the same way her legs had the last time she went two days without shaving. "I know you're nervous, darling. I won't do anything to embarrass you," he whispered.

It's a little late for that, she thought.

"Looks like you got a little sun today," he said before he did a little spin in his cowboy boots. "You know what will really help?" He turned around, still thrusting his crotch back and forth, snapping his fingers.

She was curious and figured with his tan he was probably an expert in skin care. "What?"

"Apply tons of lotion, of course. But keep your lotion in the refrigerator. The cool lotion will feel great on your burned body."

"Really? I never thought of that."

He was hovering over her again. She could see crow's feet forming around the outer edges of his eyes, and he had a scar on his neck.

"Where are you from?" he asked.

"San Diego."

His eyes lit up. "So am I! I used to dance down there. Years ago."

"How many years ago?" She wondered how long he had been stripping for.

"Twelve years."

She kind of felt sorry for him. He was like a rock star that was leaving his prime and had nothing left to do. She sensed she was probably the only lap dance he'd get all night. No one wanted him anymore. No one desired him. And stripping was his passion.

She tipped him ten dollars when it was over. "You should also try Curel lotion. It's the best, and it's really cheap, too. My dermatologist recommends it. And stay out of the sun. You're a cute girl. You don't need a tan."

She liked Cheesedick and could see them being friends, doing lunch and exchanging tips on skin products.

Val came racing over. She pulled Cate away as if she were saving her from a rabid dog. "Caaaaate! I don't know what happened! That was not who we ordered for you. I was trying to put an end to it, but Billy was pinning me down the whole time. Chrissy and Nikki are getting to the bottom of this nightmare right now."

"Val, it's okay. He was nice."

"He was *nice?*"

"Yeah. He gave me all kinds of tips for my sunburn."

"Tips for your sunburn?"

Nikki and Chrissy approached, frantic. They squeezed Cate as if she had been through an ordeal. "Cate, we are *soooo sor-ry.*" They shook their heads. "We ordered Brent for you. The one with the fireman outfit, and they mixed it up with Brett. We're getting you Brent for free."

"It's all right. Really, I don't need Brent."

"No. You're getting Brent. And your new friendship with Cheesedick is starting to worry me," Val said.

"Why don't one of you guys let Brent dance for you instead? That way we'll get two dances for the price of one."

Loni jumped at the opportunity for an intimate moment with the half-naked firefighter. "I'll do it!"

"Perfect." The waiter walked by, and Cate ordered them all a round of buttery nipple shots.

"I think we need a picture!" Val threw an arm around Cate's shoulders. They took five pictures with five different disposable cameras.

After the photo shoot, Cate went to the ladies' room. While in line she noticed that her cell phone was beeping, indicating she had messages. Excited, she dialed voice mail.

"*Hola*. I've tried to call you three times. Why haven't you answered? *Adios*."

Cate called him back.

"Where are you?" he asked.

"Olympic Gardens."

"You are? You're in a strip club. Why didn't you answer when I called?"

"I couldn't hear the phone. It's really loud in here."

"Well, I've been calling you."

"Well, I'm sorry." She sensed a little jealousy in his voice and kind of liked it. "I couldn't hear you."

"I miss you," he said.

"I miss you, too."

Her turn came for the bathroom. "Are you picking me up from the airport tomorrow?" she asked.

"Yes. I can't wait to see you."

"I know. Me, too."

She was having a great night.

The following morning, Cate felt as if she had been beaten over the head with a penis crown. When she stepped out of bed to retrieve aspirin, she noticed that Val's bed was empty. Then she remembered that her cousin had taken a hit of ecstasy and danced off to a twenty-four-hour nightclub with two of the strippers from Olympic Gardens.

In the bathroom, she rummaged through her makeup bag for her bottle of aspirin. She groaned when she accidentally dropped the bag on the floor and all of the contents scattered across the tile. She picked up the bottle and popped two pills in her mouth, drinking straight from the faucet when she washed them down.

The water tasted delicious. She found one of the only glasses Val had not mixed a cocktail in and filled it. She gulped down three glasses of water before returning to bed.

She lay in her bed, air-conditioning blasting into the room as she tried to piece together the night. Had she done anything stupid? She'd been crocked, that was for sure. But as she recalled, she'd actually been the voice of reason when two of Val's friends had gotten in a fight over Hunter, the stripping postman. Then she'd spent a solid thirty minutes helping Tina clean puke off her shirt in the bathroom. And after Cheesedick, she'd managed to steer clear of any more lap dances. That was a relief. Guilt would've haunted her for ages if she had done anything that would've potentially hurt Paul. It would have been unfair to do anything that she would be ashamed to do right in front of him.

She was drifting back to sleep when a loud crash outside the door woke her. She heard Val giggling. She listened while Val fumbled with the door handle. After a few attempts to open the door, she finally made a sloppy entrance into the room, Chrissy and Nikki in tow. They were laughing.

Val was barefoot and holding one high-heeled shoe in her hand. Her crown was gone, something red was spilled down the front of her shirt, and she was missing an earring.

"Good morning!" she declared when she noticed Cate. "My shoe broke!"

The girls erupted in laughter.

"How?" Cate asked.

"Oh my God. It was so funny," Nikki began.

Val interrupted. "We were dancing and this guy was spinning me around and the heel of my shoe hit a table and came right off. It just snapped off."

"It flew across the bar . . ." Chrissy said. They were all laughing so hard that they could barely finish the story. "The bouncer thought that Val had thrown something, and we were almost kicked out."

"Val was more pissed about her shoe than almost being kicked out," Nikki said.

Val threw her remaining heel to the floor. "Fuckin' shoes. Those cost me three hundred dollars."

She flopped down on the bed. "Thank God my flight doesn't leave 'til tonight," she groaned. "I need a nap."

After Chrissy and Nikki left, Cate decided to take a shower. The smell of cigarettes in her hair was making her hangover worse. She was dying to scrub herself. She took a long, steamy shower.

When she turned the water off, she could hear Val on the phone.

"No, sweetie. I didn't hook up with anyone last night. Did you have strippers at your party?" Cate listened while Val described a PG-13 version of the night to her fiancé. "No. We just stopped in the strip club real quick. Most of the men were completely cheesy. All my friends were flirting with them, but I didn't care." She continued to convince Jim that she could probably qualify for canonization. "I love you," she said.

Cate wondered how long it had taken for them to tell each other they loved each other. She and Paul had been dating for nearly a year and had never told each other they loved each other. Was that normal? Any time she heard Paul use the word love in a sentence her ears perked up with anticipation, and her heart skipped a beat. But he'd always been referring to something else.

Her college boyfriend, Keith, had said it after three weeks. At nineteen she thought his unbridled profession of love was premature. Even though she wasn't sure what it meant, she'd said it back. For a while she had Keith in the palm of her hand. He called her between classes and came over to watch *Friends* with Cate and her roommates. She vowed that she would never, *ever* be like the girls who sat waiting for their boyfriends to call, running to a guy when he said it was convenient to hang out.

She'd had Keith at her mercy until she lost her virginity to him. Then, Monday Night Football had taken on a new meaning for him and skateboarding with the same friends he woke up to every morning became a career. After three months of analyzing Keith to the extent of being able to provide a doctoral thesis, she threw in the towel. She held her chin high and strode on, concealing her wounded pride.

After Val hung up, she flopped down on the bed.

"Can I ask you something?" Cate said.

"No. I didn't get laid last night." She laughed. "Just kidding. Well, I mean I didn't. But seriously, what were you going to ask?"

"How long was it before you and Jim said 'I love you.' "

She thought about it. "Maybe eight months. Why? You still waitin' for Paul to say it?"

"Yeah. We've been dating for about a year now. But considering how often he travels, I guess the time that we've actually spent together has probably been more equivalent to five months."

"Just be patient. He'll say it. I was always wondering when Jim was going to say it and as soon as I forgot about it, he said it. Whatever you do, don't say it first. You'll scare the shit out of him."

"I know." She felt better hearing that it had taken Jim eight months to profess his love to Val. Maybe Paul wasn't as far behind as she thought.

Val sat up. "I feel guilty."

"Why?" Cate asked as she wrapped a towel around her head.

"Because Jim was just asking me all kinds of questions. His dad was at his bachelor party. They didn't even have strippers or anything. They just went to a Padres game and had some beer and peanuts."

"Well, you didn't do anything . . ." Cate chose her words selectively. ". . . that could ruin your relationship, right?"

"I guess not."

Neither one of them seemed convinced.

6

The Accidental Funeral

"Paul's coming to the wedding?" Her mother asked, the same way she would say, *You're wearing that?*

"Yeah. Why? Is something wrong with that?"

"No. I just thought you said he was going to Boston."

"He is. But he'll be back in time for the wedding."

"Well, you know if he's already agreed to go, it's very rude to cancel on these things. It's very important that they have a precise head count to pay for all the entrées that they order."

"I know, Mom. He's not going to flake."

It was a Friday, and they were in Cate's car heading to church. About once a month Cate attended noon Mass with her mother at Saint Mary's, then they had lunch at Trattoria Acqua.

"So, is Paul coming to the rehearsal dinner, too?"

"Yes," Cate replied.

"I thought his constant traveling was bothering you," Connie said.

"It was. But I think I'm going on some trips with him soon."

"Oh really? In the same hotel room?"

Then it happened. She was saved. A cat darted in front of the car. Glory be. Cate slammed on the brakes. Her mother screamed. They missed the cat within inches.

"That was close," her mother breathed.

"Was that cat black?"

"Oh, Cate. You shouldn't believe in superstitions."

"Did you know that black cats are actually a sign of good luck and not bad luck?"

"I don't believe in luck. I only believe in blessings."

"All right," Cate said as they pulled up to Saint Mary's. The old church was one of the simplest yet most beautiful chapels in San Diego. Cate had attended Mass at Saint Mary's for over a decade. It was a small, quaint chapel set in the midst of businesses and trendy restaurants in La Jolla. Cate liked the airy feeling inside the church, the way sea breezes wafted through the open windows and soft sunlight cast rays over the polished hardwood floors.

All the curbside parking was taken, which was unusual for a weekday mass. She could see people standing outside and wondered why they were dressed in suits and nice dresses. Weekday Masses were usually jeans and T-shirts. She drove a block away from the church and managed to squeeze into a parallel parking spot.

"Hmm. I wonder what's going on," Connie remarked.

Cate felt a flicker of joy. There might be some kind of event going on at church. Maybe weekday Mass was canceled! Being raised Catholic, she knew it was terrible to be happy about a canceled Mass, but she was starving and couldn't help it if she felt faint.

As they neared the church, Cate noticed that it was extremely quiet, with people whispering. The chapel was half full inside.

"Oh, it's a wedding," Cate said, noticing the framed photo of a couple in front of the church. Then she saw the lilies—and the coffin.

"Er, uh . . . I mean a funeral." She prayed no one heard the wedding remark. She felt as if she had just walked in on her mother wrapping Christmas gifts.

Her mother, unfazed, picked up a funeral program and proceeded down the church aisle, waving to a few of her church friends. She took a seat midchapel.

Cate slid in next to her. "Mom, this a funeral. I think we should go."

Connie shrugged. "I guess Father must have done some weird scheduling thing today. But it's still Mass. We're here to receive the Blessed Sacrament. That's all that matters."

Cate stared at her mother.

"What?" Connie said. "It's just Mass, Cate. *You* need to do penance anyway for never attending."

"Mother, do you even know this person?"

"No."

"Are you out of your mind?" Cate was trying to keep her voice low, but she couldn't help it if it had raised a decibel or two. "I mean, are you crazy?"

Her mom looked at her. "It's Mass. Anyone can come." She began to reach for her missal. "You can leave *if you want*, Cate. Why don't you leave and come get me in an hour?" Something about the way she suggested it seemed more like a guilt trip than an invitation to depart.

"You're honestly planning on staying at someone's funeral that you don't even know?"

Before she could give her stock answer of *it's Mass,* Cate reached for her car keys. "I'll see you in an hour."

She made it out of the church just as the organist began to play "Amazing Grace."

This was worse than the time her mother had confiscated all of her Duran Duran tapes when Cate was a preteen, claiming they were straight from Hell. She remembered how uncomfortable she had felt when her friends had asked what happened to her cassettes. Explaining her mother's theory that "Rio" was actually a metaphor for the devil, and "Save a Prayer" was blasphemous was too embarrassing. Even Beth's mom, the head of the San Diego Republican party, let her daughter listen to Duran Duran. Too ashamed of the truth, she'd told her friends that she'd lost all the tapes.

She was heading to her car when she heard someone call her name. "Hey, Cate!"

She spun around.

"Ethan! I keep running into you."

"I know. It's amazing how many people I've run into since I started this business. I swear I've seen more old friends." Then his smile faded. "You're not here for the, uh . . ." He pointed toward the chapel. "Fune—"

"No." She shook her head. "My mom, um . . ." *How in the hell was she going to explain this one?* "My mom's here. She . . . uh, decided to stay, and we're going to lunch after . . ." She felt clumsy with embarrassment and immediately changed the subject. "What are you doing here?"

"We're catering the reception. It's in the church hall afterwards." He ran his fingers through his dark hair. "So how have you been? Did you ever get everything sorted out that night?"

Cate remembered the ride in his van to USD, Claude held at her mercy in the men's room. "Oh, yeah. Yes. Everything was fine."

Why did she always run into him in the most bizarre moments of her life? If he only knew that she had locked someone in a bathroom for over five hours, and that her mother was attending an accidental funeral, Ethan would think she was a complete nut. Then again, he'd known Cate for a good portion of her life. When Cate had been grounded for doing something unholy like sleeping in instead of going to Mass, Ethan had help her sneak out her bedroom window. Then they would walk to the cove and sit on the cliffs, usually with a six-pack of Keystone Light.

"Anyway, I'm glad I ran into you," he said. "We're making a new menu and catalogs and stuff, and I remembered that you were a photographer. I wanted to ask if you could take some pictures for our company. We'll pay you, of course."

"Me?"

"Yeah, I remembered all those pictures you used to take in high school and the one that got the prize at the Del Mar Fair. I still have some of the photos you sent me when you were at USD. Then you were talking about photography the other night. I thought you might want to make some extra cash while you're not teaching this summer."

"Yeah, I'd love to."

"It won't be the most exciting photo shoot. It will be mostly our entrées." Her stomach growled when he mentioned food.

"That's okay. I'd love to."

She'd never had a real photo assignment before. Except for her entry in the Del Mar Fair ten years ago, the only other recognition she'd received was a free calendar when one of Grease's photos had been selected in a page-a-day contest. He'd been September 29. The picture was hanging on her wall.

"Lemme grab your phone number real quick," he said.

They exchanged phone numbers.

"I've gotta get back into the kitchen, but I'll give you a call this week."

Cate felt flattered. She couldn't believe he remembered things she'd photographed from ten years ago.

Her stomach released a loud and obnoxious growl as she walked to the car. She was tempted to grab a fish taco at Wahoo's but decided to go to Sav-On instead. Grease needed some things. Besides, she loved Sav-On. She could spend an entire day walking down the aisles, putting things in her cart.

She pushed a cart through the entrance. As she passed the rows of registers, she grabbed a Snickers bar and ate the entire thing while she walked toward pet supplies. She picked out some catnip for Grease. He was a little addict. Then she picked out two scented candles, a lint roller, a new fan for her bedroom, and a nail polish—red. At the cash register she included the empty candy bar wrapper in her purchases.

When she returned to Saint Mary's, the funeral was still in progress. She glanced at her watch. It had been over an hour. There were probably nuns that were less religious than her mother.

Cate often felt that her mother was disappointed with the way she had turned out. The only thing she had in common with her mother was the color of their hair. Cate had inherited her father's square nose, chiseled jawline, and hair that turned curly and unruly in certain temperatures. It was Cate's sister who had come from the Connie cookie cutter. Emily had grown up hearing, "You look exactly like your mother!" They shared the same cute nose that turned up like little jewels between their rosy cheeks. Their fine blonde hair was the kind that remained soft and straight, even in the most severe weather conditions.

Cate had always figured that her mother would've been smitten if Cate had been more like Emily. While Cate threatened to run away if forced to attend private Catholic schools, her sister had willingly filled out her applications to Saint Michael's and Our Lady of Peace. Even though they were two years apart, the girls grew up with a distance between them. Emily at Our Lady of Peace and Cate at La Jolla High. They couldn't complain about the same teachers or gossip about boys they thought were cute.

Emily had actually looked forward to attending catechism classes, and going to Mass was like going to an Oscar-nominated movie every week. She'd been actively involved in organizing the youth retreats for the teenagers that were nearing confirmation, while Cate had been actively involved in getting the other kids to form a coup d'état at youth retreats.

Then Emily had attended Thomas Aquinas College, a university that Cate thought was closely related to a convent. Cate remembered the way her mother had glowed with pride when they moved Emily into the dorms at TAC.

"Cate, how would you like to go to school here?" her mother had asked.

No alcohol. A dress code. Nuns as teachers. It sounded like Hell.

It wasn't that Cate didn't believe in God. She just didn't see things the way her mother and sister did. She didn't believe she was going to Hell for missing Mass or that confessing to a priest that, yes, she was indeed human, and yes, she made mistakes was going to assure her a seat in Heaven.

She believed it was the kindness people showed one another that was more powerful than all the rituals and codes her mother and sister were drawn to. She suspected her father felt the same way but never said a word, going along with his wife's religious convictions for fear that he, too, might end up losing his cassette tapes.

Cate's thoughts were interrupted when her mother appeared in the passenger side window.

"So how was it?" Cate asked as Connie slid into the car.

"Fine."

"Who was it?"

"It was Henry Fordson. I never really knew him, but I knew who he was. He was very active in the parish."

"How did he die?"

"Cancer." She reached for some Chap Stick in her purse. Two things that Cate could always count on her mother having: lip balm and Kleenex. "Oh, you'll never believe who I just saw," she said before rubbing Chap Stick across her lips.

"Ethan Blakely?"

"Yes! You saw him, too?" She smacked her lips together.

"Yes, I saw him on the way to the car, and I ran into him at Sarah's wedding a couple of weeks ago."

"He was always such a nice kid. Poor thing—being raised by those parents." She put her lip balm back in her purse. "They practically neglected him. And I think they were atheists, too."

"Atheists? Why do you say that?"

"I don't know. They just seemed like it."

Ethan's parents were both doctors and worked odd hours. Cate and Ethan had viewed Connie's notion of neglect as the best thing that could've ever happened to Treemont Drive. Ethan's house used to be the epicenter of experimentation. Pot. Cigarettes. Chewing tobacco. Driving without a license.

Ethan had an older brother who was supposed to be *watching* him, but the reality of it was that Chuck had a fake ID and used to buy them beer and cigarettes whenever they wanted.

Acqua was busy for a Friday afternoon. Cate hoped they would be seated on the upper patio. The two-story restaurant was nestled atop the steep cliffs that overlooked the La Jolla shores. It was a nice restaurant but also comfortable. If Cate came with Paul, they would get dressed up and order a bottle of wine. With Connie she could wear jeans and eat salmon and bacon sandwiches. Besides the good food, the view of the ocean was superb. Cate and Connie were pleased when they managed to score a table on the upper patio.

"Ethan wants me to take some pictures for his business," Cate said after they were seated.

"Oh, well that will be neat. Is he going to pay you?"

"I think so."

"Maybe he has some nice friends that he can introduce you to."

"I have a boyfriend—Paul."

"I know, but do you have a ring on your finger?" Her mother set her menu aside. She dipped a piece of bread in the complimentary hummus.

"Why don't you like Paul?"

"It's not that *I don't like Paul.* I just think that you're getting to an age where you should really start thinking about settling down. You know, the main reason your father and I sent you and your sister to college was so that you could find a husband."

Cate nearly dropped her bread on the ground. "What? You sent me to college so I could find a husband?"

"Well, yeah." She said it as if she were stating the obvious.

Cate wanted to scream but felt a presence at the table. "Are you guys ready to order?" the waiter asked in a chipper tone.

Cate hoped that the mortification she felt hadn't been directed toward the waiter when she peered up at him. She tried to clear the grimace from her face while her mother ordered a chicken sandwich.

"I'll have the salmon sandwich," Cate said. "And can you bring me a gin martini—large. Thanks."

"You're having a drink?" Her mother asked disgustedly before the waiter had left.

"Yes. I *need* a drink."

When Cate returned home, she listened to her messages. "Catearita! I'm just calling from Boston to say hi. I hope everything is going well. Oh . . . uh, by the way . . . I won't be able to make it to the rehearsal dinner on Friday night, but I'll be at the wedding. Talk to you later. Adios."

Irritation burned her nerves. She had already RSVPed for him.

7

Rock Off

"Where's Paul?" Val asked, loud enough for the valet parkers outside Bernini's to hear. "I thought you said Paul was coming."

No one had seemed to notice his absence at the rehearsal, but now at the restaurant it was headline news.

Cate's mother chimed in. "You didn't tell them he wasn't coming? I thought you were going to call Jim's parents and cancel for him."

Everyone was watching. Her father, her sister Emily, brother-in-law Bradley, Val's fiancé, and five people she had never seen in her life all waited for an explanation.

"I did call. I talked to Jim's mom and explained that he was tied up in Boston and wouldn't be able to make it tonight."

"Well, is he coming to the wedding?" Val asked.

"Yes. He'll definitely be here tomorrow."

Val pulled Cate aside. "I'm so stressed right now," she whispered. "The bridesmaids' gifts came today, and they didn't turn out right."

"Is there anything I can do?" Cate asked.

"No."

"Hey, I'm so sorry about Paul. I hope it wasn't too much of an inconvenience."

"Of course not. Besides, we found out that Uncle Jack is bringing all four of his kids tonight, so we needed the extra space."

"I haven't seen him since his last divorce," Cate said.

"Can you believe that idiot cheated again?"

Cate was about to throw in her two cents on Uncle Jack's notorious infidelity, when Val squeezed her arm hard enough to break blood vessels. "Oh! Loni and Nikki just got here. I *have* to go say hi!" She bopped off.

A waiter came by with a tray. "May I offer you some bruschetta?" he asked.

"Thank you." She was reaching for a bruschetta when she heard a familiar voice over her shoulder.

"Well there she is!" Grandpa shouted before he released a raspy smoker's cough.

"Gran and Grandpa!"

She abandoned the bruschetta to hug them.

"It's good to see you, doll," Grandma said. "All you girls are just looking so great. How do you keep your figure so thin, sweetie?"

"You know me. I'm such a stress case. I'm always losing my appetite."

Her grandmother kissed her on the cheek. "What's to worry about when you're young and beautiful and free? Enjoy it while you can, doll."

Cate noticed they were the only people who hadn't asked where Paul was. She loved them.

"So what have you been up to this summer?" Grandpa asked.

"I've been—"

They were interrupted by the loudest screech from a child Cate had ever heard in her kindergarten teaching life. Uncle Jack had arrived.

Four squealing kids, all under the age of ten, followed him. He wore a look of desperation and seemed eager to pawn the kids off on Gran.

Cate noticed sweat dripping down his temple when she leaned in to hug him.

"Where's the bar?" he asked. Cate pointed over her shoulder. He was gone as quickly as he had come.

The youngest child, Madison, looked uncertain about whether she should follow her daddy or not. She clutched her Barbie doll and watched as her father headed for the bar. Cate noticed that her white sandals were on the wrong feet.

"Did you put your shoes on all by yourself, sweetie?" she asked.

Madison nodded, her big four-year-old eyes peering up at Cate.

"You did a good job buckling them. Why don't we try it again? Let's switch them around this time."

"Your shoes are on the wrong feet!" Travis, a cocky seven-year-old, shouted before he shot Madison square in the forehead with his shrieking toy gun.

Cate helped her switch the shoes. Then the little girl grabbed Cate's left hand and held on to it. She stayed by Cate's side while she sampled the bruschetta.

Cate looked down at her cousin. "Do you want something to drink, sweetie?"

She nodded.

"Apple juice?"

"Yes."

Cate was ordering an apple juice at the bar when she felt a hard stick ram into her right butt cheek. A blaring screech followed. She turned around in time to watch Travis, the little shit, run off, brandishing his toy weapon in the air. Within seconds he had chosen Val as his next victim, ramming his gun into her butt cheek, mocking the sound of a gunshot with his lips. Cate watched as Val jumped, startled, spilling her cocktail on her Via Spiga pump.

Cate looked around for Uncle Jack. Someone needed to control his pack of future convicts. He was already mingling with Val's sorority friends.

Fortunately, the butt-ramming spree was cut short when a waiter asked everyone to be seated.

It was assigned seating. Cate found her place at a table shared by her sister Emily and her husband Bradley. Two other couples joined their table. She was starting to miss Paul. Besides feeling strikingly single, she wanted him to be a part of family events. Paul was an important aspect of her life. Things felt incomplete when he couldn't share special occasions with her or meet her relatives.

She looked at the place card to her right. Joanna. She was the only bridesmaid who hadn't been in Vegas. Cate was glad there was another single person at her table. "Hi Joanna. I'm Cate." She extended her hand to the fellow bridesmaid.

"Hi. It's Jo-awn-a." She was a tiny girl with a large head and big, almond-shaped eyes that resembled those of a space creature.

"Oh. I'm sorry, Joawna. Well it's nice to meet you."

"You, too," she said before turning to the couple seated on her right, leaving Cate with a view of her neatly trimmed black bob.

Cate spent most of her meal leaning back, avoiding Joanna's arm. Her skinny forearm continuously shot over Cate's plate, showing off the four-carat diamond on her hand for everyone at the table. Cate imagined the stone becoming dislodged and falling into her pumpkin bisque soup.

"I wish you guys could've all met Cody," she said as her arm flew past Cate's face. The stone could've taken out an eye if it accidentally swiped her. "He has food poisoning and couldn't make it."

Cate turned to her. "So how long have you been engaged?"

"Eight months." She pulled her pink shawl around her shoulders. "I should go call Cody and see how he is doing." When she stood, Cate noticed that she wore open-toed heels that looked a size too large. Or maybe her toes were just hanging over the edge. There was a good inch of empty space at the heels.

The other three couples at the table began to reminisce about their weddings. Bored, Cate tuned out. Her eyes wandered over the room. Gran was trying to settle a screaming Madison. The other three kids were chasing one another around the table. Uncle Jack was engaged in conversation with Loni, who wasn't even supposed to be at his table, a Bud Light held loosely in his left hand. Her mother was in some kind of moral debate with family friends. Cate could tell by the way her eyebrows were puckered in disgust. Her father was leaning back, probably not listening to a word.

"I'll tell you exactly what is wrong with this generation," Connie said with conviction, slapping her palm against the table like a gavel. "What ruined this generation . . ." Her audience waited, including Cate. "Was the invention of the birth control pill. Before the birth control pill, people waited to have sex until they got married. Now men get sex whenever they want it, and there is no reason to get married. I know this because one of my own daughters is still wrapped up in that singles life."

What! Cate wasn't even on the pill. She and Paul used condoms, rather obsessively actually. And hadn't birth control been around for decades? What the hell was Connie talking about? She couldn't hear what the other people at the table had to say about Connie's theory and decided this was probably a good thing.

After Joanna returned, Val approached their table. She held two neatly wrapped packages. She handed one to each bridesmaid. "These are my gifts to you for being in my wedding."

"Thanks," Cate said. She had gotten a little silver mirror with her initials engraved on it when she was in Sarah's wedding. She wondered what Val had picked.

Val leaned close to Cate. "Yours got a little screwed up. I just wanted you to see what it was, but we can return it and have it fixed."

Cate ripped the wrapping paper open. Inside the white box was a little silver mirror with her initials. Uh . . . no. *Not* her initials engraved on it. Instead of CAP, for Catherine Agnes Padgett, it read CAT.

"Thanks, Val. Don't worry about it. I kind of like the cat engraving. It's just like my name except it's missing the *e*."

Val patted Cate on the back. "You're such a good sport."

Joanna gushed all over Val, thanking her for the mirror and telling her how honored she was to be a part of the wedding.

After Val left, Emily asked Joanna how her boyfriend had proposed.

Joanna became alive with animation. "It was the cutest thing ever! Cody is just so creative." She pressed her left palm against her chest.

"He took me to dinner at our favorite restaurant. I could tell something was up because he kept acting so nervous." Cate noticed that she used her left hand to make all kinds of wild gestures while she spoke. Any opportunity she had to wave her ring around was not wasted. "He got up to use the rest room at least three times. He is lactose intolerant and always has indigestion, so I thought maybe that was it, but then I noticed he was sweating, and I just knew he was going to do something special." She had a horrific overbite. "Anyway, we finished eating and nothing had happened, so I began to think that maybe I was wrong." She let out a hoot and her teeth hung grotesquely over her bottom lip. "Then he kept insisting that I order dessert. I don't really like sweets, but finally, I gave in and ordered. When the waiter brought out the plate, the ring was sitting next to the crème brûlée. He got down on one knee and everything."

Emily cocked her head to the left. "Ohhhhhh that is just the sweetest thing," she cooed.

"That's really neat," Bradley said.

"He hired photographers to take pictures while he was proposing," Joanna said. "I have them with me. Do you guys want to see?"

She passed the photos around the table, and Cate listened while everyone commented on how good-looking and creative Cody was.

Cate wanted to mention that she had seen the same exact method of proposal on at least two episodes of *A Wedding Story,* but decided against it.

When the pictures came to Cate, she noticed that Joanna was wearing the same large shoes. How weird. She could even see her long middle toe dangling over the edge of one sandal.

Cate was ready to mingle with other people. She listened to a few more minutes of Joanna ranting and raving about what a catch Cody was before she excused herself. Many of the other guests had left their tables and had begun to mingle as well.

She noticed her father ordering a drink at the bar and decided to join him. "Hey, sport," he said as he put his arm around Cate's shoulders. "Are you having fun?"

"Yeah, I guess. You know . . . it's kind of exhausting . . . all this."

He squeezed her shoulders tighter. "I'm real proud of you. You're a good girl, peanut. I'm glad you're not rushing into marriage. You have all the time in the world to find the right guy."

"Thanks, Dad," she said, resting her head on his shoulder. Her father always made her feel comfortable. He'd always been the one she'd consulted with when making tough career or financial decisions. He was an attorney, and lots of people appreciated his steady advice and wisdom. So, it wasn't long before they were interrupted by a distant cousin seeking legal expertise on a traffic collision.

She was ordering a gin and tonic when she heard her mother calling, "Cate! Cate! C'mere. Bradley and I have to tell you something." When Cate turned around, she noticed that they were carrying on as if something were absolutely hilarious.

"Bradley and I figured out why you aren't married, Cate," her mother said, holding on to a sparkling water.

Bradley grinned. They both looked like they had just solved a case on *Unsolved Mysteries.*

"Okay," Cate said, waiting for their theory.

"We decided you aren't married because you're high-maintenance." They looked at each other and burst into laughter. Then her mother's face grew solemn. "No, seriously. We decided that Emily is so easy-going and you are the high-maintenance one."

"Yeah," Bradley nodded. "Men don't want to marry women who are high-maintenance."

High-maintenance? Cate was finished with this conversation and was about to head back to the bar for a double when Joanna approached.

"Is this your mother, Cate?" she asked with her alien eyes and over-bite.

"Yes. This is my mother, Connie."

Joanna proffered her left hand. "It's so nice to meet you."

Her mother perked up. "Look at that ring. Are you recently engaged?"

"Yes, we're getting married in August." She held out her hand as if it were a pointed weapon.

"What a beautiful ring," Connie said, admiring every angle of the diamond.

They talked about wedding plans until one of Val's friends hollered, "Joanna, come here. I have to show someone your ring!"

She quickly excused herself.

Connie cocked her head to one side as if admiring a cute baby. "Aren't Val's friends nice?"

She was saved from answering by Jim's father.

He was tapping the side of a champagne glass with a fork. "If every-one could take their seats that would be great. Val and Jim's mothers have put together a video and would like to share it with all of you."

All the guests went back to their seats as a waiter wheeled in a tele-vision set. The lights went dim, and Jim's father popped in the video. The angelic voice of Enya filled the room as "Valerie and James: A Love Story" appeared on the screen. The video was a pictoral history of their lives, beginning with baby pictures of each one. It chronicled their lives through adolescence, showing pictures of them with friends, pets, and various family members.

There was even a picture of Val and Cate in their preteen days. Val, of course, resembled a teen model, while Cate sported braces and a zit the size of Joanna's diamond on her forehead. Everyone laughed, Joanna the loudest.

The music went from Enya to Frank Sinatra's "The Way You Look Tonight." Photos of Val and Jim on their first date were displayed. They really were an attractive couple.

Elvis Presley's, "Can't Help Falling in Love" filled the room while photos of Val and Jim doing just about every recreational activity except sex was featured. Swimming, hiking, snorkeling, horseback riding, skiing, snow boarding, and dancing were showcased. Their mutual love was obvious by the way they looked at each other or touched each other. They were natural and comfortable, their eyes exchanging adoring gazes.

Cate couldn't help but imagine what a *Paul and Cate* video would feature. It would kick off with a photo taken the night of their first kiss at Sarah and Miles's engagement party. The kiss had happened after he'd consumed an inordinate amount of vodka. She remembered coming out of Sarah's bathroom, surprised to find him lingering in the hallway, a sly smile on his face.

"Hi, Paul," she'd said.

Then he had grabbed her waist, pulled her close, and pressed a wet, rough kiss on her lips. She'd jerked away.

"What the hell are—"

But he drew her in again. They'd known each other for three years, and she'd always found him attractive. This time she kissed him back. He drove her home that night and asked her out for the following evening. But she had plans with Beth and declined. He called her three times over the following week; each time she'd had plans.

She had one picture of their first date. A Polaroid taken at Moon-doggies by a Smirnoff girl. They were wearing complimentary red-tinted sunglasses from Miss Smirnoff. After that, they began to spend a lot of time with each other.

"I Belong to You" by Lenny Kravitz would be the background music for the next stage. She had taken loads of pictures when they'd gone apple picking in Julian. Then there were all the candids she had taken of him doing various things such as surfing, packing for his trips, and reading the newspaper.

There was their trip to Santa Barbara and pictures of them at her sister's wedding.

The later stages of their relationship would be featured while "At Last" by Etta James played in the background. She wanted a video. Then it occurred to her that there weren't any pictures of the two of them since the fifth month of their relationship. Nearly five more months had passed since the last time they had taken pictures together. Was this because they hadn't spent as much time together, or because something had changed between the two of them? She thought about how much he'd pursued her in the beginning, and how gradually the courtship had worn off.

The worry that had started to creep up on her was scared away by loud applause. The last picture on Val and Jim's video was their official engagement photo. It had been taken on the beach. They were both barefoot, wearing matching khakis and navy blue sweaters.

"That was just darling." Cate could hear her mother over the applause. "What a great idea."

One of Uncle Jack's kids screamed, and a waiter came running with a towel.

Jim's father stood. "I would just like to make a little toast." He took a deep breath. "First of all I'd like to thank all of you for coming tonight. Each one of you means a great deal to us, and we're glad to be spending this special occasion with you." Cate had met them once. "We are so thrilled to have Val become part of our family and to have Val's family become part of our extended family. It takes a lot of courage these days to take the big step, and I'm really proud of Jim and Val for having the courage to get married." He raised his glass. "To Val and Jim."

Cate felt like interrupting, stopping them all from their toast, and explaining that it takes a little more than courage to tie the knot. As if she didn't have the courage to fall in love, to decorate a house with someone, to fold boxer shorts when she did the laundry, or to cook for two. Sometimes it takes a rock.

8 • We Are Family

When Cate's alarm went off at seven-thirty A.M., she knew it was going to be a long day. Hair and makeup. Photos. Ceremony. More photos. Reception. Weddings were a routine she was becoming well acquainted with.

Hair and makeup was scheduled for eight-thirty at Val's house. She arrived, on time, with her gown covered in plastic wrap and draped over her shoulder.

Dasha, the housekeeper, took the dress. "I vill hang up for you," she said, placing it next to nine other dresses in the hall closet. "The other girls are in the kitchen."

Val's Italian greyhound, Gino, came racing over. He wore a little bow tie around his neck that read: *Groom.* Cate was leaning over the dog for a closer look at his festive attire when he lifted his leg and peed on the marble tiles right next to her Adidas.

Dasha threw her hands in the air and said something in Russian. Gino took off running.

"Do you need some help cleaning that up?" Cate asked.

"No. Go on." She motioned toward the kitchen. "Don't vorry. I'll clean up. I alvays do." She was already pulling a bottle of cleaning solution from her apron.

"Make sure you get plenty to eat," Aunt Margie said as Cate entered the kitchen. "I don't want any of you girls fainting. We have a long day."

Cate looked at the catered assortment of deli sandwiches, muffins, Brie, crackers, and bottles of champagne that were spread across the kitchen table.

Val sat in the corner, her feet propped up, while a woman painted her toes. A hairdresser stood behind her, pinning and combing her long hair into an elaborate up-do.

"Hi Cate! Grab a seat anywhere," she said. There were salon-style chairs in the kitchen. "Marcela is going to do your hair and makeup. And Ron and Cindy are going to do your toes and fingernails."

Cate noticed Uncle Jack talking to Loni in the corner.

"What's he doing here?" she whispered.

Val rolled her eyes. "He claims that Madison needs him. He says she's nervous about being a flower girl."

Cate looked at Madison. The child was giggling while Nikki demonstrated how to walk down the aisle. Cate wondered where the other kids were and who was watching them.

She took a seat next to Val and tried to forget about her loser uncle.

For three hours, a team of beauticians assaulted Cate.

Marcela put her bob in hot rollers to create soft curls around her face for a glamorous look. After that, she applied twice as much makeup as Cate normally wore. Val insisted that a lot of makeup looked better in pictures. Cate wasn't used to her fake face but thought it looked all right.

While Ron was applying a second coat of *pearl blush* to Cate's nails, Val leaned toward her.

"So, have you talked to Paul yet? He's still coming, right?" she asked.

"I haven't talked to him, but I called him this morning." She had left a message with directions and the exact time of the wedding on his cell phone.

"Does he know where to go?" Aunt Margie asked, her hair in rollers.

"I think so."

Now Cate was debating whether she should leave a message on his home phone, too. What if he didn't get his cell phone message? She remembered her mother and Bradley. Was she being high-maintenance? A high-maintenance girlfriend would call twice. She decided to wait and see if he called first. She'd give him until two. If she hadn't heard from him by then, she would call.

"Oh shit!" Val exclaimed.

"Valerie!" Aunt Margie said. "That's no way for a bride to talk."

"I wanted to give all the bridesmaids disposable cameras, and I forgot to get them yesterday."

Since Cate was finished with her makeover, she offered to run to Sav-On for some cameras.

"Would you mind?" Val asked.

"Not at all."

On the way to Sav-On, she checked her messages. Still no word from Paul. Maybe she should leave that second message. If Paul flaked, it would not only be disappointing but embarrassing as well. She felt a sudden sense of pressure. Val wanted to meet him. She could hear her mother's voice describing how socially rude and unacceptable it would be if he canceled. Even Uncle Jack had asked about him. They were all expecting him. What would everyone think if he didn't show up?

Dressed in jean shorts and a button-down top, she felt a little self-conscious walking through Sav-On with her hair and makeup done as if she were going to the Oscars. She sensed eyes following her through the store. She quickly purchased eleven cameras—one for Val, too—then headed back to bridal headquarters.

Photo mania went by surprisingly fast. The photographer was a lively Frenchman, ironically named Paul, who told continuous jokes. He kept the whole bridal party entertained and relaxed while he swept through a quick session of photos on Val's sprawling green lawn.

She took the coincidental name thing as a sign and decided to call Paul. She left a brief message, reiterating the time and directions for the wedding on his home phone.

By two-thirty they were riding in a stretch limo to Saint Gregory's. Fifteen people, including Val's parents and Uncle Jack, were stuffed in the vehicle. The scent of the gardenias in their bouquets and Val's perfume filled the limo. It was stuffy, and Cate thought she was going to pass out from heat exhaustion.

The lavender gown she wore was the best bridesmaid's dress she had ever worn. It was also the most uncomfortable. The floor-length dress was formfitting and sleeveless, with a plunging neckline. An intricate row of fifty tiny buttons traced its way up her spine. The buttons made the dress tight, and at moments Cate found it difficult to take deep breaths. She felt as if she wearing a straitjacket. The unbearable heat combined with the tight gown made her feel as if she were going to die of suffocation. Thank God Val demanded that the chauffeur turn up the air.

When the limo pulled into Saint Gregory's she scanned the parking lot for Paul's Mercedes. She didn't see the black luxury car anywhere. Perhaps he'd parked on the street. She peeled her gown from the back of her thighs as she stepped from the limousine.

Val was paranoid that Jim was going to catch an accidental glimpse of her and immediately sought shelter in the church vestibule, her posse of bridesmaids dutifully following behind.

Cate tried to steal a glance into the church. The chapel was decorated with rare breeds of lavender and white roses with orchids and greenery to match the bridesmaids' gowns. She could see Aunt Margie and Jim's mom lighting the unity candle. No sign of Paul.

It was nearly show time, and Cate felt as though she were more nervous than Val. Her cousin was quiet and collected in her strapless gown. She looked like a princess with diamonds sparkling around her neck and on her ears.

Cate's stomach pinched her insides with anxiety, and she feared she would need to run to the bathroom to relieve herself.

She was about to make a dash for the ladies' room when the wedding coordinator grabbed her by the elbow and thrust her into the single-file line of bridesmaids. "Remember to walk *slowly* down the aisle," she whispered gruffly in her ear. Garlic breath covered Cate's face. "If you think you're walking slow, you're probably not walking slow enough. Don't forget to wait for my cue. I'll tell you when to go." Cate wished she wouldn't whisper. The scent of garlic was making her stomach worse. "And don't forget to smile." She said this to everyone.

Nikki went down the aisle first. Mandy followed. Then Loni. Chrissy. Cate waited for the coordinator's cue before she shot from the vestibule. Her eyes darted across the guests on the bride's side. She noticed several of Val's friends who had been in Las Vegas. She saw Uncle Jack and his pack of brats that weren't in the wedding. One of them was scribbling with a crayon on the pages of a church Bible. A sea of faces she didn't recognize covered the chapel. She made eye contact with her mother. "Slow down!" she mouthed. Cate tried to maintain her Miss America smile. Then she saw him, seated to her mother's left. He was smiling at her.

She looked away from Paul just as she reached the altar, nearly smashing into Chrissy's back.

"You're already here?" Chrissy whispered. "I thought *I* was walking fast."

The reception followed at Val's country club in Rancho Santa Fe. Paul was waiting in front of the club when Cate arrived.

"You look beautiful," he said as he pulled her into his arms.

Val cut in between them. "Is this Paul?" she asked.

"Yes."

"Hi. I'm Val." She gave his hand a firm squeeze, then looked at Cate. "He's hot," she said, right in front of him.

Paul laughed. "Thank you. And thank you for inviting me to your beautiful wedding. I'm very glad to be here."

"I like him!" Val beamed before hopping off to the next social circle.

Cate and Paul sat next to each other at the head table. As she looked around the reception, she decided she didn't want a lavish wedding. Val and Jim barely had time to eat. And ever since their first dance with each other she hadn't seen the two of them together. It had all seemed so chaotic, worrying that flowers were in place, meeting people they'd never met before on the day of their wedding, following a time schedule from ceremony to meal to toasts to garter toss, etc. Cate wanted a simple wedding. She would have one bridesmaid, her best friend Beth. Paul could have his brother as the groomsman. They would only invite family and very close friends. No veil. No grand entrance and garter toss. It would be intimate. Weddings had this effect on her. They created the kind of atmosphere where fantasies thrived, especially for those who were single. She couldn't help but wonder what it would be like to be the bride.

She was starting to wonder if Paul ever imagined what their wedding would be like when the waiters began serving the entrées. She looked at the thick, juicy cut of filet mignon resting on a bed of asparagus and remembered the plans she had made with Ethan to photograph his food. They planned to meet at his office the following week. She noticed how the peppered yellow sauce brightened the darker meat and vegetables and the way the potatoes were cut in the shape of flowers. She'd never photographed food before. Now she realized there wasn't going to be much to her job. The food would speak for itself. If it was prepared well, it was going to look good in pictures.

After the meal, two waiters wheeled in a large white projection screen. They were going to show the Val and Jim video again, for the two hundred guests who hadn't attended the rehearsal dinner.

The lights went dim. For the second time Cate listened as Enya filled the room and watched as pictures of Val and Jim were displayed.

"Whoa!" A raucous male voice came from behind Cate's table. "Look at Val and Jim when they were young. That is a trip! Val was a little fatty when she was a baby!"

She looked over her shoulder to find out who the loud voice belonged to, but it was too dark. All she could see were outlines and shadows of heads.

"Hey! That's Val and Jim on horses. Ha! Look at them." His voice became a bad imitation of a Southern drawl. "Hi-ho Silver! Howdy! Ride 'em cowboy!"

"Shhhh!" Someone said.

Heads from all the tables in front of her were starting to turn. They all wanted to identify the drunken idiot.

"Ha! Ha! That's funny!" the unidentified voice continued. "Jim and Val as Sonny and Cher on Halloween. Look at them! *'I got you babe,'* " he sang out of tune.

"Be quiet," someone hissed.

"Look at them dancccing! Cut a rug! Whew!"

"Shut up!" someone snapped.

If it wasn't so dark, she could've pinpointed who the wedding drunk was.

"Val looks hot in a bikini! Yeaaaah, *Sports Illustrated* swimsuit model!" he yelled.

After he narrated three more pictures, there was a brief exchange of gruff whispering from behind Cate. She couldn't make out a word that was said, but the drunk was silent for the rest of the video.

When the lights came on again, she looked over her shoulder, hoping to see his face. People had already resumed mingling, and it was hard to tell who had been sitting at the table behind her. However, she felt confident that the wedding drunk would surface again at some point. He'd definitely be back.

She and Paul headed to the bar for fresh cocktails. On the way she introduced him to a few of Val's friends who had been in Las Vegas, and to Uncle Jack.

"It's a pleasure to meet you, Jack," Paul said as he gave his hand a firm squeeze. "Cate tells me you've traveled all the way from Connecticut."

"Yeah. Made the long haul with all the kids."

"I was just in Connecticut on business last month."

Paul always found something in common with everyone whom he met. Paul and Uncle Jack exchanged small talk about Connecticut.

She was watching her grandfather teach Madison dance moves that were popular in his time when, out of nowhere, a man with red hair as coarse and thick as steel wool came cartwheeling onto the dance floor. He was wearing a suit, but his tie had been loosened and his shirt stuck out from underneath the back of the jacket. The crowd on the dance floor abruptly parted. People ran in all directions to avoid being hit by the cartwheeling maniac. *Wedding drunk alert!*

After his fifth cartwheel, he landed outside the dance floor. She heard Val scream when he sprang to his feet. "The cake. *Watch ouuuuuut!*"

Apparently he didn't hear the warning, because his next flip landed within a millimeter of the table that showcased Val and Jim's five-tiered cake. He raised his arms over his head in triumph, like an Olympic gymnast. "Five-point-oh!" he yelled.

Cate recognized his voice as the drunken narrator of Val and Jim's wedding video.

"Cody!" Joanna shot across the dance floor like a bullet. *"Co-dy!"* She grabbed him by the arm as if he were a child, only she'd been too rough. In a fleeting, grotesque moment he lost his balance. He grasped for her hand. His fingers and palms becoming tight fists as he squeezed air. Backward he stumbled; down came the beautiful cake.

Well, this will be a great story over brunch tomorrow, Cate thought.

The music came to a screeching halt. Waiters ran from all directions, like secret service agents on full alert for drama.

Cate could hear Val crying. "It's okay. I'll buy you a new cake while we're in the Caribbean," Jim said.

They watched for a moment while two waiters escorted Cody from the reception. Joanna trailed behind.

"Damn. That cake looked good, too," Uncle Jack said.

So that was Joanna's catch. That was the romantic crème brûlée ring bearer? A redheaded drunk who couldn't even produce a stable backflip. A wedding wrecker.

"We don't get any cake?" A tiny voice came from beneath Cate. It was Madison, still clutching her Barbie.

"No." Cate shook her head. "There won't be any cake."

Madison began to cry, too. Cate and Connie consoled the crying child. Connie led her to a table and sat Madison in her lap, rubbing her back. Soon she had stopped crying, and Cate watched as her mother bobbed Madison on her knee, playing carnival ride with her. Cate remembered how much she used to love playing that with her mother.

A few minutes later, Val's dad was on the microphone. "Please, everyone. Continue to celebrate this occasion with us. There's still plenty more dancing to be done. Let's enjoy the night." He nodded at the band.

A drumroll sounded before they began to play "Celebration." Uncle Jack was the first to resume partying. And eventually the dance floor sprang to life again.

"Do you want to take a walk on the beach?" Paul asked. "Get some fresh air?"

"That sounds great." She was dying for some alone time with him.

"Let me just use the rest room first."

Cate waited for Paul in the lobby. She felt a sense of relief that Val's wedding was coming to a close. She'd have more free time to spend with Paul and one less wedding to stress about. She was standing alone when her grandmother approached. Gran looked worried, desperate.

"Oh Cate. Thank God I found someone." She squeezed Cate's arm as she led her to a bench in the corner of the lobby. Her grandfather sat, hunched over. His eyes were glassy, wandering slits. "Your grandfather has had too much to drink. He needs to go back to the hotel. Can you please go get your Uncle Jack? He drove us here." She started to cry. "Oh Cate. He didn't mean to do this. I'm so disappointed that he'll miss most of the night."

Cate put her arm around her shoulders. "Don't worry, Gran. Everything will be fine. I'll go get Uncle Jack."

She found Uncle Jack in the middle of Val's sorority, dancing to "Bust a Move" as if he belonged on *Soul Train*.

She tapped him on the shoulder. "Uncle Jack!" She had to yell over the music. He spun around, clapping his hands, bouncing on his feet.

"Grandpa's not feeling well!" She yelled. "He's had too much to drink. He needs a ride back to the hotel."

His palms slapped together as he hopped from side to side. Maybe he hadn't heard her. "Grandma and Grandpa need a ride back to your hotel!"

He rolled his eyes. "After this song," he said irritably before he shimmied back to the group of girls. He tossed his head back while one of Val's friends ground her pelvis up against his thigh. Another girl latched on to his other thigh, and Cate thought she actually heard Uncle Jack groan.

"I didn't know your uncle was a millionaire! And a former secret service agent for George Bush Senior!" Nikki yelled as she twirled past Cate and into Uncle Jack's lair.

"Are you kidding?" Cate yelled, but Nikki didn't hear.

Then it occurred to Cate that her very own uncle—her kin—was the freaky relative. And he was the worst kind of freak. What was so unsettling about Uncle Jack was that from the outside he looked normal. He was charming and attractive. But on the inside he was a selfish, horny, middle-aged loser who cared more about getting laid than taking care of his own parents, and his children for that matter.

She felt like announcing to Val's friends that he had just been through his third divorce and had spent a significant amount of time in a drug and alcohol rehabilitation center. He wasn't a millionaire. He sold cell phones. Secret service agent? With all of his drug abuse in the past he couldn't even get a job as a security guard. Then she noticed that there was something stuck to the back of his shoe: toilet paper, a long piece. She left him busting moves, a strip of toilet paper trailing from his penny loafer.

She hurried back to the lobby. "Paul!" She nearly crashed into him.

"Where were you?" he asked. She told him about her grandfather and Uncle Jack.

"Well, I have my car," he said. "Why don't we just give them a ride back to their hotel?"

"Do you mind?"

"No." He put his arms around her and kissed her on the forehead.

Cate and Gran helped Grandpa to the front of the hotel while Paul got the car. He pulled up in the driveway in his Mercedes and helped buckle Grandpa in the backseat. Gran wept the whole way back to the hotel.

"It's okay, Gran," Cate said. "Val and Jim are leaving soon for the airport anyway, and then the wedding will be over."

Paul pulled into the valet parking area at their hotel. He helped Grandpa from the backseat.

"Thanks so much for helping us," her grandmother said as they walked them to the room. "Paul, you are a doll."

"Don't worry about it," he said. "It's not a problem at all."

"You're a lucky girl," Gran told Cate. "This guy is a keeper."

Cate put her arm around him. "I think so, too." They both hugged Gran good-bye.

"Adios!" Paul said as they left.

"Adios, amigo," Gran called back.

They headed back to the reception. Cate was exhausted. She wanted more than anything to go back to Paul's house, slide into his cool sheets, and snuggle with him for the rest of the night, but they had to at least say good-bye.

Paul put his hand on her knee. "I've missed you," he said.

"Me, too. When do you leave again?"

"Next week."

"Where?"

"Maui. For three weeks." He glanced at her as if he were apologizing.

She was disappointed, but it wasn't odd for his trips to be long. The last time he went to Colorado he was gone for three weeks because he had to go to five different ski resorts. She could feel the warmth from his palm on her knee.

"Are you all right?" he asked when they pulled into the parking lot.

She nodded. "Just tired. Really tired."

Queen Leslie's Wedding

9 • Dollar Signs

Monday morning Cate checked her E-mail. She had one new message.

DATE: Monday, July 19
SUBJECT: Bridal fitting.

Hi girls! As you all know today is the bridal fitting. I know I already gave most of you directions to The Bridal Chateau but I just wanted to send them again in case some of you forgot.

Cate skipped over the directions.

Anyway, we're meeting at noon and you will need to bring some form of payment with you. You must pay for the outfit promptly after they take your measurements. Thanks so much girls. I am so thrilled to have all of you participate in this special occasion.

Love,

Leslie

Outfits? Cate imagined all the bridesmaids in denim skirts with matching sweater sets and heels.

Cate printed out the directions, even though she already had a sense of how to get there. She put the directions as well as a map to Ethan Blakely's catering business in her purse. She had plans to meet with him later that afternoon.

Cate was the first bridesmaid to arrive at The Bridal Chateau. Despite the fact that she had been in several weddings, she'd never actually seen the inside of a bridal shop. All of the other dresses she'd never wear again had been purchased via phone orders. She would relay her measurements to whoever took the order. Then, months later, the gown usually arrived through the mail, grossly off the measurements she had given, and in dire need of alterations.

The Bridal Chateau was more like a warehouse than a bridal boutique. Assortments of veils and gloves covered the walls. Racks filled with bridal gowns and bridesmaid's dresses lined the building. Cate noticed the princess-cut peach gown she wore in her sister's wedding on one rack.

While browsing through the dresses, she imagined which one she would pick if she were the bride. Except for a few gowns, most of the dresses looked the same to her. Some of them varied with beadwork or straps, but they all seemed to be cut from the same pattern. She couldn't imagine herself wearing a traditional gown. She wondered if they even made dresses like the one she had in mind. Simple, elegant, sexy, formfitting. No hoops, or poofs, or beads.

"There she is. Have you been waiting for a while?" Leslie asked as she approached Cate with her sister, Bethany, in tow. As usual, Leslie looked crisp and clean. She always looked put together, as if she were a very mature paper doll. She wore a white button-down blouse, each sleeve evenly rolled to the middle of her forearm, and khaki pants that looked as if she had ironed them only minutes earlier. A navy blue sweater was tied over her shoulders, and she held the handles of a box-shaped Kate Spade handbag. Not a hair of her perfectly trimmed brown bob was out of place, and her evenly distributed blonde highlights showed no roots.

"No. I haven't been waiting long. I've just been looking around."

"Good. Let me show you my dress while we're waiting for the other girls to get here." She led them to a rack in the center of the store, pushed a dozen dresses aside, and pulled one from the rack. It was an ivory dress made of the most elegant smooth satin Cate had ever seen in her life. It had a tight bodice, a deep V neck, and a long train attached.

"It's beautiful," Cate said.

"You should see it on," Bethany said. "She looks gorgeous in it."

A saleswoman approached. "Would you like to try that on?" she asked.

"I already bought this dress. I was just showing my bridesmaids what it looks like."

"Well, you're welcome to try it on so they can see, if you'd like."

Leslie shrugged. "I may as well, since we're waiting for the other girls. Also, they're here to be fitted for their outfits. So we'll need the seamstress to take their measurements. I'd like them to try them on though, just so I can see what the color is going to look like before we place the order."

"No problem. I'll go get the seamstress." She took Leslie's name and order number before she left.

"So, we're wearing outfits?" Cate asked as they walked to the fitting room.

Bethany trailed behind them, admiring some of the gowns.

"You know my sister and my cousin Veronica are a little on the heavy side," she whispered. "They were feeling self-conscious about wearing a gown, so we were looking around and we found these pantsuits. They're really dressy, and they're cute."

Pantsuits could be comfortable, Cate thought as she took a seat outside Leslie's dressing room. While she was waiting, Veronica and Sarah arrived. Cate hadn't seen Sarah since her wedding and gave her a hug.

They were talking about Sarah's Hawaiian honeymoon when Leslie came out of the dressing room.

"Wow. It's absolutely gorgeous," Cate said.

"Stunning," Sarah added.

"Who needs the fitting?" the seamstress asked.

Leslie pointed to her bridesmaids. "They all need to be fitted."

"I see," the seamstress said. She couldn't have been taller than five feet. Weighed probably one sixty. Was losing hair and had no business wearing shorts. Her legs were like two blocks of blue cheese: chunky, white, and textured with cellulite and blue threads of varicose veins. The way her glasses dug into the sides of her bulbous nose seemed painful. It looked as if the frames were cutting off the circulation in her face. She wore a name tag that read Offra.

She held up a pair of royal-blue silk pants with a matching top. The top had short sleeves, a high neckline, and zipped up the back. "Is this it?" she asked Leslie.

Sarah threw Cate a worried look. Cate prayed there had been a mistake.

"Yes, that's it," Leslie said.

"All right who wants to go first?" Offra asked.

Cate volunteered. Maybe silk pantsuits were making a comeback. And she didn't want to be late to Ethan's.

"That way." Offra pointed to a dressing room.

Cate began to close the door when Offra's fat hand shot in between the doorframe. She had yellow nails.

"Don't close the door yet. I need to take your measurements

FIRST." She spoke loudly. "Then you can try on the outfit. You just want to see what it looks like. Right?"

"Yeah, I just wanted to see how the color looked on the girls," Leslie said.

"Well, I take the measurements FIRST. I don't have time to sit around all day while you girls look at the color. I have fifteen weddings I need to prepare dresses for; one of them I have to FedEx the gowns to Maui."

Cate noticed that ever since Paul had left for Maui, she had heard the island's name more frequently. Everywhere she went: Maui. Every time she turned on the television someone was talking about Maui. She wondered if it was a sign.

"Well, can the girls still try the outfits on?" Leslie asked.

"Yes! *After* I take the measurements."

The seamstress's eyes settled on Cate, blazing from beneath her thick glasses. "Lift your arms."

Cate raised her arms. Abruptly, Offra wrapped a measuring tape around her chest. "You're definitely going to need alterations in the bust," she said. "Thirty. You'll be swimming in that top."

Now that the entire bridal shop knew that Cate had no boobs, she wondered if Offra would suggest a nose job as well. It was no secret that Cate was as flat as a countertop, but it stabbed her ego to hear someone else point it out.

Years ago she'd actually looked into implants. After minimal research, the idea of a scalpel cutting her nipple open like the top of a teakettle to insert something foreign into her breast made her gag. Instead of feeling confident, she'd end up shuddering every time she looked at the fake boobs. Furthermore, if she was going to enhance her chest, she may as well have a plastic surgeon break and reshape the beak she'd inherited from her father. Or what about her thin lips? She'd never be perfect, and she'd learned to accept her desertlike chest as well as everything else she'd been born with.

Cate sneezed, and Offra told her to hold still. As if she could help it. Maybe she was allergic to Offra.

"Next!" she hollered as she unwrapped the measuring tape from Cate's hips. Cautiously, Veronica stepped forward as if she were next in line for a prison hose down.

She wrapped the tape around Veronica's chest, then made a mark on her clipboard. "You'll be needing a size twenty."

"A twenty? But I'm a ten," Veronica said.

"Well, you have a big back, and these suits run small."

Cate sneezed again.

"Next!"

Hesitantly, Bethany moved closer to Offra. "We'll probably have to special-order for you," she said. "You're going to have a hard time with that seam in the back. With your hips it might ride up your butt."

"Well, I plan on losing ten pounds before the wedding," Bethany said.

Offra snorted. "I've heard that one before."

Bethany's lip quivered, and she clenched her jaw as tears pooled in her eyes.

Cate fantasized about telling Offra to fuck off. She imagined Offra being fired in front of everyone, her glasses becoming steamed as she cried her way out of the tulle-covered hellhole. This was intolerable. Cate was fuming, brainstorming ways to retaliate. Then she looked at Offra's legs, veiny and blue. Cate noticed Leslie staring at them, too.

"Oh wow, Offra!" Leslie said in her sweetest, kindest voice. "What happened? Are you all right? That looks painful."

"What do you mean?" she asked.

Everyone was listening.

"Your legs." Leslie pointed. "They're all bruised. Are you okay?"

Offra's eyes darted to Leslie, then back to her measuring tape on Bethany's hips. "They're from having babies," she said under her breath.

Someone had actually fucked her?

"What?" Leslie asked, cocking her head to the side, expressing mock concern. "I couldn't hear you."

"They're veins. They're not bruises. It's from being pregnant."

"Ohhhhhh. I see," Leslie said. She looked at Cate from the corner of her eye, a smirk forming on her face.

Offra didn't say much after that.

The saleslady returned and took the order, complete with all the measurements. "You know there is also a belt that goes with the outfit. It's optional. But the tops tend to run a little large so you can tie the belt like a sash around the waist. Would you guys like to see?"

Please. No sash.

"Sure," Leslie said. "Cate, why don't you try on the sample suit since you're the smallest. I think it will fit you."

"I'll go get the belt," the saleslady said.

The pants dragged on the carpet when Cate came out of the dressing room, and she hated to admit it, but Offra had been right. She really didn't have the bust to fill in the top.

Making them wear pantsuits that would've been a hit in 1982 while Leslie wore a timeless, elegant gown seemed unfair. It also seemed very Leslie-ish.

Cate thought of all the photos that Leslie had chosen to frame and hang on her walls. In each one Leslie looked her best, radiating with a ready-for-the-camera smile, not a blemish showing, not a hair out of place, and sporting the latest trend. However, all of her framed photos had captured her friends on bad hair days in the middle of winter after they'd just woken up or were on a verge of starting a diet. In one photo on Leslie's mantel Cate actually had her eyes closed. She remembered pointing out that detail to Leslie.

"Ha! I didn't even notice when I framed the photo."

Yeah, just like she hadn't noticed Sarah's three chins or Bethany's puckered face captured in midsentence. Of course she hadn't noticed. She'd been too busy looking at herself!

Cate sensed that she definitely wasn't going to be outshined on her wedding day.

The saleslady was shaking her head when she returned. "I'm sorry, but unfortunately I think we've lost the sample belt."

Yes! No belt.

"But I can describe to you what it will look like. It's thin, the same color as the outfit, and it ties around the waist. It goes over the blouse, so it makes the suit look a little more formfitting, a little more hip." Cate imagined them all walking off the set of *Three's Company*.

"Hmmm." Leslie thought about it while she looked at Cate in the suit. Then she nodded. "Yeah, go ahead and order the belts."

The saleslady penciled something on her order form.

After Leslie complained about Offra's behavior to the saleslady, she headed to a dressing room. Cate was also about to change clothes when the saleslady looked up at the bridesmaids. "Bridesmaids, are you all planning on paying in full today?"

"We don't have to pay for the whole thing today? Right?" Bethany asked.

"No. You can put down a deposit of two hundred dollars and pay for the rest later if you'd like."

"A two hundred dollar deposit?" Sarah asked. "How much is the suit?"

"The top is one twenty, and the bottom is two thirty-five so . . ." She pulled a small calculator from her pocket and punched in several numbers. "You're looking at about three fifty-five—without tax."

Three fifty-five for a freaking disco suit. The millennium had passed, for God's sake!

"Oh and I forgot the belt! So that will add another forty."

Cate had spent the past two years trying to get out of the credit card debt she had incurred in college. Today, she was plunging, head-first, right back into it. She was going to have to put in a few days of work at Beth's bead store to make extra money this summer. Ethan had also mentioned that he was planning on paying her. She'd figure out a way to pay the suit off. She paid in full. What difference did it make? She couldn't afford the damn thing anyway.

Cate hated being late. The thought of leaving someone waiting panicked her. It made her feel like an unreliable flake. Ethan might be worried, wondering if she had been in a car wreck or forgotten about him. She couldn't stand the thought of anyone waiting for her, pegging her as inconsiderate. With Offra and the disco pants, everything at The Bridal Chateau had taken much longer than she had anticipated. The manager had asked them to fill out a formal complaint about the seamstress. Cate had gotten a little carried away, writing a very detailed account of Fuck Offra's behavior, citing specific examples and quotes.

She arrived at the catering business twenty minutes late. Her cheeks were pink, and she was sweating.

All the windows and doors in his office were open, and a ceiling fan spun on turbo. The swift blasts of air felt refreshing. Ethan sat behind a desk talking on the phone.

He waved. "Have a seat."

She took a chair across from him and set her camera bag on the floor.

He wrote something on a piece of paper and passed it to her from across his desk: *"Sorry. It's the nightmare client of the summer on the phone. It's good to see you."*

She wrote back, *"No worries. I'm late anyway!"* She noticed his unshaven face again and couldn't get over the idea that Ethan Blakely could grow facial hair. In high school, he'd been a late bloomer. He'd been skinny and had always worn baggy clothes to hide his small frame.

He used to do his own laundry. Occasionally he'd accidentally throw in a red shirt with the whites, ending up with pink socks. Never stopped him from wearing them though. Or, for no explanation, some of his darks would come out with random little bleach spots. Instead of letting the cleaning lady use his black pants or shirts as rags, he'd take a marker and just color in the dots, wearing the clothes as if they were as good as new.

She wondered if he'd lost his virginity yet. Of course he had. He must've by now. Ethan and Cate seemed to be the only two teenagers at La Jolla High that had been immune to the plague of sexual obsession that had struck their classmates. Cate listened to all of her friends describe their deflowering, but she simply wasn't interested in any of the horny idiots in her grade. She was saving it for someone who mattered—like Robert Smith of The Cure. And while all the guys their age were out screwing, breaking hearts, and tallying up the number of girls they had bedded, Ethan had been more interested in building a fishing canoe and surfing. Besides, he had looked twelve when he was sixteen and would've had one hell of time trying to find a girl who would give it up for him anyway.

He took a deep breath after he hung up the phone and shook his head. "Sorry about that. This lady calls me every day about her husband's retirement party."

"High-maintenance?" Cate asked.

"High-maintenance isn't the description for her. That's being too nice." He smiled at Cate. "Anyway, it's good to see you. Why don't I show you what I have in mind? I've collected some brochures from other catering businesses, so you can kind of get an idea of what we're looking for."

For several minutes, they went over brochures of food. A tall blond guy wearing swim trunks, a T-shirt, and flip-flops entered the office. "What's up?" he said.

"Cate, this is my partner, Sean," Ethan said. "Sean, this is Cate. She's going to be taking the pictures for us."

He shook Cate's hand. "Cool. I'll go set up the stuff."

"We've already prepared all the entrées we'd like you to photograph."
They went over some ideas for photos.

"Now, as far as payment goes." His blue eyes settled on her when he spoke. "I wasn't really sure how much something like this costs, and you mentioned that you've never done anything like this before, so I called around just to compare."

She really hated discussing money with friends, but after spending nearly four hundred dollars on an outfit she would only wear once, she could really use the cash.

"How does seven hundred sound?" he asked.

Seven hundred! She had hoped for two hundred. She felt a flickering moment of greed, part of her wanting to yell, "Deal!"

Then she shook her head. "I can't take that much money from you. It will probably only cost me about two hundred for film and development with enlargements and everything."

"Well, consider the rest compensation for your time and labor."

"That's a lot, Ethan. I can't take it."

"Okay six hundred and fifty."

"Ethan! That's still a lot. I can't."

Eventually, they settled on four hundred fifty. Cate felt relieved that she would have the money to pay off the dress. On the other hand, she would've loved to have bought herself something she could've really used, or taken the wagon in to get fixed.

Ethan led her to the gigantic kitchen in the back of the building.

Dozens of side dishes, entrées, and desserts had been arranged over a burgundy tablecloth. Her stomach growled as she looked at the cuisine, tempted to shove a stuffed mushroom into her mouth while his back was turned.

She took a few different pictures of each dish, adjusting the lighting and trying different angles. She'd never had a professional photo assignment before and hoped she was doing a good job. She felt nervous.

The food looked delicious. The appetizers varied from crab pot stickers to Mediterranean bruschetta topped with feta cheese. Main courses included pesto swordfish and filet mignon stuffed with bacon and shrimp. She was dying to dig into the chocolate lava cake and apple crisp. After three rolls of film, she was finished.

"You hungry?" Ethan asked.

"I haven't eaten anything all day."

He pulled two forks from a drawer. "Let me just heat some of these things up, and then we can grind."

Cate stuffed herself with pot stickers and bruschetta. Then they shared the pesto-covered swordfish. She was stuffed by the time he offered her a piece of chocolate lava cake, but ate it anyway. After they were finished with dessert, she knew her breath reeked of garlic from the other food. But she didn't care. It was just Ethan. Hanging out with him still made her feel at ease. He was like Jill or Beth. She could let loose, be herself in front of him. During the summers of their youth they used to camp on the beach. She would sleep next to Ethan, waking up with crusty rings of sand on her face and streaks of mascara bleeding from her eyes. It always seemed natural. If she had been sleeping next to any other guy, she would've slipped away at the crack of dawn to wash her face and reapply makeup.

"What are you doing tonight?" he asked, clearing the dishes.

Beading? Talking on the phone? "I don't really have any plans."

"Sean and I and some other guys are going to The Casbah. My friend's band, King Mother, is playing. You should come. Bring some friends."

"All right," she said. They made arrangements to meet at The Casbah at nine.

10 •   King Mother

"I can't believe we're hanging out with Ethan Blakely," Beth said after she took a sip of her Jack and Coke. She pushed a stray wisp of her waist-length, jet-black hair behind her ear. Although Beth came from an Irish American background, people often assumed she had more exotic roots. She had olive-colored skin and dark, deep eyes that resembled those of a Spanish vixen. She really was a knockout, and Cate often felt like a pale little creature next to her. "Does Ethan still have a crush on you?" Beth asked.

"What? No! He never did," Cate said.

"Yes he did! Whenever you were grounded, he used to spend hours talking on the phone with you. He never did that for me when I was grounded."

"I don't know what you're talking about. Besides, I was grounded all the time. It was the only way anyone could talk to me.

"Who had a crush on Cate?" Jill asked, rejoining them with a fresh cocktail.

"Ethan," Beth said.

Jill raised an eyebrow. "Really? You never mentioned that. Does this mean that Paulo's next trip might be to Splitsville?"

Jill and Beth laughed.

Cate gave them both a look. "No."

Earlier she had persuaded Beth, Beth's fiancé Ike, and Jill to go to The Casbah with her. Now she wished she had swung it solo. All this talk of Paul and Ethan. Please. She was devoted to her boyfriend, and Ethan Blakely was practically a distant relative. Their comments were getting on her nerves.

"What's going on with Paulo anyway?" Ike asked.

"He's in Maui. And his name is not Paulo. It's Paul."

"Has Paulo been calling a lot?" Beth wanted to know.

"We haven't talked yet," Cate said. She felt an aching feeling of dismay reach out and grab her for the fifteenth time that day. He hadn't called since Monday. She had promised herself that she would not think about it while she was out. She wanted to have fun tonight. And besides, she didn't feel like boring everyone with Paul stories.

"I heard that Ethan has a girlfriend anyway," Beth said. "One of my customers was dating him." Beth owned a bead shop in Pacific Beach. She knew practically all of her customers by name. Most of them had taken her beading classes at some point.

Cate looked around the bar for Ethan. The Casbah was an old San Diego bar near the airport that had become a landmark. It was dimly lit, with bartenders who wore more tattoos than smiles. Ethan looked casual as he walked toward them, a few friends in tow. He wore jeans and a faded black T-shirt. Whatever had been advertised on the front of his shirt had long since been lost in the washing machine. He waved.

"Hey!" he said when he noticed Beth. "Wow! It's been awhile." They hugged. Then Beth introduced Ethan to Ike and Jill.

Ethan introduced his friends.

"Let's do a shot," Beth said. "A tribute to old friends."

"All right. You guys pick. I'll buy," Ethan said.

Beth wanted to do a shot of Cuervo, Jill wanted a Scooby snack, and Cate wanted a buttery nipple. Ethan ordered all three, one of each for everyone—including Ike and all of Ethan's friends.

Ike and the girls insisted on giving him money, but he wouldn't take it. Three shots and one cocktail in a matter of fifteen minutes equaled drunk for Cate. By the time the band started, she had made herself comfortable on the dance floor. Jill was front row, dead center, dancing by herself like no one was watching. Ike and Beth were dancing near Cate and Ethan, who were spinning around, Fred and Ginger style, to the rock music that blasted throughout The Casbah.

Cate loved the band and danced to every song, taking a break only to order another gin and tonic.

"Let's do another shot," she said when Ethan joined her at the bar. "I'm buying this time."

"All right. Pick whatever you want."

It felt familiar to be with Ethan again, and Cate wondered why they had ever lost touch. They leaned against the bar, chitchatting and catching up, occasionally stopping to watch some of the outlandish dancers on the dance floor.

Jill joined them, and Cate ordered a round of buttery nipples. They were wedged, closely together, in a corner of the bar.

"Your hair smells good," Jill said to Ethan. "Is that Aveda shampoo? Those are the best products."

"A-what?"

"Aveda. Did you wash your hair with Aveda?"

He shook his head. "I don't think so."

"Well, it smells good. Do you know what it is?"

He shrugged. "Soap. Irish Spring. I don't know. I just use whatever's in my shower."

Jill's face was a mixture of horror and awe.

The funny feeling of her cell phone vibrating against her leg sent little quivers up Cate's thigh. She'd put the phone on vibrate before the show because she knew she would never hear it ring inside the bar. She pulled the phone from her pocket.

It was Paul.

He said something that sounded like *Why did you?* but she couldn't make out a word over the music.

"What?"

"I said: Where are you!" he yelled.

"Oh! I'm at The Casbah."

"Where?"

"The Cas-bah!"

He said something else that she couldn't understand. She plugged her free ear with her finger and tried to listen, but it was impossible over the music.

"Hey, I'll just call you later!" she yelled. *"I can't hear you!"*

She'd been waiting for his call all week and was disappointed when she hung up. She slipped the phone back into her jeans pocket.

"Was that Paul?" Jill asked.

Cate nodded.

"Is Paul your boyfriend?" Ethan asked.

"Yes. He's in Maui."

"Surfing?"

"No. Working."

"How long have you been dating him?" he asked.

"About a year."

"Do you have a girlfriend?" Jill asked.

"Oh yeah, I heard you had a girlfriend," Cate said.

"No." He took his Jack and Coke from the counter. "We broke up." His gaze drifted from the girls to the band.

He didn't seem like he wanted to talk about it. She changed the subject by waving down the bartender and ordering them another round of shots.

Cate handed him a buttery nipple, and they popped the shots into their mouths, letting the liquor slide down their throats.

They danced for the rest of the night. When the band finished, Cate bought a CD and two T-shirts, trying to think of sobriety as she made out her check to King Mother.

Grease was waiting by the front door when she got home. He meowed until she reached down and scratched him behind the ears. She was about to dial the message center, hoping that Paul had left a phone number where he could be reached, when the phone rang.

"*Hola,*" he said.

"Don't you mean aloha?"

"Aloha. Whatever. I'm glad you answered. I've been trying to get a hold of you all night."

"You have?"

"Yeah. I wanted to ask you something."

"What's up?"

"Why don't you fly out here this weekend? Spend next week with me."

"Uh . . . yeah." She didn't want to sound too eager or drunk. "I'd love to. I have Leslie's shower though—on Saturday."

"Fly out on Sunday then."

"I guess I'll have to look into flights and stuff. I wonder if it's too expensive with summer and everything."

"Well, I think you can probably use some of my frequent flyer miles. We'll talk more about it tomorrow. We don't have to figure everything out right now. Anyway, what did you do tonight?"

Cate told him about King Mother and The Casbah.

"Cool," he said. She heard him yawn. "Well, I'll give you a call tomorrow, and we'll figure out your plans. Why don't you look on the Internet in the morning?"

"Okay. I'm excited to see you."

"Me, too."

They said good night.

"I'm going to Hawaii!" Cate screamed after setting the cordless phone in its cradle. Grease bolted beneath the bed.

11 • Burn the Sheets

Cate passed Jill on her way to the complex parking garage. Jill was dressed in an outrageously bright yellow Hawaiian muumuu, and she had three huge gardenias pinned in her platinum hair.

"You look like *you* should be going to Hawaii instead of me," Cate said.

"I'm going to a luau on Loring Street. I was just on my way up to see if you wanted to go with me."

"I would love to. Unfortunately, I'm off to another wedding shower." Why did she always miss out on all the fun when there was a wedding shower? Two months ago she'd missed the annual Pacific Beach Block Party for Sarah's shower. Val's shower had landed on the same day as the Ocean Beach Street Fair, and the year before she'd missed Street Scene in the Gaslamp for her sister's shower. That was three parties and a multitude of good bands that she'd passed up for a day of the most boring gift opening on earth.

She felt a flash of desire to cancel on Leslie's shower and hula dance the day away with Jill. She couldn't though. She remembered when Leslie had her appendix removed. Leslie had given Cate the silent treatment for two weeks because, instead of keeping a steady vigil by Leslie's bedside, Cate had only stopped by twice to visit her during her three days of recovery. Cate could only imagine the destruction flaking on the shower would cause. Besides, it would be bad manners and mean. Leslie had been waiting for this shower for her entire life.

"Well, that sucks that you can't come with me," Jill said as they headed toward the garage. "Showers are soooo boring."

"Really? I actually like watching someone open fifty packages full of plates and stemware for hours on end."

Jill squeezed her arm. "It won't be so bad. Spike the punch."

"That's not a bad idea at all."

"Showers aren't so bad if they have fun games and stuff." Jill tried to be positive.

"That is true. The games aren't bad. It's just the gifts. Someone needs to change the tradition of showers. It should be a day of games, spiked punch, and feasting on more than mini quiches!"

"There you go! I'll change it if I ever get married. Did you get her a gift?"

"No. I'm on my way to Crate and Barrel right now."

"Well, have fun!" Jill called as they got into their cars.

Cate went to the mall with the intention of purchasing Leslie's shower gift, period. She had no business buying more clothes, and she was on a time schedule. However, on the way to Crate and Barrel she noticed a sundress in the window at Bebe. Perfect for Hawaii. A hundred ten dollars later, and ridden with guilt by her impulsiveness, she was back on track to Crate and Barrel.

But when she passed The Gap she saw a cute pair of shorts she couldn't live without and a beach bag that she needed. No. She couldn't. She still had a four-hundred-dollar pantsuit to pay off and a jalopy that was in dire need of a mechanic. She felt a flicker of annoyance by the financial burden of Leslie's wedding and her piece-of-crap car. However, she was also pleased with her self-control when she passed The Gap.

She found the gift registry, entered Leslie's name, and waited for the printout. After three pages were ejected, she began to leave the registry, assuming Leslie wouldn't be able to fill another page with things she wanted. Another page flew from the printer. Then another and another . . . and another . . . Eight pages later, Cate was thumbing through the small catalog that comprised Leslie's registry. Had she gone crazy with the gun? Who could possibly need all of these things? And the two-thousand-dollar marble lazy Susan? Who did she think was going to buy her that?

Cate pulled the invitation from her purse.

Come join us for a round the clock shower!

Each guest has been assigned a time of day!
Your time indicates what type of gift you
Should buy for Leslie.

For example if you have eight A.M.
you should purchase breakfast stuff.

Your time is 3:30 P.M.

Three-thirty P.M. What do people do at three-thirty? With eight pages there certainly had to be something she could find. By the time she had scanned over the second page she had a headache. There were so many things, most of them kitchenware. None of which went with three-thirty in the afternoon. Who was the lucky devil who got eight A.M.?

She pulled her cell phone from her purse and called Sarah. She was going to the shower. Maybe she'd have some ideas.

"Hey, what did you get Leslie?"

"Oh. I had five P.M., so I got her the martini glasses and an appetizer tray she registered for. I thought that would be good for drinks and appetizers at that time."

"I have three-thirty in the afternoon."

"Three-thirty? Uh . . . let me think about that one."

"I have no idea. Everyone does something different at that time."

"Just go get her lingerie."

"That stuff is so personal, though. Besides, I don't have time to go to Victoria's Secret."

"Are there decorative things on the registry? Get her something for the house."

"That's a good idea. Thanks."

After she slipped her phone back into her purse, a salesgirl wearing an apron approached. "Hi! Can I help you find something?"

"Yeah, I need to buy a gift that could be used at three-thirty in the afternoon. And it has to be from these eight pages."

"I think that just about anything that you buy here at Crate and Barrel will go with any time of the day!"

"Well, I was hoping there would be some kind of vase or wall hanging on here. Maybe I could get her one of those." Cate handed her the first four pages. "Why don't you look over these? And I'll look over this half."

"Okay!"

They both began scanning the pages.

"There is the porcelain flowered vase for eighty-nine ninety-five on page three orrrrr . . ." The salesgirl glanced over the fourth page. "That's all I can find as far as decorations go."

Ninety dollars for a vase?

The salesgirl must've been thinking the same thing. "What's your price range?" she asked.

"Well, I really didn't want to go above forty."

"There are tons of things on here for under forty dollars." Kitchenware, stemware, dishes. Nothing that was congruent with three-thirty in the afternoon.

Cate found a set of four throw pillows at thirty dollars a pop. And that was pretty much it in the decorative department. What was she going to do? Buy Leslie one throw pillow?

She was ready to close her eyes, wave her finger around, and let it land on something on the list. She glanced at her watch: twelve forty-five. She still had to purchase the gift and drive to the shower, which was nearly forty-five minutes away.

"I'll take the vase," Cate said with a sigh.

The shower was at Leslie's aunt's estate in Carlsbad. A table full of gifts stood next to the front door of the elegant house. There was no room for Cate's vase among the mountain on the table, so she set it next to several others that had been placed on the floor. She mentally counted. Twenty-three gifts so far. Each gift—approximately three minutes. She was looking at a minimum of an hour of gift opening. God help them all.

She felt an arm around her shoulder.

"Hey, I'm glad you made it," Leslie said. She wore a pearl-colored satin suit with matching heels and had her hair and makeup professionally done. Cate was about to ask if she was underdressed when Leslie spoke up.

"Listen, I meant to tell you." She was whispering now. "My mom changed her last name after the divorce. She went back to her maiden name. So whatever you do, don't call her Mrs. Lyons. It's Van der Berke now."

"Okay."

"Oh, and my stepmom is coming. I put her at your table. You're sitting on the other side of the room from my mom. I can't even put them near each other."

"What's his new wife's name again?"

"Kim. I would really appreciate it if you could kind of keep her away from my mother. Just don't let her go on that side of the room. Okay?"

"Uh . . . er . . . yeah."

"Thanks. Listen, I gotta go say hi to some more people, but we'll talk later." She slapped on a smile and swished off.

Cate knew that Leslie's parents had gone through a sticky divorce, but she hadn't realized how bad it had been. *Van der—what?* She tried to remember Leslie's mother's maiden name. The last thing she wanted to do was create any added tension by offending the mother of the bride. *Van der Beene? Van der Kamp? Van der Berke! That was it.*

"Hi, darling! How long has it been? Two? Three years?" Leslie's mom air-kissed each of Cate's cheeks.

"It's good to see you, Mrs. Ly—Van der Berke."

She wore a canary yellow St. John suit with matching yellow Ferragamo heels and a sweeping white hat. She placed a jeweled hand beneath Cate's chin. "You look absolutely exquisite."

"Thank you." Cate thought she actually looked pretty bland in her khaki capris and white peasant blouse.

"Pour me a glass of that, will you," she said, motioning toward the open bottle of champagne on the table next to them. She held an empty glass with a gigantic bronze lipstick print on the side of it.

Cate refilled her glass. "So how have you been?"

"Oh. Much better now that the shithead I married moved out of my house."

Cate wished she hadn't asked.

"Do you know I had to burn the sheets we had, Cate?"

"Uh no. I hadn't been aware of that." She took a heavy chug of her champagne and scanned the room for Sarah. *Someone, please come to the rescue!*

"Yeah, well when someone brings crabs into the house, you have to get rid of the sheets, the towels. Everything. I mean, that's how I found out, you know? About her. She gave us all crabs."

This was way more information than she wanted to know. Way more. Crabs! For God's sake! They were supposed to be talking about the lovely china Leslie had selected.

"Anyway, that's all water under the bride . . . I mean bridge now. Ha! Ha!" She laughed at the Freudian slip. "So, how's your life?"

She tried to remember how her life was. But her mind was still reeling with shock from the crabs story.

"My life? My life is good. Yeah. Uh . . . I have the summer off," Cate said. "I've been doing some freelance photography for a friend of mine, and I'm going to Hawaii next week."

"Hawaii! I've been to every island. I can tell you all you'll need to know. Which island are you going to?"

"Maui."

"Well, you must do the road to Hana. It's a beautiful drive, and go down to Makena Beach. There is fabulous shopping over by the Fairmont."

They discussed Hawaii over champagne until Leslie told them it was time to take a seat.

Cate was seated next to Kim. Luckily, Sarah sat at her table as well as three other acquaintances from college. Since Kim was only about three years older than them, she fit right in. The only thing that made her stand out among the other women at her table was that she was nine months' pregnant, bulging with child.

"I hope I look as good as you do when I'm pregnant," Sarah said to Kim.

"Thanks. I'm an aerobics teacher, so I have an advantage, I guess."

Kim was quiet and smiled at almost anything anyone said.

Gift time rolled around, and Cate released a yawn. Leslie was unwrapping her master bedroom sheet set when her cousin, Veronica, announced that for every ribbon Leslie cut that would equal one child. So the three minutes that Cate had estimated for each gift had actually turned into seven minutes, while Leslie ripped, pulled, and fidgeted with every single freaking ribbon, doing everything in her power to avoid bringing out the scissors.

To make matters even worse, the maid of honor, Bethany—whom Cate had no reason to dislike but felt like assassinating today—stood and announced that each person had to offer advice or share a story about Leslie when she opened their gift. It wasn't a bad idea, and Cate saw the logic behind it. This way everyone would be interactively involved with the whole gift opening process instead of thinking of ways to slit their wrists from sheer boredom. But for God's sake. This was going to tack on another minute or two to each friggin' gift.

At that moment—more than ever—she wished she was married. Advice would be much easier than sharing a story. What was she going to say? *I remember the time Leslie and I got piss drunk and toilet papered her ex-boyfriend's house.*

Apparently she wasn't the only one suffering from sheer boredom because people began to chat amongst themselves, whispering at their tables, catching up.

"Do you know what you're going to say?" Kim whispered.

"I don't know. Most of my stories are rated R," Cate said.

"Mine, too. Ha ha!" She put a hand on her belly. "I don't really know Leslie that well, to be honest. She's been pretty warm toward me though. . . . I mean considering everything. I was actually kind of afraid to come today."

Cate was hoping they'd get to three-thirty fast. She didn't want to hear Kim's side. Confessions of a gold digger. No thanks.

"Her mother has put us through hell," she whispered.

Cate sensed she was going to hear it anyway.

Then a miracle. One o'clock! It was Kim's turn.

Leslie began pulling and stretching the white ribbon on the signature blue Tiffany box.

"Do you have advice or a story?" Bethany asked.

Cate felt sorry for her. The room had fallen silent. If Kim offered advice, she would look like a fool. She'd wrecked a marriage, had gotten pregnant out of wedlock, and was the archrival of another woman—the victim—sitting only feet away. And what kind of stories could she possibly have? She hadn't been there when Leslie was growing up.

"I just have some things to say," she said. "Leslie is a very special person. She has always shown me nothing but kindness, and I am sure with all of her good qualities she will have a wonderful marriage."

"Thanks, Kim," Leslie said as she continued to pull the ribbon off without asking for scissors.

Cate noticed that there was a small dent in the side of the package and a streak where some of the blue paper had been ripped. It wasn't large or noticeable, but she could see it from where she was sitting.

When Leslie finally slid the ribbon from the box, she tore at the wrapping paper. She pulled the lid off the box. "Oh! It's the frame . . ." The smile fell from her face as she pulled out the gift. "Oh no." Her voice dropped when she held up an eight-by-ten frame, the glass shattered into a million pieces.

"It's broken?" Kim asked. "I told them to put extra tissue paper in there." Her face turned red. "I'm sorry. I'll return it for you."

"Oh, it's okay. It'll take five seconds to exchange it," Leslie said. "Thank you so much though. I love this frame!"

Leslie quickly packaged up the broken picture frame and moved on to the next gift.

Cate glanced at Mrs. Lyons Van der Berke sitting across the room. If she was feeling spiteful, it didn't show. She loosely held a champagne flute as she sat watching the gift opening unfold. Her legs were crossed, and Cate couldn't help but look at her bright yellow Ferragamos. Her left leg was draped over her right knee. On the sole of her left shoe Cate could make out tiny traces of blue wrapping paper.

The Strobels in Maui

When Cate arrived at the hotel, Paul was in a meeting. A key was waiting for her at the front desk.

"Here you go, Mrs. Strobel," the hotel reservationist said as she handed Cate a key.

"Oh . . ." Cate released a chuckle. "We're not, um, actually . . ." She shook her head. "He's not my husband."

A fake smile spread across her face. "Oh. Well, that's okay, Miss— uh?"

"Padgett."

"Right. Will you need more than one key, Miss Padgett?"

"One should be fine."

Cate Strobel, she thought as she headed to her room. It had a ring to it. The Strobels. Paul and Cate Strobel. Cate Padgett-Strobel—in case she wanted to keep her last name. She kind of liked the idea of being a Strobel, of creating a life with Paul, and wondered when and if it would ever happen.

Her thoughts drifted from a possible name change to paradise as she wheeled her suitcase across the hotel grounds. Stretched over an emerald lawn, the Maui Sheraton was situated behind a crystal-blue strip of beach. Trees, lush with blooming plumeria, covered the hotel grounds. Cate reached down and snatched a fallen flower from the lawn. She breathed in the sweet scent and tucked the flower behind her ear. She paused to listen to the live ukulele music near the pool. This was her kind of Hawaii.

She decided to change into her bikini, leave Paul a note, grab a cold drink at the lounge, and head to the beach behind the hotel.

Paul had left the air-conditioning on, and the room felt crisp and dry compared to the moist tropical air outside. The king-sized bed was made, and she noticed a note sitting on one of the pillows.

Hola! I was hoping to run into you on my break, but I guess your flight was delayed. I should be finished around five, so I'll see you then. I left some snorkeling gear in the bathtub. You should take a swim out to Black Rock, the point behind the hotel. It's great! See you soon.

Paul

Perfect. She'd have plenty of time to get a base tan before Paul returned. She didn't want him to see her neon body in a bathing suit. Then she'd come back to the room, shower, blow-dry, and slip into her new sundress from Bebe before he returned.

She changed into her favorite black string bikini, then filled a beach bag with magazines, sunblock, and the snorkeling gear that Paul had left in the bathtub.

Before she left for the beach, she left a note just in case he came back.

Aloha!

I'm at the beach! Meet me for a Mai Tai!

Love,

Cate

Hawaiian music filled the outdoor lounge. The sounds of waterfalls from the pool blended with the music, creating a tropical atmosphere.

She charged a pineapple juice to the room and headed to the beach. It was crowded. She had just laid down her beach towel when two kids went screeching past, kicking up enough sand to bury her towel. She shook off her towel and sat down.

She made sure she lathered her entire body with sunblock. The last thing she wanted was a Vegas revival. For two hours she lay in the sun, occasionally flipping from back to front to even out her tan.

When she started to feel the island heat, she waded into the crystal-blue water. It felt shocking at first and then completely refreshing. She snorkeled out to the point that Paul had mentioned in the note. Among hundreds of colorful fish she saw an eel and a stingray. She snorkeled until the *Jaws* theme song began to haunt her thoughts. She suddenly became aware of her skinny legs dangling like bait in the deep water. If a shark bit her legs off, their whole vacation would be ruined. She swam with full force back to shore without looking back, the whole time envisioning a great white shark taking her limbs with one massive bite.

At four o'clock she returned to their room. After showering, she examined her naked body in the mirror. Her tan had turned out well. She hadn't lain on her stomach much because she had no one to apply lotion to her back. Her cheeks were a little red but added a rosy glow to her typically pallid face. She chose to let her hair air-dry. The wavy look was appropriate for Maui, she thought. After applying a little makeup, she put on sweatpants and a T-shirt. She'd watch television while she waited for her hair to dry.

She flipped through the channels. *When Harry Met Sally,* one of her all-time favorite movies, was on. She watched the beginning of the movie. Then at ten to five she slipped into her dress, put the plumeria behind her ear, and waited for Paul. She could hardly wait to see him, to feel his warm hugs, and to spoon with him in their king-sized bed later that night. She loved snuggling next to him. This was going to be such a fun week. The two of them in Maui, relaxing on white sand beaches, discovering the wonders of the ocean while they snorkeled together, passing the underwater camera back and forth. They would dine on shrimp cocktail in front of sunsets, growing closer to each other whenever they applied sunscreen to the other's back. She was antsy with excitement and felt butterflies in her stomach.

Six o'clock rolled around and still no Paul. The butterflies were driven away when her stomach growled. Curious to see what kind of food they served at the hotel, she searched the nightstand drawers for the room service menu.

All of it was outrageously expensive but mouthwatering. They served everything from seared ahi to cheeseburgers. There were restaurants in the hotel, too. Perhaps those were cheaper than room service. As she thought about food, she remembered that she had not called Ethan to tell him she was going to Hawaii. He'd said he wasn't expecting the photos for a couple of weeks. But she felt as if she should've at least told him she was going out of town, in case he needed them sooner. It probably wasn't a big deal, but this was her first assignment, and she wanted to be professional. She decided to call him.

She was actually kind of glad he didn't answer the phone because she would've felt stupid, explaining that she was sitting in her hotel room waiting for her missing boyfriend. She left a brief message, explaining that she was in Hawaii and that she would have the pictures for him when she returned.

After she called Ethan, she watched the local-access tourist channel. It was a complete guide to everything one could possibly do on Maui.

All she heard about for fifteen minutes was the beautiful road to Hana. Apparently, Hana was the place to be. They showed clips of a hundred-foot waterfall and a bamboo forest. She'd brought her camera and eight rolls of film. It seemed as if Hana offered a million priceless photo opportunities.

At seven-thirty she was tired of hearing about the road to Hana and was ready to find the road to a restaurant.

He was two hours late and hadn't called. She assumed he was in a meeting and couldn't get away to call her. So instead of interrupting his business with a phone call, she left a note.

Paul,
I went to the cocktail lounge for appetizers and drinks. Sorry, but I am starving and can't wait any longer. Can't wait to see you! Meet me there.
    Cate

She could've ordered three appetizers, she was so hungry. Why not? She thought. Charge it to the room. She settled on two: seared ahi and shrimp cocktail.

From where she sat at the bar, she could see rays of sunlight setting over the ocean outside the hotel. A topless Hawaiian man with a tropical-print skirt lit tiki lamps with a long, burning stick on the patio behind the lounge.

When her food arrived she immediately plucked a piece of shrimp from the plate, drowned it in cocktail sauce, and popped it in her mouth. While she worked on her appetizers, she chatted with the bartender, Chad. He had moved from Santa Barbara to Hawaii for the great surfing.

She finished her dinner and talked with Chad until eight-thirty—eleven-thirty San Diego time.

When she returned to the room, everything had been left in exactly the same position. There was no note and no sign of Paul. Her imagination ran rampant with explanations. What if he'd been in a car accident? What if he was being held at gunpoint by a Hawaiian thief? Or maybe he was just busy and hadn't had the courtesy or sense to call her. She was torn between a tug-of-war of anger and concern.

She dialed his cell phone. Voice mail greeted her after the fifth ring.

"Paul, this is Cate. I'm here at the hotel, and I'm just wondering where you are. I'm starting to get worried. Please call."

She caught a glimpse of herself in the mirror. Her lipstick had rubbed off, and the plumeria in her hair was wilted. She pulled the flower from behind her ear and tossed it in the wastebasket. She kicked off her shoes and reached for the remote. It was impossible to concentrate on the television when all she could think about was Paul's whereabouts, envisioning his abduction.

Intuition told her that he was working late. But how hard was it to pick up the phone and call? She knew that part of his being a salesman involved wining and dining his clients. Sometimes his socializing took longer than planned. But what about common courtesy?

She remembered the first few months of their relationship. He had traveled a lot, but if he was ten minutes or an hour late on returning a phone call, he provided lengthy, satisfying apologies, worrying that he'd upset her. Perhaps he was taking her for granted. Or perhaps he was leading some kind of double life that she wasn't aware of.

She began to imagine that he secretly had a girlfriend in every city that he visited, and Cate was just one of them. But then why would he invite her to Hawaii? She tried to be logical. He didn't have time to cheat on her. He was just busy, and he would be home any minute.

She must've dozed off because the next thing she heard was the front door slamming shut. Groggily, she sat up.

"Paul?"

"Hey! God. I am *sooo sorry.*" He was wearing khaki pants, a short-sleeved button-down shirt from Banana Republic, and sandals. "I got stuck with my boss. At the last minute he decided to have a cocktail mixer for this company. He said I'd be outta there no later than six, and I just got stuck. There was nothing I could do." He sat down on the bed next to her and squeezed her knee. "Anyway, it's great to see you."

"Why didn't you call?"

"I tried. I left my cell phone in the rental car, which was in valet, and I couldn't remember the damn phone number here. I feel terrible." He kissed her on the forehead. "So what did you do today?"

"I went snorkeling in that place that you suggested, and then I went to the lounge by myself for dinner." She didn't feel like discussing *her* day with him. He was over five hours late. She was irked! "I waited for you all night. I was really worried."

"I'm sorry. I really am. I had not planned on this. But we can spend more time together tomorrow, and I don't have any appointments on Wednesday, so we can spend the whole day together. We can do whatever you want."

"What kind of people do you work with on these trips?"

He shrugged. "All kinds of people. Some of them are older and some of them are just like us."

"Have you been working with a lot of women lately?"

He laughed. "No!" He turned his head to an angle and smiled. " I think somebody is a little jealous."

"I'm not jealous. I just can't help but wonder. That's all."

"Well, you have nothing to worry about." He playfully squeezed her boob. "You look cute."

She wasn't in the mood for sex, and was relieved when he stood up.

"I'm gonna take a quick shower and then we can . . ." He smiled at her mischievously. "Play."

She lay in bed listening to the drone of water rushing through pipes, and the muffled sound of Paul whistling. By the time he was finished showering, Cate was sound asleep—San Diego time.

13 •   Sampling

Paul didn't have to be at work until noon, so they spent the entire morning together. She'd forgiven him for working late the night before after he apologized profusely. Besides, he was here for business, and she'd just flown out to see him. The last thing she wanted to do was get in the way.

They ordered room service and ate it on the patio. Then they went for a long walk barefoot on the beach. Shortly after they returned, Paul was off to his appointment.

Before Cate went to the beach, she watched a little of the local tourist station on TV. Aside from the road to Hana, Hilo Hattie was the next place on her list to visit. She watched clips of a pseudofamily wearing matching Hawaiian-print skirts and leis as they browsed through the gigantic gift store, pointing out an assortment of Hawaiian souvenirs to one another. Maybe she'd go there the day before she left.

Today she planned to soak up more sun and indulge in more seafood and fruity cocktails. Paul was supposed to return by six.

As planned, she spent the day in the sun, the first part at the beach, the second at the pool. When she returned to the hotel room, the light on the phone was blinking.

"*Hola* or aloha or whatever. It's me. I have bad news. I won't be home 'til around eight. I apologize. But after that, we'll go out for some late-night appetizers. Then we have all day tomorrow. Anyway, I promise I'll be back around eight. I can't wait to see you. Adios."

At least he called this time. She still felt a flicker of annoyance but decided she would go to Front Street tonight. She'd kill her irritation with shopping. After all, Paul had paid for most of her trip, so she could splurge.

She took a cab to Hilo Hattie. She had barely set foot in the store when a Hawaiian woman approached her.

"Welcome to Hilo Hattie!" She slipped a shell necklace over Cate's head. Then she handed her a shopping basket.

"Thanks," she said, surprised by the complimentary jewelry. Maybe she should return to the store seven or eight times, and should give necklaces to her friends and family at home.

Hilo Hattie was a Hawaiian gift world. Racks covered with every variety of Hawaiian shirt, dress, and ensemble filled the store. A corner of the store was devoted to macadamia nuts. They sold every flavor known to man. There were beach towels, magnets, candles, shot glasses, hats, sunglasses, and every kind of Hawaiian souvenir one could ever want.

She was holding three sundresses and two T-shirts when she exchanged her basket for a shopping cart. She tried on eight dresses, picked out one for herself, and moved on to searching for gifts for others.

She picked out a Hawaiian-print shirt for her father, a package of stationery with blooming plumerias on it for her mother, plumeria-scented candles for Jill, Beth, Leslie, and Sarah, beach towels for Emily and Bradley, and a tiny, adorable Hawaiian-print dress for their unborn child, even though it wasn't due until November, and she didn't know if it was a girl.

She bought everyone, including herself, a box of chocolate-covered macadamia nuts. She picked out additional boxes of plain salted macadamia nuts, garlic macadamia nuts, and two boxes of chocolate caramel macadamia nuts. Beach towels and straw hats were so cheap she might as well stock up on those, too, so she tossed another towel and a cute straw hat into the cart. She loved Hilo Hattie!

She was in the checkout line when she realized she'd been inside Hilo Hattie for two hours. Paul would be back by now. She quickly paid her bill and took a cab to the hotel. When she returned, the room was frigid. The air-conditioning had been left on full blast again. She turned the freezing air off and bundled up in the blankets.

Hungry, she decided to eat some of her macadamia nuts. She set up a sampling station on the nightstand next to the bed. She lined up the boxes of plain, garlic, chocolate, and the chocolate caramel, then tasted each. She liked the chocolate-covered the best and polished off half the box by the time Paul returned. She'd been too engrossed with her macadamia nuts to be annoyed by his late arrival.

"Well, I see you did some shopping," he said when he noticed the Hilo Hattie bags piled next to her suitcase.

"Do you want a macadamia nut?" She held out the chocolate caramels.

"No. Thanks." He set his briefcase on the bed. "Let's go eat some real food." It was midnight San Diego time, and she wasn't particularly hungry. Maybe if he had been on time she would still be looking forward to dinner.

"All right," she said. "I'll go."

As they walked through the courtyard of the hotel, Cate wondered if Paul would go out to eat with her if she were four hours late.

14 • The Road to What?

They drove in Paul's rented red Ford Focus to Hana. Whoever had used the car before them had ignored the **Thank You for Not Smoking** plaque mounted on the dashboard. The car smelled of cigarette smoke and sickly sweet air freshener with a coconut twist. Paul was behind the wheel, and Cate was in charge of navigating. She held the crisp map on her lap. For several hours they drove around windy, skinny cliffs covered with gigantic tropical trees, blooming flowers, and thick green foliage. Occasionally, skinny long rodents resembling the offspring of a gopher and a dachshund ran across the road.

"Christ!" Paul yelled every time he slammed on the brakes.

They passed a poor weenie rodent that hadn't made it to the other side. Cate wanted to cry for the dead animal.

They heard the same Puddle of Mud song, "Blurry," four times in one hour. Cate was beginning to suspect it was the island's anthem.

Rain clouds dotted the sky, but the air was warm, and sunshine occasionally seeped through the clouds. They stopped once to take a picture of a rainbow on the horizon.

The tiny town of Hana was unlike anything Cate could've imagined. Settled on a cliff, it overlooked beaches covered with fine, grainy obsidian sand and white, foamy waves. Old wooden buildings and grazing cattle dotted the sprawling green pastures.

They stopped at one of only three restaurants in town, a walkup window with a menu of sandwiches and hamburgers. They ate hamburgers with fries at a picnic table near the water, listening to the waves crash behind them. In Hana, the deep seas stretched to eternity, and Cate felt as if she were light-years away from the rest of the world.

After they finished eating, they drove to the trail that led to the one-hundred-foot waterfall and bamboo forest. They changed out of their flip-flops and into tennis shoes. Right before they set out for the journey, a forest ranger warned them that the hike would take at least forty-five minutes each way. Cate couldn't wait.

The trail was rugged. Giant vines from surrounding trees created tricky and treacherous grooves in the earth. She felt giddy with excitement as she passed each priceless photo op. She took pictures of the bubbling waters of some of the smaller waterfalls and streams they encountered on the way to *the big one*. She captured the vines in the earth and the huge lime-colored leaves that grew like lily pads from the trees. She snapped at the overhangs and cliffs that plunged into deep valleys of nothing but greenery.

She was still excited when they got lost. She took a picture of the skinny trail they had accidentally wandered down.

"I know this isn't the right way," Paul said, exasperated. "And could you stop taking pictures for just one second so we can figure out where we are going?"

Eew. Someone was grouchy. "Well, let's head back down this trail. I'm sure it will lead us back to the main path."

They began to retrace their steps but ended up at the same three-way fork that had sent them on the wrong path to begin with.

"Which way?" Paul asked, as if Cate were a seasoned bushman.

"I don't know. I'm not really sure which path we were on." She felt something moving up the back of her calf. The sensation was barely noticeable, like a single strand of hair brushing over her leg. She reached down and flicked off a mosquito.

She was about to suggest a path when two long-haired, bearded men appeared. One had outrageously curly hair that sprouted dread-locks around his forehead and the nape of his neck. The other one had flowing, long brown hair that hung to his waist. They both had dirt down their fingernails and had been hiking in sandals.

"We're lost," Paul said. "Do you know how we get to the main path?"

"Yeah man, it's about ten minutes away," the blond said. Cate noticed grass stains on his pants and T-shirt. He pointed to his left. "Just keep heading down that trail, and you'll hit it, no problem."

"You guys are looking for the bamboo forest, right?" the other asked.

"Yes," Cate said.

"You're about a half an hour away."

She took a picture of them with their long beards and dirty feet.

"Would you mind taking a picture of us?" she asked, handing them the camera.

"Of course. You guys smoke? We were just about to light up," the blond offered.

She knew they weren't referring to cigarettes and was tempted to smoke whatever kind of herbal substance they were offering, but Paul answered for her.

"No. We don't smoke."

"That's cool."

She thanked them for the directions, the pictures, and the offer of weed before they continued on.

"A half an hour?" Paul asked, trailing behind her. "We've already been hiking for twenty minutes."

"The rangers told us the hike would take forty-five minutes at least," Cate said.

"Well, I guess I'm going to have to buy new tennis shoes. These are wrecked."

The path was muddy, and occasionally Cate stepped in a puddle that sent a slosh of dark water up her calves. Their Nikes were saturated with dirt and mud. However, she didn't care. She enjoyed the lush greenery and the sounds of streams and waterfalls ahead. She snapped pictures of their mud-soaked shoes and dirt-splashed calves.

She imagined them stranded on a tropical island, living off coconuts and pineapples and bathing naked together in the freshwater streams. They would have a love child and one of those weenie gophers as a pet. No more credit card bills. No more cell phones. No more piece-of-crap car. Just the two them. Tan, thin, and peaceful.

"Jesus!" Paul yelled.

She heard a loud slap and spun around. "What! What is it?"

"I'm being eaten alive." He held out his arm. "Look."

She noticed two small bumps on his forearm. "I know. I've been attacked, too. I have at least a dozen on my legs and shoulders. We'll buy some anti-itch cream when we get back to the hotel." The mosquitoes were annoying her, too, but she found no point in complaining when there was nothing that they could do about it. Besides, they were hiking in a tropical forest. She expected hazards such as these. It was all part of the rugged experience. She continued on, eager to find the bamboo forest.

They crossed a rustic old bridge, and she started to see long bamboo sticks replacing the green trees and foliage. "We're getting closer," she said.

"Good!"

Long sticks of bamboo began to envelop them as they headed forth. Gradually, the bamboo became so tall that they couldn't see the sky above them. They entered a forest of canelike sticks that stretched to the clouds. It was mystical, surreal, and otherworldly. She pulled her camera from her backpack and took pictures of the steep, hilly bamboo forest. She was already imagining ways to mat the pictures and hang them on her wall.

"Fuuuck!" Paul yelled as he slapped his cheek. "One just bit my fucking face."

She tried not to laugh when she looked at him. The corpse of a dead mosquito was stuck to his cheek. She snapped a picture of him. She couldn't help it.

"Here." She lifted the corner of her shirt and wiped the dead bug from his face.

"No more pictures, okay?" he snapped. "Do you think you can save the rest of that damn roll for the waterfall?"

"Geez. Sorry, I didn't realize it was bothering you so much."

After they emerged from the bamboo forest, they passed another young couple headed in the opposite direction.

"How much farther?" Paul asked them.

"Ten minutes, maybe," they said as they hiked off.

They headed down a steep trail covered with ominous slick rocks and deceiving patches of mud that looked like solid earth but actually had the consistency of quicksand. Cate had accidentally stepped in one of the thick spots of mud, and when she pulled her foot from the bog her shoe was covered in what resembled a ladle full of dark brown gravy. Slippery, disgusting slime oozed from the inside of her shoes and the crevices of her toes as she stepped forward. *Lotion. It's just lotion,* she told herself.

"Be careful for some of the pud—" Cate was about to warn Paul of the shoe-swallowing pools of mud when she heard a sound similar to a gigantic turd easing itself into a toilet. The plop was followed by a piercing howl. She spun around to face Paul. His left leg was submerged thigh deep in a hole as thick and dark as dog diarrhea. His arms flailed over his head as he tried to maintain balance.

"Diiisguuuusting!!" he screamed, sending tropical birds skittering from the surrounding trees. "Get me out!" His face had gone white.

She pulled on his arm. It was worse than moving furniture. "Steady yourself with the other leg," she instructed. "And pull yourself out with your other hand. See if you can push yourself up while I pull. Press on the ground with your hand."

In a flustered state of haste, he sent his hand to the earth. Instead of landing his palm onto solid terra, he missed and shoved it into the same shitty hole in which his leg resided. He screamed again as his hand and torso plunged into the cesspool of slime. He pulled his upper body out, and Cate didn't know whether she wanted to laugh or barf when she looked at the black goo that covered his arm and chest. He shook his arm as if acid rain had spilled over it.

"Ohhh Goooodd! Get it ooooff!" He screamed and shook his hand as if poison had soaked his forearm.

She still had the mush on her own foot and couldn't imagine what it must feel like to be submerged in the same crud. "Paul, relax. There is a stream ahead, and we'll wash you off. Now try to pull your leg out again."

She suddenly felt responsible for Paul's horrible situation. She was the one who had led Paul here. This had all been her idea. She had to do everything in her power to help him.

She was about to help him pull his leg from the muck again when footsteps approached. Someone was whistling. Then the lovely chords of a harmonica chimed in. A festive little jig approached them. It was the kind of music that made Cate want to jump up and clap her heels together. However, the music seemed extremely ill-fitting, considering Paul's situation.

"Whooooa! Man. Your foot is *deep* in that shit," said one of the hippies that had given them directions.

"That is fuckin' crazy," the blond added, in awe of Paul's dilemma. They beheld the scene as if they had just discovered a glorious land-mark along the trail. "How'd you get stuck in that shit anyway?"

"We were just walking, and he slipped."

They chuckled. "That is some heavy shit, Dillon," the blond said to his friend, slipping his harmonica into his back pocket.

"I have an idea," Dillon said. "Why don't we break off a branch from one of these trees like this!" He ran to a tree. "And he can grab on. We'll all pull at once."

"It's probably illegal to break the branches from the trees," Paul said. "What if a park ranger comes along and cites all of us? Those fines can be up to twenty-five thousand dollars."

Cate looked at him, his leg submerged in a hole of mire, his face as cross and irritated as an old man at a keg party. She had a hunch that they wouldn't be fined, but it also wasn't necessary to rip a branch from a tree. Paul had both arms and a leg free. With a little effort he'd be per-fectly capable of hoisting himself from his small swamp.

However, Dillon and his friend had already begun pulling, yanking and ripping a massive limb from a nearby tree. They were having so much fun that Cate hated to spoil it for them. The sound of wood split-ting filled the air as a branch the size of a flagpole dropped to the ground.

"All right, why don't you grab on to this end here," Dillon said to Cate. "And Marshall here will grab on behind you, and we'll all pull at once."

They offered the other end to Paul. "Now try to push yourself out while we pull," Marshall said, a dreadlock hanging over his forehead. "On the count of three. One. Two. Three."

They pulled with all their might. Grunts cracked from their throats as they tried to free Paul. Cate caught a whiff of patchouli blended with body odor. Paul released a yelp when his fingers tightened around the branch, as if he were holding on to a life raft. He slid from the hole like a wet fish. His leg dripped black and brown crud.

"I lost my shoe," was the first thing he said. "My shoe is still in there."

"No prob!" Dillon said. "No prob at all! We'll just fish for it with this tree branch." Immediately he submerged the branch in the mud like a toothpick in brownie batter. Marshall grabbed a nearby stick from the ground and also began to prod in the bog for Paul's Nike.

The mud was already beginning to dry on Paul's leg, crusting all over his curly leg hairs like brown spray paint. "I got it! I think I got it man!" A moment later, Paul's grime-soaked tennis shoe dangled from Marshall's stick, dripping muck all over the trail.

Cate couldn't recognize the Nike. Had they found someone else's shoe in there? Covered in muck, it was filled with brown chili, and his shoelaces hung like two long slugs from the sneaker. Now his shoes were ruined, too, and it was all her fault.

"I can't put that thing back on," Paul said.

"Sure ya caaaan!" Dillon grabbed it, turned it upside down, and began to drain the waste from it. Then he banged it on a rock, spraying droplets of mud in all directions. Cate felt one land on her face and wiped it away.

"Here. Now it's good as new." He handed the shoe to Paul.

It was eons away from new.

Paul released a deep sigh, clearly hesitant to ever wear the sneaker again.

"There is a stream right around the corner," Cate said. "I can hear it. I'll wash your shoe off there. It'll be as good as new. Just put it back on for now so you don't cut your foot." They'd had enough mishaps for one day.

"Yeah, man. That's a good shoe," Marshall said. "Hey, I'll wear it if you don't want. And you can wear my shoe."

Paul and Cate looked at his sandals. Cate had seen similar ones for sale in Tijuana. They had thick leather straps and soles that were fashioned from tire rubber.

Marshall yanked the sandal off. "Here. Just wear it, man. 'Til you get to the stream, and then we'll trade."

"It looks really comfortable." Cate tried to be positive. "You should wear it."

"Fine." Paul grabbed Marshall's sandal.

They headed toward the waterfall. A squeaking rubbery noise popped from Marshall's foot every time he took a step. The slippery mud inside the tennis shoe was still wet.

When they reached the stream, Paul immediately removed both shoes and waded into the water. They all washed their feet, and Marshall washed the Nike for Paul.

"You know if you don't want this shoe, I'll take it," Marshall said. "This is a really good shoe."

Paul looked at him as if he were from another planet. "What will I wear?"

"You can have my sandals, man."

Cate wanted to answer for Paul, to tell Marshall that he was more than welcome to Paul's Nikes. Marshall and Dillon had both been such a help that the least Paul could do was give him his shoes. She looked at Paul. "Now that your other shoes are soaked, sandals will feel good to hike in," she said. "Your feet will air out, and they won't feel as squishy."

Paul shrugged. "Let me think about it."

She could hear the waterfall from where they stood.

"All you gotta do is cross this stream and you'll hit that waterfall right around the corner," Dillon said. They had decided to stay and bathe in the stream and wouldn't be joining Paul and Cate at the waterfall.

After a few minutes of deliberation, Paul decided to make the swap. Cate thanked them for all their help before she and Paul treaded through the water. Paul's mood seemed to have gone from bad to worse. Instead of complaining, he had turned uncomfortably quiet, occasionally grunting when they went through a rough spot of water.

Cate's fantasies of cracking open pineapples and foraging for coconuts to store in their tree house had suddenly plunged into the frightening realm of reality. She had ruined their one and only day together. Worse, it was starting to become apparent that they might not have anything in common. She had looked at the hike as an adventure, each obstacle something they could share and tell stories about later. Paul had viewed this hike as hell, torturous hell. She hoped his opinion would change when they reached the waterfall. Perhaps he would think all the torment had been worth it once he saw it.

The sound of rushing water became so intense that she had to raise her voice to speak to him. It was thundering, and Cate held her breath as they stepped from the stream and rounded the corner.

The waterfall was so powerful that Cate thought it was like one giant muscle forcefully rushing down the mountainside. She'd never seen anything as strong.

The waterfall stood so grand and beautiful that it almost hurt to look at it. Its enormity and power were a combination of beauty and terror. Spray from the waterfall misted over her entire body. She let the cleansing drops cover her skin, afraid that if she took a few steps forward, she'd be blasted away.

She took dozens of pictures. When Paul wasn't sitting on a rock picking mud from his toes, she made him stand in front of the waterfall for some photos. He wore the same listless expression in each one.

They were halfway back to where they had started from when it began to pour. Luckily, Cate had wrapped her camera in plastic shopping bags. She laughed as water soaked their hair and clothes. Paul found nothing humorous or exhilarating about being caught in a tropical rainstorm and mostly bitched about his favorite hat being ruined.

When they returned to the car, he threw the sandals in a trashcan. Cate drove, and Paul propped his bare feet on the dashboard. Chunks of mud were crusted beneath his toenails.

They took a different route back to the hotel, driving over rocky dirt roads the whole time. The car bounced over each crack and bump. Cate wanted to pull over and take pictures of the beautiful horizon. To the left, jagged cliffs collided with the kind of white, foamy waves that were too dangerous for swimming. And on the right of the Focus, endless hillsides of wheat-colored grass and weeds extended to a horizon where the sun was about to drop into its cradle for the evening. They were covering an exceptionally rocky stretch of the road when a loud bang sounded. "Shit! What was that?" Paul yelled, sitting up.

Cate looked in the rearview mirror to see something resembling a hubcap bouncing away, stirring up gravel in a cloud of dust behind them.

"I think we lost a hubcap," she said, slowing down. "Should I pull over?"

"No," Paul groaned. "I bought insurance. We'll just deal with it later."

She sensed that he wasn't going to pull over for pictures either. At this point she just wanted to return to the hotel as well. The tension in the car was thick. Neither one of them had said much, and she felt as if they needed their space.

"Paul, I'm sorry about everything that happened today," Cate said. "I thought it would be fun."

"It's okay." He squeezed her knee. "It wasn't that bad."

She felt a little better but still considered the day to be a complete failure.

They were filthy and exhausted by the time they returned to the Sheraton. They quickly examined the tires. Sure enough, the front driver's-side tire was minus a hubcap.

"Fuck it. Insurance will cover it or I'm suing," Paul said before heading to the lobby.

It seemed as if they had traveled around the world and back. They walked through the plush hotel, tracking dirt across the tiled foyer.

When they returned to the room, they showered separately, then fell into deep, sound slumber.

Signs of Life

A torrential downpour hit the island. Paul had to work all day, and Cate was bored out of her mind.

That morning she took a cab to the nearest minimart, where she purchased a tube of anti-itch cream. She and Paul had both been eaten alive by mosquitoes in Hana. They each had awakened several times in the night to scratch various parts of their bodies. She had one on her tush and couldn't figure out how a mosquito had managed to break through the barrier of her shorts *and* clingy granny-style underwear to suck the life out of her.

Apparently Paul was allergic to mosquitoes. Some of his bites had swollen to the size of golf balls, and he'd broken out in hives on his face.

At the minimart she also bought a book from the minimal selection. It was a legal thriller written by an author she had never heard of.

After she returned to the hotel, she applied the cream to all of her bites and tried to ignore the itching that plagued her entire body. Out of boredom, she counted the bites: twenty-five in total.

She wished she had brought some beads with her to the island, so she could at least make a necklace. She decided to give the book a try but found that she couldn't stay focused and that her mind wandered off the pages and onto Paul.

She had hoped this trip would bring them closer, but she had never felt more distant from him. His lack of consideration when he'd left her waiting two nights in a row bothered her, and she was beginning to wonder if they were even compatible. The hike in Hana had been a real eye-opener. She'd known Paul had always been a little anal. The travel candles and his impeccable cleanliness had been indications of this, but now she wondered if his uptight tendencies clashed with her personality.

However, everyone had his or her flaws, and she didn't know any couples who were perfectly compatible. Example: Leslie and Russ. She was the most precise person that Cate had ever known, and her fiancé, Russ, was so easygoing he had actually forgotten his own birthday one year. From the outside Beth and Ike appeared perfect, but Cate knew that Ike's failure to express his feelings and Beth's constant need to be open with hers created friction in their relationship. Even her parents had their differences, and they had been married for thirty-two years. Her poor dad had been nodding his head and keeping his opinions on politics and religion to himself for over three decades, just to avoid lengthy debates with his wife. But he still took her to nice dinners once a week and they did their crossword puzzles together every night. Every now and then, Cate would catch her father looking at her mother when she told a story. She could see a little glow in his eyes, the corners of his mouth turned up in one of the most satisfied smiles Cate had ever seen.

She was wise enough to know by now that perfection didn't exist. Perfect relationships only existed in fairy tales. She wondered if the things that bothered her about Paul could be overlooked. Could she live with their differences?

Around two o'clock she was dying to leave the room. She couldn't sit there, dwelling on Paul all day. It wasn't healthy, and it was driving her nuts. She decided to locate the business center in the hotel so she could check her E-mail. All of the occupants of the Sheraton must have had the same idea, because she had to wait twenty minutes to use a computer.

She had twelve new messages. For the first time in days she realized how isolated she had felt. There were people out there whom she missed and wanted to talk to.

Disappointment hit when she realized nine of her messages were advertisements. Of the other three, one was from her supervisor at Tierra Bonita Elementary School.

From: Marcia Strauss
Subject: Home visits

Hi Cate,
    Attached is your class list for the fall. All of your students'
phone numbers are enclosed. Home visits should probably
begin no later than next month. Hope you are having a great
summer. If you have any questions please leave a message on
my voice mail. I check my messages regularly.
    Marcia Strauss

Home visits were her least favorite part of being a kindergarten teacher. Most of her students had never been to school before. Although home visits made the first day of kindergarten much easier for everyone, the meetings were time-consuming and nerve-racking. Driving around from house to house, introducing herself over and over again, and talking to children clinging to their mother's legs was draining. At least she got paid.

Next message:

FROM: Leslie Lyons
SUBJECT: Nail polish

Hi Bridesmaids!

Just wanted to let you know that I've picked out the nail polish that I'd like all of you to wear for the wedding. I'm going to send it to all of you, Priority Male. I'd like it on both your toes and fingernails. It would probably be best to make appointments for a manicure and pedicure. I think a professional job just looks better. Also, please do this no earlier than the day before the wedding. I'd like it to look fresh. Make sure your manicurist applies two coats so we all have the same amount of color. I'll remind you all again when it gets closer. I am so glad to have all you be a part of this special day with me. Each one of you is such an important part of my life.

Love,
Leslie

A manicure: at least fifteen dollars. A pedicure: at least eighteen. Another thirty-three dollars she could tack on to the cost of being Leslie Lyons's bridesmaid.

She wrote back.

FROM: Cate Padgett
SUBJECT: Nail polish

Dear Leslie,
Thanks for buying us nail polish!

And learn how to spell, she wanted to add.

> Love,
> Cate

She couldn't resist. Besides, Leslie would never notice the sarcasm. Next message:

FROM: Connie Padgett
Empty subject box

Her mother had E-mail access?

Cate-
    Emily and Bradley just taught me how to use E-mail. Isn't it neat? Anyway, I hope you are not having an early honey-moon with Paul. I know all of your friends are engaged or married but you're not. I still think it is inappropriate for you to be visiting him on business trips and staying in the same hotel room with him. However, I've decided that is between you and God. Be safe and good. I said a novena for you today. Talk to you when you return.
    Love,
    Mother

Cate sent a brief reply to her mother, saying that she hoped the new E-mail account was useful and that she would be back tomorrow.
    Rain still poured when she left the business center. It was a warm rain, and she didn't mind if her hair got a little wet. When she returned

to her room, she decided to check her voice mail. She used her calling card so the phone calls wouldn't be billed to the room.

"Hi. It's me." Jill. "I know you're in Hawaii, but I felt like calling you anyway. I've been taking good care of Grease. We miss you! See you soon."

"Hey, Cate. It's Ethan. I was just wondering if you were back from Hawaii yet. I wanted to see what you were up to this evening. No worries about the pictures. I told you I wouldn't need them for a couple of weeks anyway. Give me a call whenever you get a chance. Take care."

She called Jill first. "Aloha!"

"Cate! Are you calling from Hawaii?"

"I am. It's pouring, and Paul's at work, and I'm bored. How is everything there?"

"Oh fine. Grease is great. Nothing really exciting has happened. How's Paul?"

She sighed. "He's fine. He's just been working a lot, so I feel like we haven't seen much of each other." Cate wanted to tell Jill that she was having a mediocre time, that there was something missing with Paul, that she felt empty, but she had called for company and to cheer herself up, so she didn't go into it. "Anyway, it's probably costing me ten dollars a minute to talk on this phone so I should go, but you're picking me up tomorrow, right?"

"You bet."

After she said good-bye to Jill, she called Ethan.

"Hey! What's up, Cate?"

"I'm actually still in Hawaii, with Paul."

"That must be nice. I'm jealous. What have you been doing?"

She told him about Hana and the bamboo forest and waterfall.

"That is the best hike ever. I did that a few years ago with a couple of my buddies."

"I took tons of pictures," she said.

"I bet they're great. I took a bunch with a disposable camera, and they were terrible. I'd like to see yours."

"Well, I'll bring them when we meet to look at the catering pictures."

They made plans to meet the day after Cate returned from Hawaii. After she hung up, she'd never felt so lonely.

At six A.M., Paul's cell phone cracked the silence. He had one of those custom rings that played a classical music fugue.

She pulled a pillow over her head while he took the call. After he hung up, he slipped in next to her. "I wish you didn't have to go," he said as he pulled her into spoon position.

"You do?" She sat up.

"Yeah. It's been great having you here."

They had spent no more than fifteen waking hours together since she had arrived four days ago. What had been great? Knowing that she was waiting for him at the hotel?

"Did you have a good time?" he asked.

Good question. She looked at his swollen face, still puffy and red from the mosquito bites. If she hadn't known any better, she would've thought he had gained five pounds and had a bad sunburn. But she answered, "Yeah. I like Maui."

"I wish we could've spent more time together." He kissed her on the lips. "I'm sorry I was so busy."

"It's okay. I'm glad I got to come to Maui."

He pulled her closer, and his boner stabbed her leg. Morning sex. It meant breathing through the nose to avoid any exchange of dragon breath, no foreplay, and praying that Paul didn't notice the crust in her eyes.

The romp lasted about one minute. She wasn't surprised. He was usually a champion in bed, but morning sex was another story. He couldn't control himself.

"I'm sorry," Paul said as he pulled out. "I have to pee really bad, and I just couldn't last."

He always used peeing as an excuse for his morning quickies. She felt edgy from unsatisfied arousal as she packed her suitcase. Luckily, he made up for it an hour later in the shower. She left the hotel with a wet head.

At the airport Paul pulled up next to the curb. "I wish I could go inside with you," he said. "But I have to get to work."

"I know. It's okay."

He pulled her suitcase from the trunk of the Ford Focus. Then he hugged her. "I'll talk to you later," he said.

She nodded. "All right." She watched the Focus pull away from the curb. Mud was still caked in streaks along the red paint. It looked like a neglected jalopy with its missing hubcap. As she walked away, she wondered what Paul had meant by *"later."* Would she hear from him tonight? Tomorrow? Next week? Part of her didn't care.

16 • Details

Cate weaseled her way through the horde of people who filled the front of World Famous restaurant. It was one of the most popular restaurants in the Pacific Beach area. This was in part because of its prime location, mere walking distance from the ocean and only a step away from the boardwalk. Furthermore, the food was outstanding. She was thankful that she didn't have to wait in line and hoped that Ethan had managed to snag them a table. It was always jam-packed on Mondays for half-off appetizers.

"Cate!" He was already seated, motioning for her from a table with a view. Long rays of sunlight filtered over the crown of his head. Just in time for sunset, she thought. This was her favorite time to come to the beachside restaurant.

He stood up and hugged her. "It's good to see ya. You're pretty tan. I can't wait to hear about Maui."

She didn't want to talk about Maui. "How on earth did you ever manage to get this table?" she asked as she took a seat. Gold and red bursts of light settled on the ocean behind them. Two surfers, emerging from the waves, headed toward the boardwalk. They were soaking wet and held their boards beneath their arms.

"I left work early," he said. "I was gonna grab my board and surf for a little bit, but I've never managed to get a good table at this restaurant, so I thought I'd try." He motioned for the waitress. "Do you want something to drink? I'm having a Corona."

"I'll have a Corona, too," Cate told the waitress.

"Are you hungry?" Ethan asked.

"Starving."

At World Famous, Cate could never just order one appetizer. Especially on Mondays. She had to order all of her favorites. They ordered the nut-crusted Brie (of course), seared ahi (a must), and the firepot Tai grilled jumbo shrimp.

"So how was your trip?" he asked after they ordered.

"It was nice. Maui's beautiful."

"Besides Hana, what did you do?"

"Well, Paul was busy most of the time with his work, so we really only got to spend a couple of days together."

He must've sensed her disappointment. "How is everything going with him?"

Part of her wanted to pull the catering pictures from her purse and drop the subject of Paul. However, she felt tempted to discuss him with Ethan. A male perspective might be what she needed. And who better than Ethan? He was sharp and insightful and had always been the best listener. He was the only male she knew who would spend more than five minutes on the phone with her. It was hard for her to talk to her girlfriends about Paul because most of them either loved him or hated him. Jill and Beth resented him because he was a flake. Sarah and Leslie liked Paul because he was a good friend to both of their significant others. They were all biased. Cate needed a fresh opinion.

She shrugged and looked toward the sunset. "He's all right, I guess."

"What do you mean?"

"I guess I'm just a little confused. I don't know what to think sometimes."

Ethan waited for her to explain.

"I'm just starting to feel like there are two Pauls. There is the flaky Paul who doesn't call when he says he's going to or goes days without calling for no good reason. He acts aloof and elusive and inconsiderate. Then there is the prompt, sweet Paul who is enthusiastic and excited to see me and calls on time and acts the way a boyfriend should act." She shook her head. "He wasn't like this in the beginning. But now he just throws me for a loop all the time. I don't know what to think of him anymore. He's hot and cold and enthusiastic and indifferent all at once. I don't know what he wants."

She also wanted to mention that she didn't even know if they were compatible anymore. But that was a whole other can of worms.

Ethan took a swig of Corona before replying. "It sounds like he doesn't know what to think either. He might be just as confused."

"But I don't treat him that way. How can *he* be confused? I'm always consistent."

He shrugged. "I don't know. I don't know the guy, so I don't know what he's thinking. I will tell you though that a lot of guys are pretty big idiots when it comes to relationships. I don't think most of them know how to act half the time. In fact, I think most guys figure it out when it's too late."

For a moment she remembered Claude, living with the regret of losing Sarah. Regretting acting like a fourteen-year-old when he'd been twenty-two. But that wasn't Paul.

"Well, he's had other girlfriends," she said. "I feel like he should know by now."

"Girlfriends? Everybody has had a girlfriend. I'm talking about a relationship."

"I guess there is a difference between a relationship and a girlfriend or boyfriend."

Had she ever really been in a relationship? She'd had other boyfriends before Paul. There had been Keith in college. He'd also been a roller coaster of love and indifference. After college she'd been selective, cautious about whom she became involved with. There was a brief tryst with Devin, who seemed perfect with his high-paying job and good solid family background. He'd shocked the hell out of her when he confessed that he actually had a girlfriend who'd been studying abroad in France and was due to return in a week.

Then there had been Joe. Without any explanation he'd simply stopped calling after four months of courtship. She'd driven herself crazy trying to figure out what she had done to make him disappear. Had she been mean, needy, too distant, too clingy? Had she farted in her sleep? As soon as she stopped caring, he started turning up sporadically on her answering machine at three in the morning. She wasn't interested in his explanations or suggestions of a late-night booty call and never answered.

Had she ever been in a situation where she felt entirely comfortable with a guy?

"Look," Ethan said. "Like I said, I don't know the guy. But this is something you might want to consider. Most dating situations don't work because the people are in different places."

"You think I'm way ahead of Paul?"

"I'm not saying that. I'm just saying that he might just be in a different place. Maybe he's immature. Maybe he's afraid. Maybe he isn't ready. Or maybe he is madly in love with you and doesn't know what the hell to do, which could very well be the case. That's why you gotta talk to him. You have to ask *him*. Do you like the guy a lot?"

"I do. But I'm getting fed up. When I left Maui I didn't even care if he called or not."

"Then you gotta just say, 'Look, Paul, I like you a lot. I really want to be more involved in your life, and I want to know if you want the same thing.' Wait 'til he comes back from his trip though. It's never good to deal with this shit over the phone."

"You're right. Thanks for all the advice." She felt the subject was getting stale and reached for her purse. "So, I brought the pictures with me," she said as she pulled the catering proofs from her bag. She handed him an envelope full of three-by-five photographs. She'd had them developed at her favorite photo lab in Hillcrest.

"Wow. These are good," he said as she studied each picture.

Their food arrived, and they feasted on the assortment of appetizers. Ethan ordered them each another beer.

Cate remembered that she had to meet with two kindergartners tomorrow and probably should keep her drinking to a minimum. But the drinks just kept coming.

When the tab came, Ethan insisted on paying. "Please," he said as Cate vigorously attempted to shove a twenty into his hand. "I'm buying." His voice was firm.

"All right," she said. "Then you have to let me buy you a drink at the Fox." Even though she had to meet with some of her future students tomorrow, she suddenly had an urge to go out and could feel this turning into a spontaneous party night.

"I could go for a drink at the Fox," he said.

They drove separately to Cate's apartment, where she parked her car. Although she lived in walking distance from the bar, Ethan offered to drive them in case they decided to go somewhere else. His Ford Explorer smelled like a closet full of old clothes. Except for a couple baseball caps and a few sweatshirts that were strewn across the backseat, Cate couldn't find a wardrobe. Crumpled gas receipts and CDs were scattered across the center console and floor.

"Sorry about the mess," he said, before throwing an empty paper cup and several empty bags of potato chips into the backseat. "I would've cleaned my car, but I didn't know you would be riding in it."

"No worries. We're just going around the corner." Within minutes they were parked across the street from the bar.

The Silver Fox was unusually quiet when they entered. On weekends the bar provided standing room only, and bouncers with shaved heads and tattoos guarded the entrance like pit bulls. No one was working at the door tonight. There were two guys with mullets playing pool and an old woman wearing ankle socks and flip-flops sitting at the bar. Ethan ordered their drinks as they sat down on cracked and battered brown bar stools.

"Shall we put some music on?" he said as he pulled some dollar bills out of his wallet.

"Yes! I've never been able to play music here because there are always a zillion songs waiting to play on the jukebox."

They scanned through the songs, picking out dozens. Everything from Johnny Cash to Madonna. They played five dollars' worth of songs. They sang along with Frank Sinatra when "Fly Me to the Moon" played.

The more they drank, the better the music sounded. "Patience" by Guns n' Roses came on, and Cate attempted to whistle with Axl but couldn't seem to produce a note.

"I went to a Guns n' Roses concert in high school," Ethan said. "I still have my shirt that I bought. They played with Soundgarden."

Cate laughed. "I remember when you went to that with your brother. Do you remember when we went to The Cure concert? And my mom dropped us off and waited in the parking lot until the concert ended."

"Yeah. You wanted to go backstage so you could meet Robert Smith after the show."

"Did you know that I was actually planning on moving to London after high school so I could marry Robert Smith? I really thought I had a chance," she said.

"You know what I always remember about you?"

She groaned. "Oh God. What? My braces or my black lipstick?"

He was serious. "No, really. It's not bad. But every time I think of you—even now—I think of it."

"What?"

He reached over and lightly touched the top of her cheek, right beneath a corner of her left eye, near her temple. "That freckle," he said. "I always think of the little freckle next to your eye."

"My freckle? I've had this since birth."

"I know. You have the most flawless skin, and then there is that one little mark. It's so unique."

"You're kidding?"

"No. I'm not. Every time I think of you, I think of that little freckle."

"No one has ever complimented my freckle. Ever."

His brows shot up. "Really?"

"Never. When I was little I used to call it a birthmark, but my mom said to call it a beauty mark. That's all anyone has ever said about it."

"It's you."

"I think that is the best compliment I have ever received in my entire life."

He shrugged. "It's just the truth." Then he set his empty glass on the bar.

He was so sweet she wanted to cry. As a preteen, she'd felt self-conscious about the freckle. Despite the fact that no one had ever mentioned it, the freckle had been the first thing she noticed in pictures. Then when Cindy Crawford had made moles seem in, she felt she had a beauty mark. Still, no one had ever said she reminded them of Cindy. She'd gotten so used to the little detail on her face that she'd practically forgotten its existence.

Whether it was the alcohol making her sentimental or Ethan's kind words, she couldn't help but want to be closer to him. She watched as he tapped his fingers on the bar to the beat of the music, oblivious that she was studying his face. He had the kind of eyes that babies had: innocent, sweet eyes that never told lies. He was so different from anyone she had ever been attracted to. Paul turned heads when he walked into a room. He was tall and lean and had a face that could be in movies. Ethan was smaller, less muscular, and rarely combed his hair. But for a split second she felt like she could be attracted to Ethan. God no. What was she thinking? She could never touch him the way she touched Paul. Ethan wasn't sexy. He was her friend. Her childhood friend.

"I think I'm ready for a shot. You?" he asked.

She had forgotten that she was staring at him and snapped out of her alcohol-induced trance. "Yes! I'd love one!" She didn't know what had gotten into her. Tomorrow began the first day of her home visits, and she was getting crocked with Ethan at the Fox.

"Two buttery nipples," Ethan said to the bartender.

She was nearly stumbling when they left the bar. "Ethan, I just want you to know that you're such a good friend. You're practically family. Really, I mean it. You are. You are just the greatest." She squeezed his cheeks. "Les go get another drink."

Ethan had resorted to water over an hour earlier. "It's two, Cate," he said between his cheeks that Cate held together like a sandwich. "I think the bars are closing."

"Les get a burrito then."

"Okay. *I'll* drive."

She tried not to step on the pile of CDs near her feet and grabbed a few of them.

"Pick out whatever you want," he said. "Sorry about the mess. I need to organize my car."

She rifled through some of the CDs. They'd already listened to a lot of them at the Silver Fox. She picked an Elton John CD, then sang at the top of her lungs to "Daniel."

The restaurant was brightly lit and painted. Its red and yellow decor was outdated by a few decades, but festive.

"Thank God for twenty-four-hour Mexican food!" Cate said as they entered.

Although Ramone's had some serious shady qualities, it was her favorite place to eat. It was the kind of dive that a tourist would never set foot in. However, all the locals overlooked its outdated, rundown facade and appreciated the mouthwatering authentic Mexican food. At the counter she ordered a carne asada burrito with sour cream, and Ethan ordered five rolled tacos with guacomole.

While they waited for their food, Cate challenged him to a game of Destroyer. She played the video game with an aggressive assault and determination. It was a close match, but Ethan ended up beating her. She challenged him to five more games, ignoring her burrito and finally beating him on the fifth.

She grabbed the paper bag that held their food, and more hot sauce containers than she could carry. She left a trail of hot sauce behind her as she headed to the Explorer.

Somewhere between Ramone's and her apartment, her head began to spin.

17 • The Obvious

When daylight hit, Cate's mouth felt like a bowl of Cream of Wheat that had been left on the kitchen table all day. She tried to rub her tongue over her lips to create moisture, but it was no use. Her first thought was that she had suffered a blow to the head because she'd never felt such severe pain. Her stomach threatened to erupt in her throat, and she was in the same outfit from the night before. She even had one sandal still strapped to her left foot.

Grease sat no more than a hair away from her face, as still as a statue, watching her. He was purring and wore the look that cats sometimes get when they confuse themselves with royalty.

She limped to the bathroom in one shoe. A glance in the mirror revealed the most severe bed-head in the history of mankind and splotches of mascara that had dried down her cheeks. She caught a glimpse of the clock in the mirror and nearly jumped out of her sandal. Ten-twenty. She was due at her first home visit at eleven. With force she kicked off the shoe, turned the shower all the way to hot, and stripped naked. She washed her hair, face, and body all with shampoo but failed to shave her legs or condition her hair. She still felt drunk. A lack of clean clothes created a major dilemma when it was time to find an outfit. Pants were her only option, because her legs resembled creatures from *Wild Kingdom*. However, all her pants were dirty. She tore through the pile of stuff on her wicker chair, looking for something to wear, tossing her bridesmaid's dresses from Sarah's and Val's weddings on the floor. Both gowns were horribly wrinkled and now resembled fur coats because of all the white cat hair they had collected.

She ended up in wrinkled black pants, a blouse she hadn't worn in two years, and a pair of blue suede loafers that were probably inappropriate for the occasion. She was bolting into the kitchen to feed Grease when Ethan rose like a blow-up doll from the couch. His bed-head was worse than hers.

"Ethan!" she gasped. "I didn't know you were here!"

He scratched his head. "I'm sorry. I crashed on the couch. You were pretty faded last night. You puked in front of the building, and I was worried about you."

"I'm still drunk, Ethan. And I have to meet with two students' families this morning."

"Come here."

She moved closer to him.

"Say something," he said.

"What are you doing?" she asked as she leaned in closer.

He shook his head. "You don't have alcohol on your breath."

She grabbed her purse and car keys. "Will you feed Grease for me?"

He shrugged. "Sure."

"You're a doll."

*   *   *

Timothy Sickle was first on her visit list. His mansion was situated in the hills of Huntington Gate. Rumor had it that a player from the Padres lived on his block. She wondered what his parents did for a living.

Getting into houses such as these was always a pain in the ass. There was usually some variety of a gate with an elaborate code or intercom system. In the Sickles' driveway, she couldn't reach the button on the gate. She put her car in park, opened the door, and leaned closer to the intercom, her left leg grounded on the asphalt. When she pressed the button, an awkward buzz burped from the intercom. A moment passed before a childlike giggle came crackling from the speaker.

"Hi there!" Cate said in her Miss Padgett voice.

"Who is it?" the child asked.

"It's Miss Padgett. Is this Timothy?"

The child squealed and said, "Go away, Miss Pis—"

The intercom burped again and went dead. Did he just call her Miss Piss? The intercom had been scratchy, and she must've misunderstood him. She pressed the button again and waited while the sun pounded into every pore of her body.

Sweat beads trickled down her neck and back. She didn't know which was worse, her pants stuck like wet lettuce to the back of her thighs or her sweaty feet, dying for air inside her suffocating loafers. A few minutes passed before the intercom burped again, and the gate opened.

She noticed that her car was making its usual rattling noise as she pulled in next to a Mercedes. She'd look into it later.

Timothy's mother answered the door with a golden retriever at her side and a baby on her hip. "Hi, I'm Karen Sickle, Timothy's mom." She looked fortyish and was sunburned. "And this is Marla." A stream of bubbly drool ran down the baby's chin and onto the collar of Mrs. Sickle's shirt.

Cate extended a hand to Mrs. Sickle. "I'm Miss Padgett. It's nice to meet you."

Mrs. Sickle's hand felt limp. "Come in. We were just finishing lunch. Timothy is in the kitchen."

Cate noticed a full glass of apple juice on the counter and wanted to suck it down in one gulp. She would've paid a king's ransom for a glass of water. A large bowl filled with pasta salad and two serving spoons also sat on the countertop. She could see black olives and rotini dripping with olive oil and seasoning. Greasy, salty. Perfect hangover food. Her stomach growled, and she thought of how nice it would be if Mrs. Sickle offered her some of that salad.

"Why don't we go into the living room?" Mrs. Sickle suggested. Then her voice suddenly became high-pitched. "Timothy, this is your teacher. 'Member when we talked about kindergarten?"

His eyes darted to Cate. "I don't want to go to kinnergarter. I just want to make pancakes with my mom."

His mother let out a screech of a laugh. "Timothy! When was the last time you made pancakes?"

He crawled beneath the table.

Mrs. Sickle released a tired sigh and set the baby in a high chair.

"Timothy, I have a lot of things planned for kindergarten," Cate said. "We're going to do things that are even better than making pancakes." She looked under the table. "Why don't you come out from under there so I can tell you all about it."

He shook his head.

Cate crouched down on her knees. He was a cute kid with a blond bowl haircut and blue eyes. "Do you like play dough?" she asked.

He ignored her.

"We're going to make play dough and alphabet cookies that you can spell your name with."

He looked at her with skepticism.

"I can start showing you how to spell your name if you come out. I'd love to—"

He started to lean forward when Mrs. Sickle's hand shot beneath the table. She waved a Fudgsicle at him. "Here! You can have this if you come out from under there."

Timothy shot from beneath the table like a cat after a bird. Cate wished she hadn't bribed him. It only reinforced his fiendish behavior.

Mrs. Sickle picked up the baby and led Cate and Timothy to the living room. They were about to sit down on the couch when the shocking sound of an atomic fart filled the room. For a second it wasn't clear who was responsible. Cate didn't think such a small child would be capable. Mrs. Sickle?

Timothy giggled then yelled, "I tooted!" taking full ownership for the gaseous blast. He began to sing, *"Beans, beans, the musical fruit"* at the top of his lungs.

His mother laughed even louder than the fart. "Timothy!" she hooted. He did it again, this time sticking his butt out as if he were about to take a seat. Cate tried to laugh with them, but it smelled, and she didn't want him doing that in her class.

The baby began to cry. "Timothy, that's enough," Mrs. Sickle said, still smiling. She looked at Cate. "I'm so exhausted. Our nanny went back to Mexico, and I haven't been able to find a replacement yet."

Cate was dying of thirst and felt salt-deprived from her hangover.

The baby was cranky and began to wail even louder. Cate's head pounded.

"She hasn't had her nap yet," Mrs. Sickle said.

"You can go put her down," Cate said, hoping she didn't sound eager to get rid of her. "I'll just spend a few minutes getting to know Timothy, then I really have to get going to my next appointment."

"All right."

"Juice!" Timothy yelled as his mother left them. "Bring my juice."

"You've had enough juice today. You can have water."

"Juuuuice!" He threw himself to the floor. "Joo-hoo-hoo-ce!" he wailed as he flung his limbs in all directions. He sounded as if he was crying, yet Cate didn't notice any tears. "Give me joo-hoo—"

"All right! Fine," Mrs. Sickle snapped.

Cate waited for Mrs. Sickle to offer her a drink, but she had already disappeared to the kitchen. She returned with a plastic cup for Timothy. He sat up as if the mini-tantrum had never occurred and began to suck down the sugary drink like a starving piglet.

"Happy now?" Mrs. Sickle said.

His blond head bobbed up and down.

Then Mrs. Sickle was gone again, the dog following her.

She hadn't been gone for thirty seconds when Timothy turned to Cate and stuck his tongue out. Then he grabbed his juice and took a giant chug.

"So, Timothy, what do you like to do for fun?"

He ignored her.

"I bet you have a favorite toy. Why don't you show me your favorite toy?"

He shook his head.

"Well, do you like finger painting?"

He stuck a little forefinger up his nose. He twirled his finger around, digging into the depths of his nostril, shamelessly prodding away for something disgusting.

"You really shouldn't do that," Cate said. "You're going to get a bloody nose."

He plucked his finger from his nose and produced a juicy booger. He suspended his finger in the air, pointing it at Cate. She sensed he meant trouble. Her heart pounded as she tried to reason with Timothy, praying that he wouldn't come any closer with his loaded finger.

"Timothy, if you go get a Kleenex, I'll tell you a secret. I'll tell you something that none of the other kids will know before the first day of school." She had no idea where she was going with this. "It's a very special secret, and you'll be the only one—"

He moved closer, holding his forefinger up to her temple. "Timothy, please," she whispered, scared to death of his green booger.

"Timothy! What are you doing, for heaven's sake? What's on your finger?" Mrs. Sickle yelled.

"Nothing," he said as he moved away from Cate and hid his hand behind his back.

Cate stood. "I should really get going. I have a full schedule today."

Although she wanted to flee from the Sickle residence, she was still dying of thirst. She used the bathroom and drank straight from the faucet before bidding a quick farewell to the spawn of Satan. As she drove away, she swore she saw Timothy flipping her off from a window.

After her visit with the Sickles she debated darting over to El Ranchito for a burrito and a water before her next visit. However, she didn't have time. She was due at Ariana Gomez's house in three minutes.

They lived in the neighborhood across the street from Huntington Gate, High Valley. This was also a nice neighborhood but more rural. Most of the houses varied in size and were set on at least five-acre plots of land. Horse rings and stables covered the yards.

She had one hell of a time trying to locate the Gomez home. High Valley was a maze of winding roads that led to unpromising paths. The wooden street signs were faded and nearly camouflaged amid the sagebrush. When she finally found the house, the address number did not match the last name on the gate. It read *The Banks Family* rather than *The Gomez Family*. Maybe there was a divorce or something.

She pulled onto a ten-acre lot with a sprawling horse ring surrounded by one of the most beautiful emerald lawns she had ever seen. A woman atop a white horse, wearing an English riding habit, stopped next to her car. "Can I help you?" she asked. She looked too old to be Ariana's mother.

"I'm looking for Ariana Gomez," Cate said. "I'm her kindergarten teacher, and I'm supposed to meet with her today."

"Oh." The horse's tail swished from side to side, swatting flies. "They live in the trailer behind the property." She pointed to a skinny dirt trail encased in avocado trees before trotting off.

When Cate stepped from the car, dust swirled around her pants and settled on her blue suede loafers. She could hear the sound of sprinklers in the distance. Water sprayed over several blossoming yellow and red rosebushes that surrounded the gigantic ranch-style home. She was still dying of thirst and wondered what the Bankses would think if she drank straight from their sprinklers. She walked past their home and headed toward the dirt trail.

A trailer that had probably been a real beauty for someone in the 1970s stood at the end of the path. One of the windows was cracked. Another was held shut by duct tape. She knocked on the door. A man at least five inches shorter than Cate answered. He had a mustache, and his black hair had been parted and slicked to the side. He wore a pair of brown pants, cowboy boots, and a button-down shirt that looked as if it had also been around for a few decades.

He nodded. "Hi."

"Hi. I'm Cate Padgett. I'm Ariana's kindergarten teacher."

"*Sí. Sí.* I am Eduardo, Ariana's father. Come in, Mrs. Cate. We've been waiting for you."

"Oh, I'm sorry. I hope you haven't been waiting long. I got lost."

"No. It's good. Very happy to meet you. Very good."

An audience awaited her. Five faces under the age of twelve looked up at her, and a tiny Mexican woman wearing a white dress and sandals smiled anxiously at Cate. Her hair was pulled into a tight bun.

"Please. Meet family," Mr. Gomez said. The trailer was immaculately clean but tiny. The kitchen area was not even half the size of Cate's bathroom. All the children sat around a small table. There were four bunks in the front end, one of which Cate sat on, and what appeared to be a tiny bedroom in the back.

"This is my wife, Lupe."

The woman smiled shyly and nodded.

"And these are our children. Please be welcome to our home." He pointed to each child, Enrique, Reuben, Oscar, Maria. Finally a little head emerged from behind one of the older boys. "This is Ariana. Come say hi, Ariana."

She was dressed in a ruffled white dress that Cate imagined was probably her most valued possession, and black sandals. A neat braid hung over the back of her tiny neck. She looked up at Cate with huge, round brown eyes.

"Hi, Ariana." She knelt down in front of the child. "I'm Miss Padgett. You're going to be in my class this year."

Her eyes wandered shyly to her father.

"I've been teaching her some English. She's getting some, but she's shy. I want her to do good in school. It's very important."

Mrs. Gomez stood and walked to the small kitchen. She opened the refrigerator, and all the children's eyes darted to what she pulled out. "We have soda," she said to Cate. "Please have drink with us."

"Oh thank you. I really appreciate it."

"Which one?" She pointed to a liter of Sprite and a liter of Coke.

"Sprite would be great. Thanks."

Then Mrs. Gomez pulled out a plate filled with tamales, a bowl with refried beans, a basket of freshly baked tortillas, and another bowl of salsa. Mr. Gomez said something to the other children in Spanish, and they moved from the table and took seats on the cots. He pointed to the table. "Please have a seat. My wife prepares food for us."

Cate took a seat at the table, and Mr. Gomez slid in across from her. He pointed to the empty spot next to Cate, and Ariana took a seat.

She thought about Karen Sickle and how she had offered her nothing. She thought of how bratty Timothy had been, and how she knew it was going to take some work to get him on the right track. In a strange way, this was part of the reason she liked teaching so much. She loved meeting a variety of kids and seeing the way they developed throughout the school year. She knew that Timothy would be difficult to control at first. But as soon as she put all the kids on behavior modification contracts, rewarding them with stickers when they were good and taking the stickers away when they were bad, Timothy would live to impress her.

Although Timothy and Ariana came from such different backgrounds, Timothy would learn something from her. When he watched Ariana get constant rewards for good behavior, he would want to follow in the same path. Cate was willing to bet that he would grow into a different child by the end of the school year. That was what she loved, watching these kids from unique backgrounds intermingle with each other and grow into different people.

Mrs. Gomez set a glass filled with Sprite and a heaping plate of food in front of Cate. The smell of Mexican food made her mouth water. The rest of the family was served before Mrs. Gomez took a seat next to her husband.

The food was delicious. She could've eaten three tamales but didn't want to be greedy after Mrs. Gomez had already dished a second round of food on her plate. She spent over an hour with them. She asked the kids questions about their ages and what they liked to do. Some of the older children were nervous about attending school. She told them what they could expect at Tierra Bonita.

She thanked them profusely for the meal, and they thanked her a dozen times for visiting with them. The entire family followed her to her car.

She was just about to step inside the Volvo when Ariana tapped her on the leg. Cate looked down at her little face. She pulled something from behind her back. It was a drawing done in pencil, on the back of an ad that had probably been left on someone's car in a parking lot. It was of a schoolhouse with two huge clouds and a sun overhead. On the bottom in the childlike writing that Cate had become familiar with over the years was written Miss Padgett.

*   *   *

Cate practically collapsed when she returned to her apartment. After putting Ariana's drawing on the refrigerator, she fell into a deep, sweaty nap for three hours.

She probably would've slept all night if Grease hadn't been determined to kill a spider that had crawled behind her dresser. His constant clawing at the slim space between the dresser and the wall had forced her to wake up.

The first thing she did was call Ethan, so he could fill in the blanks from the previous night. She prayed that she hadn't made a *complete* ass out of herself. She hated the postdrinking nervous ache she got after a night of binge drinking. This was why she always tried to remember her limits. Unfortunately, Ethan wasn't available to provide details. She left a message.

Then she realized Paul still had not called. She tried not to think about No Call Paul and fell into a beading frenzy. She beaded like a maniac, making bracelets, and anklets, and necklaces, and little inventions like beaded pinky rings and key chains.

Ten rolled around and still no word from Paul. Her imagination went wild with possibilities. He was cheating on her. He was mad at her. He was a jerk. Why was she like this? Her moods and emotions were at the mercy of Paul's phone calls. She felt pathetic. But she couldn't stop herself from dwelling on him.

Love meant that you called someone when you were out of town. Love meant that you wanted to hear someone's voice, even if you had nothing to say to her.

Then a horrific thought flashed through her mind the same way lights on top of a cop car glared in her rearview mirror the last time she'd been pulled over for speeding. Paul didn't love her. He'd never said it. He wasn't in the same place—like Ethan said. She was speeding.

She needed some fresh air. She walked to her mailbox in sweats and flip-flops. Fog had rolled in over the ocean, and the air outside was moist.

Disappointment hit when she pulled her Visa bill from the box. She didn't feel like looking at it tonight. There was a thank-you note from Leslie Lyons, acknowledging the *"wonderful pancake warmer"* Cate had given her at the shower. Pancake warmer? No. Cate had given her a ninety-dollar vase. Emily Post would've died.

She could hear her phone ringing from the hallway. The mail nearly scattered from her hands when she darted for the front door. *Paul! Please be Paul!* She dropped the mail on the floor and took a deep breath before she answered.

"Hello."

"Hey!" It was Leslie. She always sounded excited on the phone. "What are you doing tonight?"

"Nursing a hangover."

"You went out on a Monday night?"

Cate's engaged friends had all forgotten that Monday nights qualified as a Friday when you were single. "Yeah, it was one of those spontaneous things. I ended up two sheets to the breeze with my friend Ethan— the one I've been taking pictures for."

Leslie's voice turned to an excited whisper. "Did you hook up with him?"

"No! I have Paul. I would never do that to him."

"How *is* Paul?"

Cate sighed. "Fine."

"What happened?" Leslie asked. "I can tell something is wrong."

"He hasn't called in two days."

"Where is he? Is he still in Maui?"

"No. He went straight from Maui to San Francisco."

"Well, two days isn't that long. He's been traveling. Give him a break. Maybe he's busy."

"True. But he does this to me constantly. You know how he is. Hot and cold and up and down. I just get bummed because I think if you really care about someone, you call just to hear her voice. I mean, doesn't Russ call you every day? Doesn't he *want* to talk to you?"

"Yeah, but we're getting married."

"Paul and I have been dating for almost a year. Don't you think he should be calling every day by now?"

She was quiet for a moment. "All guys are different. It takes some a little longer to become more attached. And besides, guys get busy and they just forget. They're stupid. Don't worry."

"How long was it before Russ started calling you every day?"

She thought about it. "Well, hmmm. A while. I used to get pissed, too. It takes guys a while to catch on. They're like dogs. Most of them need training."

Cate imagined herself guiding Paul to the phone with a leash.

"Sometimes I think I should just date other people."

"Maybe that's what he needs. When Russ was acting like a flake, I started talking about this guy, Alvin Youngkin, that I worked with. I always said how cute and great he was. Then I would flirt with him when Russ was around. It really made Russ jealous, and then he started behaving. I whipped his ass into shape."

Cate wondered if that was how Leslie had coerced Russ into marrying her, always making him feel threatened. "I don't want to have to play games like that. I like Paul. I don't want him to feel insecure. I want him to love me."

"Well, don't make any drastic decisions tonight. Give him until midnight. If he hasn't called by then, you can start to worry."

"Why midnight?"

"I don't know. Just so you don't worry." She changed the subject. "Anyway, I was just calling to tell you a little bit about the wedding. It'll all be in the itinerary, but I just wanted to let you know some of the details. It's going to be at the Laguna Cliffs Marriott. The hotel overlooks the harbor. It's gorgeous, so everything will be held outdoors. I can't wait to show you my table linens!" she exclaimed. "My mom and I saw a pattern we loved on a gown at Neiman Marcus. We bought the gown and took it to the garment district in L.A. to see if they could make thirty-eight tablecloths and four hundred matching napkins with the same pattern."

"There's four hundred people coming to the wedding?"

"Well, we're inviting five hundred, but we figured that only four hundred will show. Anyway, we found someone who could make the table linens. But they had to send everything to China. So right now all of my table linens are being made in China!"

"Great." The last thing that came to mind when planning a wedding was table linens, let alone custom-made ones from China. Cate imagined children slaving over the tablecloths and napkins in a sweatshop. "So what kind of ceremony are you having?" she asked.

"Since Russ is Jewish and I'm Lutheran, we're going to have a minister and a rabbi."

"Really? You found a minister and a rabbi who will do that?"

"Yeah. It was hard, but we found them. Anyway, you guys are all going to walk down the aisle and then I'm going to come in on a horse."

A burst of laughter nearly exploded from Cate's throat before she realized that Leslie was serious. "Your dad isn't walking you down the aisle?"

"Yeah. He'll be leading the horse by a rope."

"Oh. That should be . . . nice."

"Yeah. I wanted a whole fairy-tale feeling to the wedding. We looked into horse-drawn carriages, but there wasn't enough room at the hotel with four hundred people coming, so we thought a horse would be just as pretty. It's going to be a white Arabian horse with a long mane and tail. And Russ is going to lift me off the horse when I reach the altar."

Cate was just glad that *she* didn't have to ride a horse down the aisle. She tried to picture everything. The bridesmaids in their disco suits. Leslie in her strapless ivory gown on a horse. Mr. Lyons holding the rope. It was a horrendous episode of *A Wedding Story*. Who was she to judge, though? She was unengaged and sitting at home alone waiting for Paul to call.

After she hung up with Leslie, she flopped onto the couch. She decided not to dwell on Leslie's advice about Paul. Leslie was no expert when it came to relationships.

Cate had met Leslie her freshman year of college, and from the very beginning of their friendship, Cate knew that Leslie's lifelong goal was to get married.

She'd been one of those girls who'd always had a boyfriend. Since she was thirteen she hadn't been without a relationship. If she saw the romance going south, she had one boyfriend lined up before she dumped the other. *Father of the Bride* was her all-time favorite movie. She watched it religiously in the dorm room they shared. She lived for episodes of *Celebrity Weddings,* jotting down notes of things she wanted to replicate at her own wedding. Cate remembered her describing her wedding dress, cake and, if memory served, her bridesmaid's *dresses* to her friends after her second date with Russ. There had been no mention of suits.

After several years of continuous nagging, she'd finally convinced Russ to take her to Zale's, where she picked out the three-carat ring surrounded with little diamonds that she'd had in mind for nearly a decade. She just wanted to make sure that she liked the ring, since she was going to be the one wearing it for the rest of her life. Cate thought that picking out your own engagement ring was perhaps one of the most unromantic things she had ever heard. Then again, maybe she should listen to Leslie. She was the one getting married. She must be doing something right.

The phone rang again. *Paul! Paul! Please be Paul!* It was Ethan.

"I just got your message. I was going to call you anyway to see how you were feeling."

"Today was horrific. Heat and hangovers just don't go together. It must've been a hundred and ten in Poway."

"I know what you mean. I was a little hung over, too."

"I wasn't too much of a pain. Was I?" she asked.

"No. Not at all. I had a good time last night."

"You did?"

"Of course. We'll do it again."

"Next time I won't behave like Mötley Crüe."

He laughed. "What's wrong with partying like a rock star?"

"Nothing, if you're actually a rock star."

"Let's grab dinner or something this week," he said.

They made plans for dinner and said good-bye. She watched an hour of mediocre television and popped a zit on her forehead that was barely visible but would probably create ten more pimples now that she had attacked it. Finally she decided to call it a night. It was midnight, and he hadn't called. She felt like crying but was too tired.

She washed her face, then doused the zit with enough rubbing alcohol to fuel a car. Even though she knew she wouldn't be able to get a sound night of sleep without hearing from Paul, she wanted the warm, safe feeling of her comforter over her body. She had barely turned off the light when the phone rang.

"*Hola*, sweetie," he said.

"Paul."

"How are ya?" he sounded happy to hear her voice.

"I'm good. What have you been doing?"

"I've been swamped. This whole week has just been crazy with meetings, luncheons, seminars."

"You had a meeting this late?"

"No, I just ended up sitting in the hot tub at the hotel for like two hours and didn't feel like getting out. How are ya?"

Didn't feel like getting out! She'd been on the verge of hysteria, and he didn't feel like getting out of the freaking hot tub to call her? "I'm tired," she said. "And I've been a little worried, Paul."

"Why?" He didn't have a clue.

"I called you two days ago and never heard back. I was starting to wonder if something was wrong." She felt like saying, *I want an explanation for your damn hot and cold confusing personalities,* but she maintained control.

"Soooorry! I didn't know you were so worried. I honestly didn't mean to make you worry."

"Well, it would help if you could just return my calls when you get them."

"All right. Geez."

She absolutely loathed herself. She hated sounding like the worried, needy girlfriend. What was she becoming? She let it go.

"So what have you been up to?" he asked.

"I went out with Ethan last night and then—"

"Oh yeah," he sneered. "That caterer."

"Yes. He is a caterer." *And he promptly returns all my phone calls and is interested in my life and my hobbies,* she wanted to add.

"Humph. Anyway, go on."

She sensed a jealous tone in his voice and remembered Leslie's story about how she had made Russ jealous over a coworker. Perhaps she should take Leslie's advice. Maybe she could use Ethan to her advantage. She could talk about how *wonderful and fabulous* he was, and what a *great* time they had together. But Ethan really was wonderful and fabulous, and she couldn't use him to get back at Paul. Ethan meant more than that.

Instead, Cate began to tell him about her hungover morning with Timothy Sickle and Ariana Gomez. She was getting to the part about the tamales when she heard a steady liquid stream in the background. "Are you peeing?" she asked. Abruptly, it stopped.

"Sorry, I couldn't hold it. Like I said, I was in that hot tub forever, and I had to take a piss." She heard a flush. "I'm beat," he said, seemingly uninterested in the rest of her story.

"So am I."

"I can't wait to come home," he said.

"You're coming back Friday?"

"Yes. My flight gets in around four, I think. Oh! I meant to ask you. Some of my friends are going to be in town from Los Angeles. I told them I'd meet them for drinks in the Gaslamp on Friday. Do you want to go?"

"Sure."

"Good. I'll see you on Friday then."

"Okay." Good-bye was on the tip of her lips when she remembered something. "Hey, I have a question for you."

"Yeah?"

"What do you think of the freckle right next to my left eye?"

"What freckle?"

"You know. The only one on my face that sort of stands out."

"Where is it? On your cheek?"

"Never mind."

"You know that everything about you is cute, Cate. I'm sure your freckle is cute, too."

"Thanks," she said but didn't mean it.

Bailey Goldsmith had been Cate's last appointment on Friday. She was a tiny thing with a vocabulary that seemed too large for her little body. Cate had liked her. She was inquisitive and interested in school. Her mother had also volunteered to be a helper in Cate's classroom, which was always a bonus.

She had just stepped into the Volvo when the piercing sound of her cell phone filled the car. She was glad that it hadn't rung inside the Goldsmiths' home. That would've been unprofessional.

Paul.

She hadn't been expecting him to call for at least another hour or perhaps even five minutes before they were scheduled to hang out. That would've been more like him.

"Did you just land?" she asked.

"I sure did, and you're the first person I called."

So, he was Prompt Sweet Paul today.

"Really?" She acted surprised.

"Yes. I'm in a cab right now. I can't wait to see you."

"Are we still going to the Gaslamp?"

"Yeah. We're going downtown, so just dress like you're going downtown."

That meant dressed up. Going downtown meant that Cate would bust out a black cocktail dress and heels. Downtown meant a little more makeup. It wasn't like Pacific Beach. People didn't drip salsa and spill beer on their jeans in the Gaslamp. They drank ten-dollar martinis and valet-parked.

"What time are you coming over?" she asked.

"Be ready at eight."

When she returned to her complex, there was a small package from Leslie Lyons waiting in her mailbox. Inside the box was the promised nail polish. It was a dark gray color called Slate. Cate pulled out a note.

Don't forget! Two coats each! Russ and I are so honored to
have you share this special day with us.
  Love,
  Les

Cate tossed the note and package onto her wicker chair.

When Paul arrived, she was still in her robe. She'd finished blow-drying her hair. She'd even borrowed Jill's flatiron and had straightened the hell out of her bob for a slicker look. She had applied eyeliner and eye shadow, which she only wore if she were in a wedding or going downtown.

"You look sexy in that little robe," he said as he kissed her neck. She looked down and noticed that his erection had formed a tent in his pants. Actually, it was more like a circus tent. He was huge. She was about to reach for it when he pulled away. "We're actually in a hurry. I told them we'd be there by eight." It was five to eight.

"Should I wear black pants and this burgundy halter top or this black cocktail dress?" She held up both outfits.

He pointed to the dress. "The dress. I love the dress."

"Do you know which club we're going to yet?"

"We're actually going to Little Italy. I can't remember the name of the place. I have to call them on the way."

"Little Italy? Maybe I should go more casual."

"No. You're fine, and we're just meeting there, anyway. I think we'll end up at The Onyx Room or On Broadway."

The Onyx Room and On Broadway were definitely meant for black cocktail dresses.

En route to Little Italy, his friends phoned with a meeting place.

She was excited to meet Paul's friends from home, never having been exposed to that aspect of his life. She'd heard about his friends and family from Los Angeles but had not met them.

The Whaler's Pub was an English pub in the middle of Little Italy. Its specialty was fish and chips and the beer from their own brewery. Several men were involved in a dart tournament when they entered.

Cate almost landed her black heel into a basket of fries that someone had left on the floor when they walked to a table in the corner.

"Paul!" someone roared.

Approximately ten people were seated around a table. They wore jeans. The guys all resembled other versions of Paul with their short hair and sharp shirts.

He shook hands with his guy friends from Los Angeles and kissed Meredith, the only girl, on the cheek. She was a tall blonde with a tiny nose and fair skin. She reminded Cate of Nicole Kidman. She had a tendency to turn her head to an angle when she spoke and she looked at Cate as if she were a cute two-year-old when Paul introduced them.

Even though Cate was confident that her outfit was the essence of vogue, she felt painfully uncomfortable in her dress and heels. She stood next to Paul, fidgeting with her purse, while they all said hello.

She was dying to hide in a booth.

She and Paul found seats at the end of the table. At first he spoke to his friends about their trip to San Diego, the weather in Los Angeles, and a bunch of other crap that no one really cared about.

Cate ordered a gin and tonic that had been hopelessly watered down and listened while Paul reminisced with his friends about home. His elbows rested on the table as he leaned closer to his friends. They spoke of people she didn't know. Johnny Pierce was getting married. Mandy O'Neill was having a baby. Bryce Sommers was gay. Paul hung on every word. It was all irrelevant to Cate. She ordered another gin and tonic. If there was any alcohol, she couldn't taste it.

She was thinking about complaining to the bartender when she noticed Paul had moved to the other side of the table. He was now seated next to Meredith, his back turned to Cate.

"So what are you doing now?" Cate heard him ask her.

"Pharmaceutical sales." She had a way of saying *pharmaceutical sales* that made it sound cute.

She couldn't hear much of what they said because they were about five chairs away. She looked at the people across from her. They were laughing at a joke someone had just told. "So how long are you guys in town for?" she asked.

No one heard her. She leaned closer to the table and said it again, louder. They weren't paying attention and continued to talk amongst themselves. She tried to appear preoccupied and searched through her purse for nothing in particular. She found a mint that had been in her bag since she'd gone to World Famous with Ethan. She wished she were with Ethan or her girlfriends instead of the jerks she was sitting across from. She undid the wrapper and popped it into her mouth. Ethan would never hang out with people like this or, if he did, he would never leave her out. He would be the perfect boyfriend, and she wished she felt the same kind of sparks she experienced when she looked at Paul.

What seemed like a decade passed, and she still didn't feel a buzz from the cocktails. Again, she tried to make conversation with Paul's friends.

"So how long are you all in town for?"

A silence fell over their little group. She felt as if she had a giant piece of spinach stuck in her tooth. "Just 'til Monday," one answered.

"What do you all do?" She was really beginning to wonder if something was stuck between her teeth.

"We're all in pharmaceutical sales," another said. Then he turned to his friends. "Did I tell you that I ran into Mike Walters last week?"

"Really?" they all said with enthusiasm.

Without telling anyone, she left for the bathroom. She felt like announcing to all those who were staring that she had not planned on going to a pub and thought she was going dancing instead.

In the bathroom she shut herself into a stall and called Jill on her cell phone. Jill was having dinner with Beth and Ike in Old Town. Cate actually considered walking the ten plus miles to meet them.

"Where are you?" Jill asked.

"I'm having the worst night," she whispered.

"What? I can't hear you."

She raised her voice but was careful not to speak too loud. "I'm having the worst night."

"Are you with Paulo?"

"Yes. We're at some pub in Little Italy with like ten of his friends. He told me we were going to the Gaslamp, so I'm dressed up and they're all in jeans. His friends are kind of assholes, and I honestly wish I had just stayed in."

"Hold on," she said. Cate could hear the sound of an accordion and a Spanish singer in the background while she waited. She wished more than anything she was sipping on properly made cocktails with them. "We're coming to get you," Jill said.

She couldn't just leave. That would be rude. But, hell, leaving your girlfriend alone at the end of the table when she doesn't know a soul to go chat with some other girl is rude. "Do you mind?"

"Not at all. We'll be there in ten minutes."

"I'll be waiting outside."

She turned off her phone before slipping it back into her purse. When she came out of the stall, Meredith was standing in front of the mirror, fluffing her hair. "There you are!" she said. "We've been wondering where you went."

"Oh. My phone rang, and I thought it would be rude to talk at the table." How long had Meredith been standing there for? Cate prayed she hadn't heard the part about Paul's friends being assholes.

"Paul was wondering where you were." She put her arm around Cate. Her camel-colored boots looked good with her Levi's. "C'mon. Let's go back to the table." She said it with zest.

Paul looked concerned when they returned to the table, and Cate wished that Meredith would remove her arm from her shoulders. "Hey! There you are," he said. "I was starting to wonder where you went." He pulled an empty chair in between him and Meredith. "Here. Why don't you sit with us?"

She sat down. "Jill called," she said quietly. "She's coming to get me."

"You're leaving?"

"Well, they're just right around the corner, and I'm tired. It's been a long day. Besides, I think it will be good for you to catch up with your friends."

"Why don't you have Jill come in for a drink?"

Jill would be bored to tears after three minutes with this crew. Cate shook her head. "She's just swinging by to grab me. I don't think she's planning on coming in."

He seemed confused. "Well, let me walk you out then."

"No really. It's okay." She didn't feel like making a production and wanted to quietly slip away from the table. "I'll just talk to you tomorrow."

"Are you sure?"

"Yeah. It's fine."

"Well, what are you doing tomorrow? Don't forget that I leave again Sunday night. Let's do something tomorrow."

"I'm working at Beth's store all day. Why don't you call me on my cell phone? We'll figure something out for tomorrow night."

"All right." The truth was, she didn't really care if she saw him tomorrow. She was tired. She was sick of chasing after him and waiting for No Call Paul to be the Prompt Paul. She was sick of feeling like she had half a boyfriend instead of feeling like she was part of a couple. She was over it.

She quickly said good-bye. Thankfully, it wasn't a production, and no one seemed to care that she was leaving.

The cold air outside sent prickles up her bare back and legs. She wrapped her arms around her chest as she waited and tried to keep from shivering.

She'd been having a nightmare that she lost the nail polish for Leslie's wedding when the phone rang. Groggily, she answered on the third ring.

"*Hola.*"

"What time is it?" she asked.

"Two-thirty." She could tell he was on his cell phone by the subtle crunching in the background. "I'm standing outside your door. Come let me in."

She sat up. "You're outside?"

"Yeah, I want to talk to you. Please let me in."

She hung up the phone and walked in the dark to her front door. He was still in his clothes from the Whaler's Pub. The scent of cigarettes, cologne, and fresh air came in with him. He seemed nervous. "Why'd you leave?" he asked.

She flipped on a light as she walked toward the couch. "I was tired."

"Is something wrong?"

She debated continuing with her tired excuse, going back to bed, and preventing the boat from rocking. After all, he did care. He was worried and had shown up in the middle of the night. "Yeah, Paul. There are things that are bothering me." She felt her hands shaking, the boat tipping.

He sat down on the couch.

She stood across from him. Her arms were folded over her old T-shirt.

"What's wrong?" he asked. "Tell me."

She didn't know where to begin. Did she start with his consistent failure to call? Or with the fact that they spent about four days a month with each other? Or how much he'd changed since the beginning? "I guess sometimes I just feel like we're not in the same place." She shook her head. "I don't really think you want a serious girlfriend. And if you don't, that's fine. But I need to know."

He stared at her. "What do you mean?"

"You honestly haven't noticed the way things are between us?"

His hands shot to his sides, palms facing up. "No."

"Paul, we're not like other couples. Yeah, we say we're boyfriend and girlfriend, but there are all kinds of things. You don't call when you say you're going to. It seems like you don't care if we don't speak to each other. You're not interested in my life. I don't feel like I'm a part of your life. For a while I thought it was your job that was preventing us from becoming closer, but now I realize it's more than—"

He interrupted her. "You know how busy I am. I don't mean to blow you off."

"I just need to feel like I'm part of your life. I need to feel like I can count on you. I need more." She thought carefully about what she said next. "If you don't want that, then maybe we should start seeing other people."

The release felt intoxicating. For months she had been scared, holding everything in, tiptoeing around the fact that they were drifting from each other. Now she didn't know why. It felt liberating to unload. She didn't care if the boat tipped over and sank.

He walked toward her. His hands felt damp when they cupped her wrists. "I'm sorry. I really am."

She felt herself shaking again. She couldn't tell if he was saying good-bye or making amends. What exactly was he sorry for?

"I didn't realize I was being that way," he said. "I'll make more of an effort. I want this to work. Do you?"

She nodded. "Yeah, I do. But there have to be changes. I want us to be closer. I can't feel like I'm in the dark anymore. I can't go on feeling like I am last on your list of priorities."

"Don't worry. You won't." He squeezed her shoulders. "I'm sorry I made you feel that way." He pulled her close and hugged her harder than he ever had.

All night, he held her in his arms.

Paul fell asleep quickly, his body securely cupped against hers. She could feel his ragged breath on the back of her neck, the prickly hair on his thighs rubbing against her shaved legs. She was restless and uncomfortable. The more pressure she put on herself to fall asleep, the more insomnia seized control. She debated getting up and watching television in the living room for a while.

Instead, she lay awake, wondering if Paul would really change. Uncertainty clouded her thoughts. She still considered the notion of seeing other people. She hadn't planned on suggesting it, but now it didn't seem like a bad idea. He couldn't expect her to rely on him if he was going to be flaky and inconsiderate.

She didn't fall asleep until the wee hours of the morning. Her alarm clock cut the silence only a few hours later. She pulled out of Paul's vicelike embrace.

"Come back," he said affectionately. "Can't you stay for a few more minutes?"

"I have to be at Beth's store in an hour."

He pushed the covers off. "I'll make you breakfast."

She felt as if she'd just witnessed her mother take the Lord's name in vain. "Okay."

He walked to the bathroom in his boxers.

She brushed her teeth while he took the longest piss in history. Then he headed off to the kitchen. "I think I have some bagels in the cabinet next to the fridge," she said.

She went through her ritual of getting ready. Shower. Light makeup application. Blow-drying. Wardrobe. She picked out denim cropped pants, her Adidas (with peds) and the King Mother T-shirt she had purchased at The Casbah.

Paul was waiting for her in the kitchen. He stood next to a bagel covered in cream cheese and a tall glass of orange juice. She hardly recognized him.

"Here you go," he said as he pulled out a bar stool for her. He even handed her a napkin.

"Thanks. This is great."

She quickly ate the bagel, then fed Grease. He put on his clothes from the night before and walked to the parking lot with her. "Call me from the bead store," he said. "Let me know how things are going."

"Let me know how things are going?" She hadn't heard that since the first month of their relationship.

He opened the car door for her and smiled affectionately at her before she pulled away.

She wasn't sure whether she should be glowing with romantic bliss or completely pissed off.

19 .   Dining In

Beth was waiting at the store when Cate arrived. Her long, jet-black
hair was parted down the middle and hung loosely over her shoulders,
settling right beneath her breasts. She wore faded jeans that hung low
on her waist, a black tank top, and matching bracelets with various
shades of blue seed beads on each wrist. "Thanks so much for working
today," she said.

"Oh, hey, thank *you*. I need the money."

"I know." She seemed like she was in a hurry. She and Ike were
driving up to Los Angeles to spend the day with his family. "Anyway,
here are the keys. You know how to close, right?"

"Yeah."

She quickly reminded Cate which keys went to which locks, and
how to turn the alarm on. "Okay, so everything is set. You remember
how to use the cash register?"

Cate nodded.

"If any customers have questions that you can't answer, just tell 'em to leave their name and number, and I'll give 'em a ring when I get back on Monday. Oh! Anthony is stopping by to pick up some things. He knows where they are, so you don't have to worry about finding anything."

That was a bonus. Days spent working at the store tended to be a little long. Beth's cousin would make great company. "Don't worry," Cate said. "Everything will be fine."

"Have you talked to Paul since you left the bar last night?"

"Yes. It's a long story. He came over last night and we talked about everything."

"Really? How did it go?"

"Good. I guess. He's acting different now."

Beth reached for her purse.

"I know you're in a hurry," Cate said. "I'll just tell you everything later. I need some good Beth advice."

"All right. Love ya, honey. I'll call you tonight."

"Love you, too," Cate called as she walked toward the door.

"Help yourself to any beads you want, and call me on my cell phone if there are any emergencies." The door swung shut behind her.

The morning was slow. Cate picked out some seed beads in various shades of red and pink and made a bracelet on Beth's loom. A few customers came in, and she showed one girl how to use the crimping beads.

Around noon she was bored and hungry. Maybe Paul would bring her lunch. She tried to call him, but his cell phone went straight to voice mail.

He didn't answer at home, either. She left him a message. "Hey, Paul. It's me. I was just calling to see what you were doing about lunch. Give me a call on my cell when you get a chance."

She checked her messages and found one from Ethan. She called him back.

"I was gonna see what you were up to. Maybe see if you wanted to grab a sandwich at E-Z Jay's," he said.

God, that sounded delicious. "I would love to. But I'm working at the bead store and can't leave. I'm the only one here."

"Have you had lunch?"

"No."

"How 'bout I bring you a sandwich. You've gotta be hungry." He was such a sweetheart.

"You would make my day if you brought me a sandwich. I will pay you back as soon as you get here."

"No worries. What do you want?"

"Ham and turkey toasted."

"You got it."

E-Z Jay's was her favorite sandwich spot in the world. One hung-over Sunday, she and Jill had driven there before it had even opened. Instead of going to the other various restaurants that actually served breakfast, they waited for twenty-five minutes outside and were the first people served that morning. She suspected that Ethan wouldn't arrive at the bead store for at least another hour. The line alone would take twenty minutes.

She was picking out beads for another bracelet when Anthony arrived. "Hey, gorgeous," he said. "When Beth told me you were working today, I decided I *had* to stop by." He was an outrageous flirt.

He pulled her into a bear hug. "You look great," she said, flirting back. He wore one of the most beautiful suede jackets she had ever seen and brilliant turquoise jewelry that he had undoubtedly made himself.

"You like my jacket? I got it in L.A."

"I love it. I love the smell of new leather."

"Me, too."

He was the same age as Cate and Beth. When they were growing up, Cate had sometimes wondered if Anthony might be gay. He cared about his appearance, and he could pull off wearing edgy things. He also loved to engage in lengthy phone conversations about clothes, food, and what great style Julia Roberts had.

The more Cate had gotten to know him, the more convinced she was that he was definitely straight. She'd watched Anthony date women who resembled supermodel Claudia Schiffer, and then watched as his heart had broken when it didn't work out. He was the type of guy that practically smothered women with love and attention in relationships.

She remembered the day when Paul ignorantly called Anthony her *"gay friend."* Instead of laughing, her blood had run cold. His cavalier attitude had bugged her. "No. He is definitely *not* gay," she'd said, flashing him the look of death. He'd never said it again.

The thing with Anthony was that he wasn't afraid. He didn't care if people thought he was gay because he liked to watch movies like *Moulin Rouge* and had a passion for jewelry. Those were the things that he liked, and he only cared about what his real friends thought. Anyone else could go to hell in a handbasket.

"So, have you decided what you're dressing up as yet?" he asked.

Cate had forgotten that Anthony was standing up as a bridesmaid in Beth's wedding. They had been inseparable growing up. He was a silent partner in Beth's store and had taught Beth everything she knew about beading. "I'm not sure," she said. "You?"

"I was thinking about going as a gangster or a paramedic."

"Hmmm. They're so different."

"Well, my girlfriend's brother is a paramedic, so I was just going to borrow his uniform."

"That's a good idea. A gangster would be cool, too. Like Al Capone."

"Yeah, I was thinking kind of prohibition era."

They brainstormed ideas for Cate's costume. He thought she'd look good as Carmen Miranda or an Olympic gymnast.

"Anyway, I should probably get going. I'm off to the track today.

Wish me luck!" He took the beading supplies he'd come for and left the store.

Twenty minutes later, Ethan arrived, holding a paper bag from E-Z Jay's and two large drinks.

Her stomach growled at the sight of food. "Thank you so much for bringing me lunch. And for curing my boredom. I'm sure you'd rather be at the beach."

"No. I already went this morning."

"There's another stool on this side of the counter. Why don't you come sit down over here?"

They laid out the sandwiches on the paper bag and ate next to each other at the counter.

"So, what happened with Paul?" he asked. "Did you talk to him about all that stuff that was bothering you?"

"I did. I got really fed up last night, and I just felt like it didn't matter anymore. I felt like I had nothing to lose, and I told him everything. I even told him I wanted to see other people if he didn't think he could change."

"And?"

"He said he would change. And he's suddenly kissing my ass."

"Good. When you bring up something that's bothering you, the most important part is how the person reacts. He obviously got your message."

"I don't know, Ethan. It's kinda funny. I'm not that happy about it." She dabbed a napkin at her lips before she continued. "I feel like he's acting like the boyfriend he should've always been because he felt threatened last night. Obviously, he has always known how to treat me right. He just didn't *want* to treat me right."

Ethan thought it over. "That could be true. Maybe you scared him, though. Maybe you gave him the reality check he needed."

"I don't feel like I should have to give someone a reality check to make them be considerate. I'm confused."

"You'll figure it out."

He stayed at the shop with her for the rest of the afternoon. They talked about old times and listened to the radio. She taught him how to make a key chain using bone and shells. Shortly after he left, the phone rang.

"The Beadroom. This is Cate."

"*Hooolaaa.*"

"Hey."

"I just got your message. I went to the beach with some of the guys you met last night. Anyway, I would've loved to have had lunch. I'm so sorry I missed your call. Let me buy you dinner."

"All right. I'm leaving here in about an hour."

"Good. I'll see you at, let's say . . . six."

Cate was dressed and ready for a dinner date when Paul arrived at six. He held a picnic basket. The aroma of garlic filled her foyer.

"Are we having a picnic?" she asked, impressed.

"Sort of," he said. "Why don't you make yourself comfortable on the couch?"

"Okay." She played along.

He began to pull candles from the basket. He set a pair of ocean-scented ones on top of the TV. Then he placed another on the window-sill and a few others in various spots around the floor. One by one, he lit them. Then he pushed the coffee table away from the couch. He pulled out a red checked quilt from the basket and spread it over the floor.

"Do you need some help?" Cate asked.

He shook his head. "No. I'm fine. I have everything under control. You just sit back and relax."

Maybe she should tell him she wanted to date other people more often.

He pulled out plates, forks, place mats—everything. He had

brought a bottle of wine and a five-course meal from Fillipi's. She was smitten.

They stuffed themselves with salad and lasagna and garlic bread. Then they indulged in tiramisu for dessert. They had more fun that night than Cate could recall having in a long time. It was like old times, when they had first started dating. When Paul cared about winning her over. She wanted to enjoy all of it, the way she had in the beginning. She loved being courted and pampered. However, an ache of uncertainty dwelled in her chest. She couldn't help but wonder how long all this would last.

"So how is Paul, anyway?" Jill asked when she noticed his postcard from New York City on Cate's refrigerator.

"Great," Cate said. "He's been sending me postcards. He's called twice every day since he's been gone just to say hi. He's really changed."

"Good. Well, continue doing whatever it is you're doing, because it's working."

Cate thought about what she had been doing. She'd been distant and cool, busy, and a little less interested in him.

She was unsure how to respond to her new boyfriend. Most of her confusion came from the notion that as soon as Paul was comfortable again, he would go back to No Call Paul. She felt cautious around him, afraid to be herself or to pour herself into the relationship.

Was this what she was going to have to do to have him treat her right? Be a bitch? It didn't make sense. She shouldn't have to be walking on eggshells, worried that she was being *nice*.

When she went out with Jill and Ethan for sushi one night and was too tired to call him back before she went to bed, he'd called at three in the morning, frantic.

"Why didn't you call me?" he asked.

Interesting, the tables being turned.

"Sorry. It was five A.M. your time when I got home, and I didn't want to wake you."

"You could've woken me up. I was so worried."

"I'm sorry. I truly didn't mean to scare you." She felt terrible. The last thing she wanted was to worry anyone.

She let go of her concerns about his personality lapses and felt as if she was falling for him all over again.

Three days before he was due to return, she left him a sweet message. "Hi, Paul. I was just calling to tell you that I miss you, and I can't wait to see you when you get back on Friday. Miss you. Talk to you soon!"

After that, he went two days without calling.

By Friday, she hadn't had much time to dwell on Paul. She'd met almost all of her kindergartners and had been busy. However, she knew one thing for certain. When he returned that afternoon, they were going to have a *long* talk. Their relationship was a game, and she was sick of keeping score.

Her last kindergarten appointment had been with Tyler Chan, a quiet little boy with a cowlick and a stay-at-home dad.

When she returned from the meeting, her bridesmaid suit was waiting on her doorstep in an enormous white box, marked Priority Mail.

Inside her apartment, she pulled the outfit from the box. Cate remembered Leslie saying something about the belt. She rummaged through the tissue inside the box and pulled out a stringy strip of royal blue satin. There was a note safety-pinned to the strap in Leslie's handwriting, *"Don't Lose This."* It looked like a cheap, satin shoelace. Grease batted at the dangling string with his paw, and Cate pulled it away.

The phone rang.

"What are you doing?" her mother asked.

"I'm trying on this ridiculous four-hundred-dollar suit I have to wear for Leslie Lyons's wedding."

"Four hundred dollars! That is *just* terrible. When I was your age, the bride was responsible for providing all the accommodations for the bridesmaids. You didn't ask people to be in your wedding and then ask them to pay four hundred dollars!"

"No, Mom. It's not just four hundred dollars. By the time I've bought the shoes, paid for an up-do, and blown a small fortune on her bachelorette party, I will have spent about eight hundred dollars. And that's not even counting the gifts for the shower and wedding."

Her mother gasped. "That is awful. We didn't do that to Emily's bridesmaids when she got married."

"I know."

"Anyway, I was just calling to see how all of your appointments have been going."

"Good. I have a pretty good class this year."

Her mother was the only person who truly cared about listening to kindergarten stories. She had a genuine interest in Cate's job and appreciated the funny and cute things the children did. Connie had also been a good shoulder to lean on and a great listener when Cate had spent hours venting about the bratty kids and unruly parents she had to deal with.

They chatted some more about the upcoming school year, then said good-bye.

She tried on the outfit, complete with belt. Why did Leslie want her to wear this? Cate had paid for the damn outfit. The least she could do was make the belt optional.

She was starting to feel hostile when the doorbell rang.

Jill stood in the hallway with a bottle of Tanqueray and a lime. "It's Friiii . . ." Her voice trailed off when she looked at Cate. "What are you wearing?"

"My bridesmaid's *suit.*"

"That is really fucking ugly."

"Guess how much it cost me?"

"I wouldn't have paid more than three dollars for that at PB Thrift and Resale."

"Try four hundred."

Her mouth dropped. "I didn't even think you hung out with her that often."

That was true. Ever since Leslie had become serious with her fiancé, their friendship had drifted. Occasionally, they hung out, but only if Russ was sick or watching a football game.

Jill shook her head as she walked in the kitchen. "Well, if I ever get married, I'll let you pick the dress."

"Thanks."

She began mixing them cocktails. "Anyway, how's Paul? Has he called yet?"

"No."

"Are you all right?"

"I'm not upset. I'm just fed up." She shook her head. "This whole thing—it isn't right. I shouldn't have to play the unavailable bitch to win his attention. I just want to be myself." She began to untie the belt as she spoke. "You know what else I've been thinking? All this time I thought it was Paul that had changed throughout our relationship, but it was me that really changed. In the beginning when I was indifferent, he was chasing after me, and as soon as the indifference wore off and I fell for him, he became distant. It's the same thing now. Why does it have to be that way with guys? Why do you have to make them chase after you to make them want you? If that's the way it is, I'd rather be alone. I don't think it's going to work out anymore."

"Are you thinking about breaking up with him?"

She nodded. "He comes back today. I'm going to have to talk to him." She began to walk toward her bedroom. "I'm going to change out of this."

"A cocktail will be waiting when you return. Hey, I was thinking we should see what Ethan and his friends are doing."

"All right," Cate said. "Call him. His number is on the fridge."

While she was hanging up the suit, she remembered that she hadn't checked her E-mail since yesterday morning. There was a possibility that Paul had written instead of calling.

She shoved the belt into a corner of her desk next to a half-empty glass of water and a pair of toenail clippers.

While drinking a Tanqueray and tonic, she checked her E-mail.

FROM: Leslie Lyons
SUBJECT: Outfits and shoes

Hi Girls. By now you should've all received your suits. I hope they fit well. You're all going to where the belt, so make sure you put it in a safe place. It's probably best to just keep it with the suit. I've ordered shoes for everyone. You can just make the check out to me for one hundred and eighty dollars. I had to pay in advance so I would appreciate if you could send the checks soon. Thank you. I am so happy to share my special day with each one of you.

Love,
Leslie

She had another message from her mother wanting to know if Leslie had been raised with any manners.

Cate turned off the computer. Matching shoes? She was going to have to take out a loan for Leslie's *special day.* Had Leslie forgotten that most of her friends fell into the lowest tax bracket in the country?

She was a teacher, not a pitcher for the San Diego Padres. She thought of all the things she could spend one hundred eighty dollars on. Her car problems. Supplies for her class. Three weeks' worth of groceries. A pair of shoes she would wear more than once—two pairs for that matter. And who was going to notice their shoes anyway? Weren't their friends attending the wedding to see the marriage of Leslie and Russ?

She shut off her computer and returned to the living room. Jill had taken control of the remote control and was flipping through stations.

"I'll mix us another drink," Cate said, taking Jill's empty glass from the coffee table.

A few minutes later, Ethan arrived with another bottle of Tanqueray and a spinach salad covered with bits of meaty bacon. "I thought you guys might be hungry," he said as he handed Cate the salad bowl. "I just whipped this up."

Cate thanked him for the food.

"I'm starving," Jill yelled from the couch.

They ate the salad on the coffee table, their laughter and voices growing louder with each drink. After doing a significant amount of damage to the first Tanqueray bottle, Jill teamed up with Ethan and convinced Cate to model her hideous bridesmaid's outfit.

"All right. All right," Cate said. "But I can't wear it for long. Leslie will have my head on a platter if something happens to it."

While Cate dressed, she could hear her friends rummaging around her cabinets in the living room, occasionally laughing then lowering their voices into hushed whispers. She wondered what kind of mischief they were up to.

After changing into the pantsuit, she found a pair of old white pumps and a bright pink headband in her closet. She put them on for an added touch. She took one step into the living room when her Culture Club CD came blaring from the speakers of her stereo. She'd purchased the CD when CDs were first invented, back in the eighties. Her friends had been rummaging through her CDs and had chosen to play "Karma Chameleon," a song entirely fitting for Cate's attire.

They all burst into laughter as Cate busted into a series of dance moves similar to something out of a Cyndi Lauper video. Ethan grabbed her by the hand and spun her across the room. Then he grabbed Jill by the other arm and the three of them locked elbows.

"We're *Three's Company!*" Jill yelled.

"I have to get out of this thing," Cate said as the song ended. Even in her buzzed state, she had rational visions of gin and tonic spilling down the front of her bridesmaid attire.

"You mean you don't want to wear that to the Silver Fox?" Ethan asked.

"I'd like to show my face in the Silver Fox after tonight."

Cate hung the outfit in the closet and set the belt in a loose pile on top of her dresser. When she returned to her friends, they relocked elbows, feeling comfortable and warm with one another. On her way to the bar, Cate realized that Paul had been home for three hours and still hadn't called.

21 • End of the Rope

Paul called the next day at three. Any reservations Cate had about talking to him were eliminated. He'd been home for nearly twenty-four hours and hadn't bothered to pick up the phone.

She was curt when she took his call.

"I was thinking we could go down to the cove and have a bottle of wine around sunset," he said.

He lived to confuse her.

"All right," she said.

"Good. I'll pick you up around five."

"Sounds good," she replied, already thinking about how she was going to break up with him.

"Well, if it isn't the elusive Paul Strobel," Cate said as he entered her apartment.

He released a nervous laugh and pressed a dry and awkward kiss to her forehead. "Shall we go to the cove?" he asked.

"Yeah, let me just grab my sweater."

"Do you have any wine?" he yelled as she headed to her bedroom.

"I think there's a bottle of red on the counter."

When she returned, he was putting the bottle of wine and two coffee mugs into a brown paper bag. "Ready?"

They spoke mostly of Paul's trip on the car ride over, the weather in New York City, and the shitty chicken he ate on his return flight.

Cate glanced at him. "You got a haircut," she said.

"*Sí.*"

"And highlights? Did you color your hair?" She reached out to touch a piece of his hair, and he jerked his head slightly to the side. Then, as if he had noticed his spastic reaction, he moved his head closer to her again.

"Yeah, I put some color in it."

"Oh." He'd never highlighted his hair before. "It looks nice."

He fiddled with the radio dial. "I like this song." He stopped on a song Cate had never heard.

Her stomach ached when she thought about what she was going to say. She'd never broken up with someone. Most of her other relationships had amicably fizzled out. She went over it in her mind. *It seems like you don't really want a relationship with someone right now. It's probably best for both of us if I move on.*

Deep down there was a slight flicker of hope that Paul's response would be: *What do you mean? I love you. Of course I want a relationship. I've just been busy, and I had no idea how much this was bothering you. Let's get married!* Cate had a feeling it would be more like: *I'm sorry, Cate. I am too busy to be in a committed relationship. Maybe it's better if we're just friends.*

The cove was crowded when they arrived. Tourists tossed Frisbees on the grass over the La Jolla shores, and other couples sat on blankets, waiting for the sunset over picnics and wine. Paul and Cate were lucky to find a parking spot within walking distance of the grassy cliff. He grabbed the wine and mugs before they headed for the cove.

A Suburban pulled up next to them. "Hey, Paul." It was an older couple that Cate had never met before.

"Well, hello," Paul said.

"Just here for the sunset?" they asked, glancing at Cate.

"Yeah." He looked at Cate from the corner of his eye, and she noticed that he was holding the paper bag with the wine and mugs behind his back. "This is my friend, Cate," he said. "Cate, this is John and Nicole Ducheck. I work with John."

Cate was too shocked that he called her his "friend" to give them a warm greeting. She politely waved. Paul said good-bye to the Duchecks. Then they headed down to the cove, her nerves on edge.

Friends! She was fuming. Friends don't drink wine in front of a sunset. Friends don't date for a year.

They found a spot on the grass with a good view of the horizon. The sun had already begun to inch its way toward the ocean and had cast brilliant golden rays off the sea-green water.

Paul pulled the wine and a corkscrew from the bag. He poured the Merlot into the mugs. They talked about things that Paul had done while he was on his trip, and his upcoming plans to go to London. The whole time, Cate waited for an opportunity to bring up their relationship. After two glasses of wine, she noticed that the sun had begun to hit the horizon. It looked as if it were melting into the water, bleeding orange and red all over the choppy sea.

"Paul, we need to talk about our relationship." She hadn't planned on blurting it out, but the wine had made it easy.

He looked down at the grass, ripped a healthy chunk of green blades from the earth, and spilled them in a little pile between them. His gaze turned to the sunset. "You must not be very happy with me right now," he said.

He knew? "No, Paul. I'm not. I'm not happy at all." In a way, it was a relief that he knew. She wouldn't have to explain. On the other hand, irritation consumed her when she realized that he'd known he'd been treating her badly all week and had continued to do so.

He looked at her. "Cate, I think you are a great person, and everyone I talk to loves you. You're a phenomenal girl, but I can't do this anymore." He shook his head. "I just can't do it." He continued to pick at the grass, creating a substantial heap in between them. "I wanted it to work. When we got together, I wanted it to work out so bad. I had been thinking about you so much, and I had to find out if you were the one. I had to know if I could marry you. I prayed about it." He pressed on the mound of blades with his palms, then looked up at her. "I realized you're not the one. I'm not in love with you, Cate. I never was."

Being hit by a car and landing in a giant pile of dog shit would've been better. He didn't love her. *He had prayed about it?* She was incapable of forming sentences. He should've just slapped her; it would've been less shocking. And in public! Over a bottle of wine and a sunset! What the fuck was wrong with him?

She had a burning desire to grab the bottle of Merlot and break it over his stupid fucking highlights. A fleeting vision of wine and glass spilling over his head popped into her mind. It wasn't like there was much to damage.

She glanced at the bottle, then at him. He was actually smirking, waiting for her to say something.

"Cate, I wish it could work. I think you're a great person. The best. You're pretty. You're—"

She held up a hand. "Enough." He'd humiliated her to the lowest level in the middle of La Jolla. She didn't need his pity on top of it. "Paul, I don't need to hear how great I am. In the future, if you have these feelings, break up with the person right away. Don't try to send them messages and blow them off until they get frustrated, and for God's sake, do it in private."

"Well, I talked to all my friends, and they told me to just stop calling."

Icing on the fucking cake. "You talked to *all* your friends about this?" Her voice was loud. People stopped throwing Frisbees and tossed her a look.

"Well?" He turned his palms out. "I needed some advice."

"You told all your friends! We know all the same people, and I have to see them at Leslie's wedding next week. These are people I know, Paul! And they all knew before I did that you were going to dump me!"

He squeezed her arm. "Cate, they all love you. They couldn't understand why I wanted to break up with you. Everyone thinks I'm crazy."

"Does Leslie know?"

"No. I swear. She has no idea."

She stood up. "All right. I just want to go home."

He grabbed the paper bag, the mugs, and the rest of the wine. "Cate, please don't be mad. I think you're a great girl, and I still want to hang out with you. Promise me that we can do brunches at the Brockton and go see those foreign films you like."

She turned away from him. "Not now, Paul. Not now."

The car ride home seemed like a five-hour drive through the desert. When they reached her complex, Paul leaned over the center console and hugged her. She would've rather hugged a bum who had recently pissed on himself. He handed her the paper bag with her mugs and the rest of the wine. "You take care," he said.

"You . . . drive safe, Paul."

She didn't look over her shoulder as she walked to her building. She could hear the engine idling behind her all the way to the gated entrance of her complex. Everything had happened so fast. Overwhelmed, she turned right and headed to Jill's. Thank God she was home. Cate needed to tell someone. She needed to hear the words come out of her mouth. She couldn't quite comprehend what had just happened.

Jill's head was covered in Saran Wrap. Fushia strands of hair peeked out from beneath the plastic. A stick of magnolia incense burned on the coffee table.

"Come on in," she said. "I'm dying my hair pink. I'm so glad you came over. I need your . . ." Her voice trailed off when she looked at Cate. "What happened? You look terrible."

"Paul just dumped me." She sat on the couch and buried her face in her hands.

"What? I thought *you* were dumping *him*."

"He beat me to it."

"Asshole." She pulled a pack of cigarettes from the pocket of her bathrobe. "You're going to need a smoke while you tell me this."

Cate grabbed a cigarette. She took heavy drags while telling the La Jolla Cove Dumping Story.

"Cate, he is an idiot! I mean it! What a fucking moron." Jill's voice became a goofy drawl. "Hi, my name is Paul. Or, no, excuse me: *Hola*. I'm Paul, and I'm a fuckin' idiot. I had to break up with Cate because I'm stupid. I asked my friends, and they said to just stop callin', but I had to take her to a public place and get drunk on wine before I could do it because I'm a big fat coward!"

Cate laughed. She looked down at Jill's feet. "Did you stay at the Ritz Carlton?" Her white slippers had the Ritz Carlton monogram on them.

"No. But it looks like I stayed there. I bought them at a thrift store. Aren't they a find?"

Cate smiled. "Yes."

"Anyway, Cate, you can do so much better than Paul. So much better!" She lit another cigarette and offered Cate one as well. Cate smoked a second cigarette. "I'm going to set you up with that guy I was telling you about, Nick."

"Isn't he a tattoo artist?"

"Yes, I'm telling you he's so cute and sooooo nice. He's perfect. In fact, I'll call him right now."

She hopped up from the couch. Cate wished she wouldn't. She really had no interest in dating a man who made people bleed every day.

Cate paid no attention to Jill's conversation with Nick. She smoked a third cigarette and poured the remaining wine into a mug. When Jill returned, she was holding a photo album. "I just talked to Nick," she said. "We're going out with him and this other guy, Ted—that guy I like—tomorrow night. Okay?"

"Okay," Cate mumbled. She didn't care.

"You're going to love him." She glanced at the album in her hand. "Oh! I have a picture of him!"

Cate looked at the picture of Nick. He was actually pretty cute. She stayed there until Jill was finished dying her hair a blinding shade of bright pink.

"See you tomorrow around eight," Jill called as Cate left.

"All right."

Darkness filled her apartment. She reached for a light switch before she threw her purse on the couch. She kicked off each shoe and headed to her bedroom. Moonlight spilled through her bedroom window. She could see Grease's outline on the floor near the end of the bed. He was chewing on something.

"What do you have there, Grease?" she asked as she crouched down near him. He bolted, his toy trailing from his mouth. It was long and thin.

Cate flicked on a light. "Grease, come here," she said. She found him in the living room, perched on the coffee table, a royal blue satin strap dangling from his mouth.

Rearranged

Cate woke up at six in the morning. Before she opened her eyes, she remembered that Paul had dumped her. Her chest felt painfully empty. She wished she could sleep all day, but she was too emotional.

There would be no future with Paul. No wedding. No mutual real estate investments. No shared holidays. It was over. Deep down, she'd sensed that they weren't meant for each other, but part of her had always longed for him to change. She had wanted him to see how much she appreciated him. She'd been waiting for him to realize what a devoted girlfriend she was, and then he wouldn't be able to live without her.

Now she was going to have to start from scratch. For a moment she felt a flash of relief. Paul was gone. Everything would be new, and she would no longer have to worry about No Call Paul. There would be no more analyzing and guessing where he was and what he thought about her. He was out of her life. But then she realized that nothing would ever be new. She'd just have to find someone else to play the game with.

It wasn't the loss of Paul that necessarily made her sad. Most of her sadness stemmed from her wounded ego combined with the bitter reality that the world was filled with Pauls. All the nice guys were either taken or not her type. She would never find anyone and was destined to be alone. Someone had to be the old maid. There was one in every group. It had to be Cate. Jill didn't count. She wasn't normal.

She wanted to call Beth and tell her what had happened. She knew Beth wouldn't be up this early on a Saturday. Leslie and Sarah? No way. She needed to talk to someone. Her mother. She was always up by six.

Connie answered on the second ring. Her voice sounded confident and bright.

Cate came right out with the news. "Paul dumped me, Mom."

"He did?"

"Yes, it was terrible." Cate briefed her on the wine, the sunset, and the brutal words that made her ache just repeating them.

"I knew he wasn't right for you anyway. And your dad never liked him."

Was this Share Your Shocking Revelations with Cate Padgett Week or something? "Dad didn't like him?"

"No. He thought he was a real asshole."

It sounded hilarious whenever her mother cussed. It felt good to laugh. "Dad called him an asshole?"

"Yes." Her mother sighed. "Forget about him. Move on. He's not the right guy for you. Besides, he wasn't Catholic. And he drank a lot."

"No, he didn't." The last thing Cate wanted to do was defend Paul. He *was* an asshole. However, if anyone had more than one drink at dinner, her mother assumed they were an alcoholic.

"You can do better," her mother said.

You can do better was just a stock response people provided when they didn't know what else to say. Cate knew this because she had said it to a dozen other friends while consoling them after a breakup.

"I can't do better," she said. "They're all alike."

"No, they're not. There is one special jewel out there that God has already picked out for you. He's probably dying to send him to you, but couldn't because Paul was in the way. Just forget about Paul and focus on your photography and the upcoming school year. That guy is going to come your way. I know. I've been praying about it."

How the hell was she supposed to focus on anything? "I'm so humiliated."

"I know how you feel," Connie said.

"You do?"

"Yes. I had my heart broken once, too."

"Really?"

"Yes. But I got over it. I stayed busy and I dated other people."

"Well, what happened?" Cate was curious. She could not imagine her mother ever having a love life, even with her father.

"I used to date this guy, Patrick McCourt. He was so cute. We dated for several months. I went on vacation with my family, and when I came back, he was dating my best friend."

"You never told me that story."

"Well, I got over it. I let myself be sad for a few days, and then I moved on. Have you been to church lately?"

"What does that have to do with Paul?"

"Well, you might feel better if you go to church."

Or bored, Cate thought.

"Maybe that's why all these things are happening to you. Because you don't have a relationship with God."

Why did she have to do this every time they were starting to bond? Cate hated to think that God was punishing her for missing a man-made ritual every week. What kind of God did that? She felt like asking her mother, but the last thing she needed was to get into a religious debate. She changed the subject. "Can you recommend a good seamstress?"

"There's one on Poway Road that I used to go to years ago when we lived out there, next to the used book store."

"Thanks," Cate said before they hung up. She was going to need a genius seamstress who was borderline magician to fix the belt. Grease had nearly bitten it in half, and the fabric was punctured with kitty teeth marks in various places. She'd take the suit to Poway later.

She remained in bed for the rest of the morning, watching shows like *Blind Date* and *Trading Spaces*. At eleven, it occurred to her that she hadn't eaten anything all day.

She threw on a pair of sweatpants, a hooded sweatshirt, and her running shoes. She decided to take the belt and outfit to Poway. After all, she did believe in miracles.

She found the seamstress in the exact spot that her mother had described. She brought the whole outfit because she needed the bust line taken in. The seamstress was a friendly Asian woman with a heavy accent.

"You try on," she said to Cate.

Cate slipped into the outfit.

"Very nice," the seamstress said when Cate stepped out of the dressing room. "You go to homecoming?" she asked.

"No. I'm twenty-six. I'm actually in a wedding."

"Ahhh. My son married."

She didn't even ask Cate where she wanted alterations. She immediately began inserting pins around her chest, pulling the fabric tighter, and mumbling things that Cate couldn't understand the whole time.

When she was finished, Cate pulled the damaged strap from her purse. "Can you repair this?" She waited for the seamstress to keel over and die. "My cat got a hold of it, and I have to wear it with this suit."

She threw her head back and released a screeching burst of laughter.

"It's that bad?" Cate asked. "You can't repair it?"

"No! Cat got hold of it! That funny." She had a wide smile.

"So you *can* fix it?"

She snatched the strap from Cate's hand. "Yes. I repair. When you wanna pick up?"

Cate shrugged. "Next week sometime."

"I see you Tuesday."

Instead of going straight home, she drove to her favorite photo lab in Hillcrest. She needed to place an order for the pictures that Ethan had picked for his brochure.

"Hi, Sam," she said as she entered the store.

"Hey. How you doin', Cate? Here to pick up your pictures?"

"Pictures?" Then she remembered she had dropped off her film from Hawaii the previous week. God, she didn't want to look at those. "Oh yeah. I . . . guess I'll pick those up. I also need to place an order."

"All rightey!" he said as he handed her three envelopes full of Maui.

She placed the order, then spent a small fortune paying for pictures she didn't want. On the way back to her car, she quickly thumbed through the Hawaii photos. Laughter surprised her when she saw the photo she had snapped of Paul in Hana, the mosquito corpse dangling from his grimacing face. Maybe she should put that on the fridge when she got home. She didn't look at the rest of the pictures and threw the envelopes in the backseat of the Volvo before heading home.

There was a message from Jill when Cate returned to her apartment. "Hi, girl. It's me. I just wanted to see how you were doing and tell you that we're meeting Nick and Ted at the West End. All right? Call me when you get in."

Cate didn't feel like going out. She wished it were March. She craved Girl Scout cookies. She wanted to eat Thin Mints and Samoas and watch eighties movies on cable TV all night. Then she remembered that she had a box of Thin Mints in the freezer. She was five minutes into *Some Kind of Wonderful* and halfway through a box of frozen cookies when the doorbell rang. She expected to see Jill and was surprised to find her mother standing in the hall, a loaf of banana bread in her hands.

"Hi. I just made some banana bread and thought it might cheer you up."

"Thanks!" Cate said. She loved her mother's banana bread. She made it special with little chocolate chips and cinnamon sprinkled over the top.

"Listen. Don't be sad about Paul." She threw her arm over Cate's shoulders. "You're going to find someone much better. I've been praying about it."

"Thanks, Mom," she said.

They walked to the kitchen with their arms around each other.

"Well, I can't stay for long. Your father and I are meeting the Coursons for dinner. But I just wanted to stop by." She pulled an envelope from her purse. "And here is a little something to cheer you up."

"Oh. Thanks."

Her mother set the card on the counter. After she was gone, Cate opened the envelope. It was a card with a cat that bore a striking resemblance to Grease painted on the front. Inside was a check for four hundred dollars.

Just thought this might help pay for Leslie's wedding.
    Love,
    Mom

Immediately she called her mother and left a message thanking her for the money. She was beyond grateful. The kind gesture had brought a small amount of relief to her overstressed nerves. Now she could get her car fixed.

After she hung up, Jill called. "Are you getting ready?"

"No. I don't want to go out."

"Get your ass off the couch and get in the shower. You need to kiss a cute guy tonight."

"I don't need another man in my life. I hate them."

"Cate, if you're not down here in an hour, I'm going to have to drag you out. Oh and I made something for you. I'm coming over."

"Fine."

She did next to nothing to improve her appearance. She applied a coat of lipstick, failed to put concealer over the zit that had formed on her right cheek, and picked out a pair of comfortable jeans and a T-shirt. Who did she need to impress? Another jerk?

Ten minutes later, Jill let herself in. She carried a strong scent of perfume and wore a denim skirt, cute platforms, and a funky top with butterfly sleeves.

"Here. I burned you a CD. It's a breakup mix." She handed her a CD with "Breakup Mix" written in black across the front of it. "I thought this might help you get over Paul. Every song is meant to make you feel like one bad bitch. Screw Paul."

"Thanks," Cate said as she took the gift. "Am I underdressed? We're just going to the West End, right?" The West End was not a place to dress up for. Although the bar packed in crowds of people, it was a borderline dive with its pool tables and jukebox.

Jill looked at her. "A little. Let's find something else for you to wear." She began to rummage through Cate's closet.

Cate popped the CD into her stereo. When "Survivor" by Destiny's Child blasted from the speakers, Cate couldn't help but smile. The woman singing sounded stronger without her man. She wasn't gonna give up. Cate wanted to be like her. The CD was already making her feel a little better. If Destiny's Child could recover from a disastrous breakup, so could she.

Jill picked out an outfit. She handed Cate a pair of pointy heels that Cate rarely wore, a pair of whisker-washed jeans, and a tank top. Then she began to work on Cate's hair and makeup.

"Now. I want you to try to something," she said.

"Okay." Cate waited for her to suggest a bold shade of lipstick.

"Every time you start to think of Paul, I want you to envision yourself with someone else. Whoever you want. I mean anyone. Tom Cruise. Brad Pitt . . ." She brushed blush across Cate's cheeks. Aretha Franklin's "Respect" played in the background. "It doesn't even have to be a celebrity. Make up your own fantasy man if you want. Give him all the qualities you like. Looks, career, personality, family background. When I broke up with Danny, I imagined myself with a rock star that looked like Jared Leto and wanted five kids and a tattoo with my initials on his forearm. I imagined us going grocery shopping, picking out a puppy at the Humane Society, running into Danny—whatever. Open your eyes wide please."

Cate stretched her eyes while Jill applied mascara.

"Focusing on someone else will help you think about the future instead of the shitty, depressing situation you're in right now. It will help you to realize that there are other fish in the sea."

She created a fantasy man in her head. He had the looks of Viggo Mortenson, the loyalty of Forrest Gump, the charm of Rhett Butler, the courage and heart of Mel Gibson in *Braveheart*. A real stud. No more idiots who travel with candles and highlight their hair.

They listened to more songs on the CD while Cate imagined her ideal guy. He would carve the turkey for her family on Thanksgiving and enjoy weekly getaways to Mexico, where they would devour lobsters and drink margaritas, drunk on love and cheap tequila. She didn't care if he tattooed her initials on his forearm. She just wanted someone who would appreciate her.

Jill stood over her, ironing her hair, singing at the top of her lungs to Limp Bizkit's "Rearranged." She set the flatiron down. "Isn't this a great song?"

"Yes." Cate said. "Thanks for making me this CD."

"Eye of the Tiger" by Survivor, "No Scrubs" by TLC, and Alanis Morissette's "You Oughta Know" were just some of the songs that were meant to make Cate feel strong again. Jill and Cate were both singing Pat Benatar's "Treat Me Right" when they decided to leave for the bar.

Nick turned out to be much cuter than Cate had remembered from the pictures. He was tall, soft-spoken, and flashed dimples on both cheeks whenever he smiled. "So Jill tells me you're a teacher," he said.

Cate nodded. "Yeah, I teach kindergarten. I heard you're a tattoo artist."

"Yeah, I'm an artist. I've been trying to break into graphic design for a while. I had a roommate that was into tattoos. He taught me everything, and eventually I picked it up. It was easy money." He seemed too gentle to work in a tattoo parlor.

"Who do you practice on when you're learning?" she asked. "I mean, who's willing to be the guinea pig? What if you screw up?"

He laughed. "I practiced mostly on potatoes." He lifted his shirt and exposed his forearm. "I did this one on myself when I was learning."

It was a geisha, her gown filled with shades of red, blue, and green. "It's good," Cate said.

"It's not bad. I'd like to improve it a little." He took a swig of his drink, washing ice into his mouth. "You want another drink?"

"No, thanks. I'm fine."

She was feeling better, glad that she'd gotten out of the house, but she still felt a dull ache in her heart. Ted and Jill joined their conversation. "Do you guys want to play pool?" Ted asked.

"Sure!" Jill said. "Nick and Cate can be a team, and we'll be a team."

Cate sucked at pool. She just didn't get it. No matter how hard she tried, she couldn't figure out the dynamics of the stupid stick. After one game she suggested that the boys play by themselves.

"So what do you think of Nick?" Jill whispered as she handed Cate a gin and tonic. She took one sip of the cocktail, then set it aside. Waking up heartbroken and hungover didn't seem appealing.

"He seems nice. But it's too early."

"Early shmearly. Will you have fun tonight?"

"I am having fun." She could feel her feet sweating in her heels. She knew there was a reason she never wore those shoes.

They fiddled around with the jukebox for a while, playing old Fleetwood Mac and Rolling Stones hits.

"Hey, do you guys feel like getting something to eat?" Ted asked.

Cate realized that all she'd eaten in the past twenty-four hours was a box of Thin Mints. "I could go for Mexican food," she said.

They walked to the Mexican restaurant around the corner. It was a walk-up window with a couple of picnic tables outside. There were already people at each table, so they ordered their burritos to go.

Cate couldn't wait to eat her food, and was tempted to take a cab home alone. But before she knew it she was in a cab headed for Nick and Ted's in South Mission Beach.

Their apartment was typical South Mission. It was older and looked as if countless raging parties had been thrown in it throughout the years. Their furniture had a bachelor garage sale appeal to it and posters of local bands were pinned to the walls. Cate devoured her burrito within a matter of minutes.

Jill and Ted disappeared into Ted's bedroom, and Cate wondered how on earth she was ever going to leave with Jill in Love Land. Nick offered her a beer, and she declined.

He sat down next to her. They looked at photo albums of people he had tattooed. Then, before she knew it, they were kissing. He was a decent kisser but tasted like Bud Light.

She pulled away. Their carpet needed steam cleaning. There was dog hair on the furniture, yet she hadn't noticed a dog anywhere. And the couch had a stain that resembled blood on one of the cushions. She missed Paul. She wanted to feel her bare feet on his hardwood floors and smell the clean scent of his sheets. She had to go. Immediately, she sprang up from the couch. "Do you mind if I call a cab?" she asked.

"No. You tired?"

"Exhausted."

"Sure you don't want to stay and have a beer?" he asked as he handed her a cordless phone.

"Positive."

Waiting for the cab to arrive seemed like an eternity. She was so anxious to get home that she thought of everything she wanted to do when she returned to her apartment in precise order. First she would take off her shoes. She couldn't wait to rid herself of the slick feeling on her feet. Then she would take off the outfit Jill had picked out, put on her favorite T-shirt, wash her face, brush her teeth, and watch the tube until she fell asleep.

When she got home, it took all her strength to stick to her plan. She forced herself to keep from picking up the phone and calling Paul.

23 • Shine

The final pictures for Ethan's brochure turned out better than Cate had expected. She was excited to show him. They met at the China Inn, an old restaurant in Pacific Beach with dim lighting and booths that made Cate feel as if she were going to pop off of them every time she sat down. The last time Cate had been to the China Inn was two years earlier at the Pacific Beach Block Party. She'd gotten so soused off their fancy cocktail menu that she had actually left the restaurant holding a cocktail glass.

"These are great," he said as he shuffled through the photos. He reached into his wallet and handed her a check for the negotiated four hundred fifty dollars.

"I still feel funny taking money from you."

He shook his head. "Consider it your start as a professional photographer."

"I have been thinking a lot about looking for more work." She didn't mention that she had written a rough draft for an ad to run in *The Reader*.

"You tired of teaching?"

"No. I like to teach. But I do think I have a passion for photography. I just never thought I could make money doing it."

"So how has everything been going?" Ethan poured steaming green tea into her little porcelain teacup.

"Fine. School starts Monday. Oh. And Paul dumped me."

"What?"

"Yes, Paul dumped me."

"*He* dumped *you*?"

"Yes. It's really a horror story."

"What happened?"

"He drove me to the La Jolla cove for a bottle of wine to watch the sunset and told me he wasn't in love with me and could never see us getting married. It was lovely—being dumped in public." Her teacup felt warm against her palms as she raised it to her lips.

"I'm sorry, Cate." He shook his head. "If you don't mind, I just have to tell you that he is an idiot. You can do so much better. What guy wouldn't appreciate you?"

"I'm starting to wonder. I mean, if I'm so great, why did he want to dump me?"

"Because he's a guy."

Cate laughed. "Are all guys idiots?"

"It means he can't handle you."

"What do you mean?"

"I'm saying he's just another stupid guy, Cate. You are a catch. It takes somebody a little more mature to realize that."

"You're just being sweet to make me feel better." Cate wrapped lo mein noodles around her fork.

"No, I'm not. I'm serious. Believe me, I can't imagine being a woman."

"Why?"

"Well, it's hard enough to find a good girl in this world. And knowing how my friends are, and how most men are, I imagine it has to be even worse for women. It must be harder for them to find a decent guy."

"You have a hard time finding nice girls?"

"Yeah, it's hard to find a girl that I can actually hold a conversation with."

"I just want to find someone who is mature, focused, spontaneous, and down to earth," Cate said. "It's not like I'm asking for an heir to the royal throne or something." She didn't want to talk about her hard luck in love. "Anyway, I need your help with something."

"Oh yeah?"

"I need you to help me decide what to wear to Beth's wedding."

"Oh, that's right. It's on Halloween." He thought about it. "Hmmm. It's gotta be good. Original."

At this point she was actually glad that she could create a costume instead of spend another small fortune on a dress she'd only wear once. She had no idea what she was going to be. She'd been a black cat two years in a row. She had enough vintage clothes to go as any decade.

She also had a closet full of bridesmaid's dresses. She could wear one of her dresses and go as the bridesmaid from hell. She could rip it and put fake tattoos all over her body and smudge black eyeliner around her eyes and let her bra strap show, and wear ugly shoes that didn't go with the dress. Then she realized Beth probably wouldn't think that was funny.

"I was thinking maybe Cleopatra."

"That would be cool. What about Marilyn Monroe? You've got that little blonde bob of yours. I think you'd make a good Marilyn."

"Me? Marilyn Monroe?"

"Yeah, why not? I'll help you find the costume."

"In case you haven't noticed, I have no boobs."

"So? Stuff your bra."

She thought about it. "That's a good idea. I could go to PB Thrift. I bet they have lots of fifties stuff, and Jill could do my hair. It's settled. Marilyn Monroe."

When they were finished eating, the waitress brought the bill and a little plate with two fortune cookies.

Ethan handed Cate the plate. "You pick first."

She had to get a feel for which one she wanted. She looked at both cookies and let intuition guide her to the one to her left. Ethan snatched the other cookie. They cracked the cookies open and pulled the little white fortunes from the crusty shell.

"What does yours say?" he asked.

She shrugged. "It is better to shine than to reflect."

"No way. That's what mine says, too."

She reached across the table and pulled the fortune from his hand. "Let me see." She read his fortune. "It does. We have the same fortune."

"That's kinda cool," he said.

"No, it's not. It means there aren't enough fortunes to go around."

"No. I think it says something about our friendship."

"I think it means that not many people have a unique or special future. What the hell does *shine rather than reflect* mean, anyway?"

"It means you're supposed to put forth your best effort and shine instead of pulling inward and reflecting. Just do it, is what it means."

"Hmmm. I was thinking that it meant like a window when it's clean is better shiny than reflective."

"Yeah, it could be that, too."

She was disappointed. She wanted something different for the future. She was destined to turn out like all the other single people roaming the streets of Pacific Beach, getting drunk and taking cabs home alone. While the rest of her girlfriends had children and socialized with other families, she'd simply be weird Aunt Cate with a neurotic cat. And Paul—he would probably end up happily married to supermodel Heidi Klum and own homes in La Jolla and the Caribbean.

She wanted to sleep until noon and eat Mexican food three meals a day. She wanted to lie on the couch with Grease curled up next to her feet and the remote control settled next to her hand. She wanted to make bracelets and take pictures at her own free will. But she couldn't do these things. She was forced from bed by the rude sound of her alarm clock.

On the first day of school, she took the kids to the playground for recess. They were giddy with the excitement of school starting. They needed to run around the playground for a while, burn off some steam.

The kids had been racing around like dirty little hooligans for ten minutes when Timothy Sickle tapped her on the leg. She looked down at him.

"Teacher?" he asked. "I need to go poopy."

"What's my name, Timothy?" She asked in her singsong kindergarten teacher voice when she really wanted to grumble, *It's Miss Padgett, you little farter, and didn't your mother ever teach you any manners?* God, she'd been in a foul mood ever since Paul had dumped her.

"Teacher," he said, genuinely convinced that Cate had been given the name Teacher at birth.

"No, Timothy. My name is Miss Padgett, and the polite way to say you need to go potty is to ask if you may please use the bathroom."

He stared at her as if she were explaining foreign stock trade.

"Can you try asking again?"

He shook his head.

"Timothy, this is how you ask: 'Miss Padgett, may I please use the bathroom?' Okay? Now I want you to try."

"I need to go potty."

She gave up when she noticed Mackenzie Hurwitz throwing sand at Caitlin Miller. "All right, Timothy. The bathroom is right around the corner. You may go. But when you return, we're going to have a talk about manners."

She ended the sand war and made Mackenzie sit in time-out for the rest of recess. By the time recess was over, she'd been pegged by a cherry ball, removed gum from Parker Carson's hair, and sent one child to the nurse's office for a skinned knee.

She blew her whistle. "All right, class! Recess is over. I need each of you to please quietly line up in a straight row next to the wall." Obediently, the children lined up, single file. "We're going to have a quiet contest on the way back to the room," Cate said. "Those of you who remain quiet the whole way back to the room will get a star on your progress report. When you have ten stars on your progress report, you get a smelly sticker."

She was just about to head back to the classroom when she noticed that Timothy Sickle was not in line. "Has anyone seen Timothy?"

They all shook their heads.

"I want you guys to stand really still, just like little statues for a minute. Do you guys know what statues do?"

"They're quiet!" Mackenzie yelled.

"They're quiet, and they don't move. They're just like a rock. Those of you who can be little statues for me will get two stars on your progress reports."

She entered the boys' bathroom. It smelled stale and dank. Dots of petrified bubble gum covered the tiled floor. "Timothy?" she called. There was no answer. "Timothy!" She peeked under the stalls. Beneath the third stall she could see his small pants bunched up around his sneakers. "Timothy, I can see you in there. Why aren't you answering me?"

A long silence followed. "Timo—"

"Teacher, will you wipe me?"

In all her years as a teacher, she'd never been asked to wipe a child.

"No, Timothy. You are a big boy. You are in kindergarten now, and big boys don't need help going potty. I am not your mommy or your baby-sitter, and I'm not going to wipe you. Now hurry up. The other kids are waiting."

Five minutes later, Timothy came out of the bathroom. Cate told him to go to the end of the line.

When Cate got home that evening, she had two new messages.

"Hi, Cate. It's Nick. 'Member? I met you the other night with Jill. Anyway, I just wanted to see what you were up to."

Thank God she hadn't been home. He'd already called four times since they'd gone to the West End, and she hadn't returned any of his calls. She kind of felt bad. His only downfall had been not being Paul. It had been too soon to try dating someone else, and she made a mental note not to get involved with the rebound game again.

The next message was from Beth. "Just wanted to tell you that I just saw Paul at Sav-On. I think he might be gay. Call me back."

Cate snatched up the phone. *Paul! Sav-On! Gay!* She needed the whole story—pronto!

The line was busy. None of her friends had run into Paul since they'd broken up. She wondered if he looked sad, or if he had said anything about her. The curiosity was killing her!

Again, she pounded Beth's number into the phone, praying that it wasn't busy. Still busy.

She played Jill's CD and sang along with Pink's "There You Go." She listened to the disc at least three times a day. The compilation of songs made her feel as if she were not only better off without No Call Paul but also thrilled about losing his flaky ass. Cate sang it with attitude, loud and unashamed.

She turned up the stereo and began to move her shoulders from side to side the same way that Pink would. She danced toward the mirror and tossed her head back, singing at the top of her lungs. She was nearing the chorus when she heard a loud bang coming from beneath her. Startled, she stopped dancing and spun away from the mirror.

"Turn that shit off!" her downstairs *male* neighbor yelled. He'd been banging the ceiling with something, probably a broom.

She rolled her eyes and turned the music down, annoyed that her little concert was over and slightly embarrassed that she'd been performing for the apartment complex.

While she waited for Beth to call, she checked her E-mails.

FROM: Leslie Lyons
SUBJECT: Bridesmaid Itinerary

Hello girls. We're getting down to the final days now! As most of you know I am extremely busy, so I don't have time to take phone calls. I have all of your shoes and will distribute them to each of you at the rehearsal dinner. Cate and Sarah, I still need your checks.

Oops. The check for one hundred eighty dollars was sitting in a stamped and sealed envelope somewhere beneath the free Humane

Society calendar she had received in the mail and a pile of clothes on her wicker chair.

> I have attached the itinerary for the weekend. My wedding coordinator says that it is impairetive that you read it and follow it. Please follow **ALL** instructions. If one of you is late it will mess up the schedule and push everything back for the entire wedding party and all the guests. I am so happy and honored to have each one of you in my wedding. Can't wait to see you this weekend!
>
> Love,
> Leslie

Cate opened the five-page itinerary. As she glanced over the itinerary she realized she was no longer a bridesmaid, but instead a bride's slave.

Rehearsal Dinner:

Rehearsal will begin at 5:30 p.m. at the Laguna Cliffs Marriott. Please dress **appropriately**. This is the most important day of my life. No flip flops, etc. Dinner will follow at Café Marseilles. Dates and significant others are welcome. Just tell me ahead of time if you are bringing someone. If you tell me the night of the rehearsal dinner I will not be able to accommodate them.

Wedding Day:

Hair begins **promptly** at 9:00 a.m. Again, if one of you is late it will ruin it for everyone. Please get a bight to eat before arriving at the salon. We will not be eating again until that evening.

Bight? Cate had read enough. She was too anxious and absorbed with hearing Beth's Paul info that she didn't bother to read the following four pages. She closed the computer screen and dialed Beth's number for the third time. "Beth! I just got your message. What happened?"

"Well, I was in line at Sav-On when all of a sudden I see this impeccably dressed man two carts in front of me wearing Prada loafers and, you know that whole look. He was putting Kleenex on the conveyer and he turned around and it was Paul. He popped out of line for a minute and gave me a hug and asked how I was doing and then he asked how you were doing—"

"He did! He asked about me?"

"Yes. He seemed nervous. He was like, *'So how's Cate'* and kind of turned his head to an angle as if you'd just been through some kind of trauma."

"Ugh! He thinks I'm depressed about him. That egotistical jerk!"

"Don't worry. Listen to what I said." She started to laugh. "I told him you were doing fabulous." She had to stop because she was laughing so hard. "And then I told him you were dating a stockbroker."

Cate screeched. "But I'm not!"

"So? He doesn't need to know that."

They were both laughing now.

"What did he say?" Cate asked.

"He seemed kind of surprised and then he was like, *'Good. That's great because she seemed kind of mad about everything.'* I was like, 'Mad? Cate mad? No. I've never seen her happier.' "

The thought of Paul being burned in the middle of Sav-On by Beth's harsh news was delightful. Then something occurred to her. "What am I going to do? He'll be at Leslie's wedding, and now he's going to tell everyone I'm dating a stockbroker."

"Just say you went out with someone a couple of times. No one has to know. Besides, why aren't you dating anyone? What's going on with Ethan?"

"Ethan? He's fine."

"No, I mean, why haven't you *dated* him?"

"Dated him?" Cate was mortified. "He's just a friend. I told you that already. Why does everyone keep saying these silly things?"

"He's so cool and cute, and I just think you guys would be perfect."

"You think he's cute?"

"Yes."

"Really?"

"Yes. And he would treat you so well."

"I know. I just . . . *No.* It would never work. He washes his hair with bar soap!"

"I know. That's great!"

"No. It's not like that with him. I can't see him romantically. It's too weird."

"You've just made up your mind that you're not attracted to him. I think you should give him a fair chance. Just give the guy a chance."

"I've known him forever. Do you know how bad I would feel if I hurt him?"

"What makes you so sure you're going to hurt him? What if he ends up hurting you?"

That was a good point, and this conversation was treading into deeper waters than Cate was prepared to swim in. She changed the subject.

They talked for a while about the Halloween wedding before they said good-bye. After Cate hung up, she couldn't help but imagine herself with a stockbroker.

Grand Exit

Cate picked up her suit the day before Leslie's wedding. The belt had been repaired. She was prepared to sign over her savings account to the seamstress and was elated to learn that the miracle was only going to set her back five dollars. It was the alterations in the bust that cost a small fortune.

The following day went by quickly, and she left for Laguna Beach straight from school.

When Cate arrived at the hotel, she noticed that the chuppah, a wedding canopy for the bride and groom to stand beneath during the ceremony, had already been set up on the lawn outside the hotel. Rows of white folding chairs had been situated in front of the chuppah. Near the chairs stood a giant white tent for the reception.

She checked in to the hotel, found her room, then changed into something *appropriate* for the occasion. Rebellion nagged her, and for a fleeting second she considered wearing a thong bikini and her reading glasses just to spite Leslie. She remembered that she didn't even own a thong bikini as she headed to the chuppah.

Luckily, Paul had not been invited to the rehearsal dinner. That was one less night that she was going to have to see his face.

Leslie was waiting near the chuppah with a cell phone next to her ear. She grabbed Cate's arm, took the phone away from her face, and let her voice drop to a whisper. "Don't mention my stepmom in front of my mother, okay? Don't ask where she is or anything. Don't even mention her name."

"Okay."

It would probably be best to avoid Leslie's mom altogether. Simply steer clear of any STD stories. Cate was en route to the chuppah when Ms. Van der Berke rushed toward her, waving her hands in giant circles. As if Cate would miss her in her flaming red and gold St. John suit.

"Cate! So glad to see you!" Leslie had mentioned that she had Botox injections, and Cate could definitely see a change. Her face didn't move when she spoke. Her boobs seemed much stiffer as well. She wore a number of jewels, including a giant ruby on her French-manicured hands.

"It's good to see you, Ms. Van der Berke," Cate said. "How have you been?"

Her eyes darted over the street each time someone new arrived. "Thank God my asshole ex-husband isn't coming with his bastard child and that whore of a wife he took."

"Oh."

Cate noticed a man at least ten years Ms. Van der Berke's junior standing behind her. Cate wanted to shout, "More power to ya, mama! Rob the cradle!" but didn't think she was at that level with Leslie's mom yet. Her gentleman friend was wearing a navy blue suit and had a boring haircut. His hands hung stiffly at each side. She waited for an introduction, but Ms. Van der Berke ignored him. Cate felt bad for him. She remembered the way she had felt when Paul took her out with all his friends and they ignored her.

"Anyway, it's good to see you, darling." She squeezed Cate's arm.

"Thanks. You, too."

Cate noticed her back grow stiff and her gaze fixate over Cate's shoulder. Mr. Lyons had arrived. His pudgy face was as red as a raw steak, and he dabbed at his forehead with a handkerchief.

"Excuse me," Ms. Van der Berke said. She turned to her gentleman friend and began to whisper something.

Cate wondered why Ms. Van der Berke couldn't be happy with her boy toy. So what if he looked like a young Sam Donaldson? She could make him her slave.

Leslie grabbed her arm. "I need to give you your shoes *and* I'd like to introduce you to someone." She led Cate to a corner of the lawn. A large brown box was filled with smaller shoe boxes. "Seven, right?" Leslie asked as she rummaged through the box.

"Yes. I'm a size seven."

"Here you go."

Cate was dying to see her hundred-eighty-dollar shoes. She didn't recognize the designer name on the box. Nestled in the tissue paper inside the box were two powder-blue satin sandals with matching satin flowers sewn to the front. "Oh. Wow," Cate said. "They have flowers on them."

Leslie beamed. "Yeah! Now. Don't lose those. Put them in a safe spot."

She pulled on Cate's arm. "Now let me introduce you to the guy you're going to be walking down the aisle with. He's a great guy, Cate. He's rich. He owns his own computer company. He has a nice four-bedroom house in Newport, a BMW, a Range Rover, and a boat."

They passed a frail-looking man with a long beard, wearing a yarmulke. He was conversing with a heavyset younger man wearing clerics. The rabbi and the minister. Then she led Cate to a group of people situated near the chuppah.

"Cate, this is George." He was shorter than Cate, which meant that he had to be about five-five. He was slightly overweight and had a strikingly upturned nose.

Cate shook his hand. "It's nice to meet you, George."

She was in no mood for small talk and thanked God when Sarah and Miles interrupted.

Most of the rehearsal was spent planning for the Arabian horse that would be dropping Leslie off at the chuppah.

"I want Russ to pick me up right under my arms like this," Leslie said, cupping her hands under her armpits. "Then I want him to lift me, kind of in the air like in the ballet, as he pulls me off the horse."

Leslie was five-seven and had been trying to knock off twenty pounds for as long as Cate had known her. Russ was maybe an inch or two taller and probably weighed less. How was he going to hoist her around like a ballerina? This wasn't *The Nutcracker*.

The rehearsal became complicated when Ms. Van der Berke told the coordinator she didn't want to sit on the same side of the grass as her ex-husband.

"Well, he's the father of the bride. He'll be escorting her down the aisle," the coordinator said.

"I don't care who he is. Figure out a way to keep him at least thirty feet from me. I have a restraining order."

A sharp whizzing noise came from Ms. Van der Berke's territory. Cate turned to see Leslie's mom stretching a tape measure across the lawn. She was crouched down in her Ferragamo heels, instructing her boyfriend to pull on the other end.

"Thirty feet and three inches," he called.

Ms. VDB's eyes locked on the coordinator. "Well, I guess he's lucky."

Leslie inched closer to Cate. "I'm so embarrassed." She looked drained. "This is supposed to be the happiest time of my life, and my parents have to stay thirty feet away from each other."

Cate put her arm around Leslie's shoulders. "It *is* the happiest time of your life. I think if they knew how much pain it caused you to see them this way, they would be more civil. Just focus on the life you're going to start with Russ, and let them worry about their problems."

She squeezed Cate's hand. "You're right. Thanks for being here."

The dinner that followed was a blur. Cate sat next to Sarah and Miles, who ordered martinis as if vodka would be officially banned tomorrow.

She drunk-dialed Ethan somewhere between dinner and dessert to tell him that his food was better than the garbage they were eating at this rehearsal dinner. He wasn't there but she left a lengthy message, reiterating that he was the best caterer she had ever known and a great friend at that.

She received a monogrammed mirror that Leslie had given as gifts to her bridesmaids, then later lost it somewhere at the restaurant. It didn't matter though. She had two others just like them in her purse.

George had been seated somewhere to her left. By the time dessert came he had asked Cate if it would be all right to E-mail her. Smashed, God only knew what she'd written as her E-mail address on her napkin.

The phone rang, and Cate groggily reached for the receiver, ready to hear the Marriott wake-up call.

"Hello," she said, noticing that her voice sounded as if she were a chronic smoker.

"Cate! Where the hell are you!" It wasn't the hotel wake-up call she'd been expecting. It was Leslie.

Cate bolted up. "What time is it?"

"Eleven-thirty!"

"Oh my God. I didn't get my wake-up call. I can't believe this." She had committed a wedding felony.

"Didn't you read the itinerary? We're supposed to be back at the hotel *in an hour* for pictures!"

"Do I still have time to get my hair done?"

"Hurry!"

Cate jumped out of bed. She endured ten seconds of a freezing cold shower, barely dried off, then dressed in something that didn't match before sprinting from the hotel.

"Finally!" Leslie said while her hair was getting the finishing touches.

"I knocked on your door this morning," Sarah said. "You didn't answer, so I assumed you were in the shower."

A hairdresser smelling of cologne approached Cate. "Hi, are you Cate?"

She nodded.

"I'm Michael. Come with me. If we hurry, we can still do your hair." He pointed toward a revolving chair. "Why don't you have a seat?" Once Cate sat down, he immediately began running his fingers through her hair. "Since we don't have much time, I think we should just put your hair in hot rollers and go for a nice curly effect." He spoke to her reflection in the mirror. "It will take too long to pin up your bob."

Cate remembered Val's wedding. The hairdresser had used curlers, and it had come out looking nice and wavy around the face. "That sounds great."

Leslie complained about the way her veil looked, loud enough for people in the shopping center across the street to hear. After the poor hairdresser readjusted the veil for the eighth time, Leslie said good-bye and gave Cate and Sarah specific instructions for the rest of the afternoon.

Michael turned out to be an interesting character. He loved to talk about himself, which was perfectly fine with Cate. His tales of a porn star sister and cocaine parties kept her hanging on his every word while he rolled away. After he'd covered her head in rollers, he set her under the dryer.

"Just stay here for about ten minutes. I'll be right back," he said. "I'm going to go smoke." She wished he wouldn't leave her.

Sarah was finished with her hair by then, a nice classic French twist. She sat down next to Cate and they took a personality quiz in *Cosmo* together.

They were reading their horoscopes when Michael returned. "I'm going to the bathroom," Sarah said. "I'll be right back."

One by one the rollers came out. She started to feel alarmed when she noticed that the curls looked like an explosively bad perm. They were tight, boingy—obnoxious. Complaining seemed premature at this point. She figured it was probably safe to assume that he had other plans for her hair and wasn't finished. She was petrified when he ran his fingers through her hair, doused it with hair spray and said, "All done."

She looked like Shirley Temple on crack. This couldn't be happening. Words escaped her as she gazed at her reflection in the mirror. She didn't want to hurt Michael's feelings. However, she sure as hell was not walking out of the salon looking like a wired poodle. Paul was going to be there.

"Can you—um—flatten it a little? It's a tad more poofy than I'm used to."

Michael looked at her with little expression on his face. Then he shrugged. "Sure. We can flatten it a little."

She breathed a sigh of relief. He smashed his hands over the curls as if he were stuffing a turkey. A thick cloud of hair spray choked her as he pushed the fro against her head. "Is that better?"

Cate was coughing. She couldn't tell him, "No. It is definitely *not* better."

She could see Sarah's reflection behind her. Cate sensed that she was just as horrified. "Cate, we were supposed to be there twenty minutes ago."

Cate was panic-stricken. "Michael, I'm sorry, but I'm not really comfortable with . . ." She motioned her hand around her head. "This. Is there anything you can do to change it? Just get it back to how it was before."

"Yeah." Sarah nodded. "Do you think you could just run a flattening iron through it or something? Straighten it out a bit?"

He released a deep sigh. "We'll have to start all over. I can wash it and blow dry it if you'd like."

"We don't have time." Cate stood up. "Just forget it. It's fine." She'd figure something out in the car. At this point she just wanted to leave the salon. Her temples had begun to pound from holding in a flood of tears. If she looked in the mirror for another minute, she would start crying. She quickly paid Michael fifty dollars for doing nothing but embarrassing the hell out of her.

"I hate my hair!" Cate yelled as soon as they were outside.

"It's not bad." Sarah was a terrible liar. "It's just *really* curly."

"Sarah, we have to do something. I cannot go to the wedding looking like this."

"You mean you don't want to wear an afro in your royal blue disco suit?" They both began to laugh as Sarah smashed Cate's hair with her hands. "Geez, he put enough hair spray on here. I can't even get it to budge."

"I know. I could render someone unconscious if I accidentally bumped him with my hair."

"We'll see what we can do when we get back to the hotel," Sarah said.

Nothing could be done when they got back to the hotel. All the other bride's slaves were dressed in their outfits, waiting for Cate and Sarah.

Ms. Van der Berke closed in on Cate. "You need to go get dressed immediately," she said. "The other girls have already begun taking pictures."

Leslie glanced at Cate when she passed. "Your hair looks . . . curly."

She felt like crying.

She spent a frantic five minutes in the bathroom doing everything in her power to salvage her image. Combing her hair only made it worse. The tight curls turned to frizzy blonde poofs when touched with a brush. She even wrapped her head in a towel while she changed into her outfit. She was minutes away from Paul. He was supposed to be sorry he'd broken up with her, not glad. For weeks she'd envisioned herself greeting him with an Academy-award-caliber up-do and flawless makeup.

Ms. Van der Berke knocked. "Everyone is waiting for you!"

They spent a hellish hour taking pictures that Cate hoped were destroyed.

All she wanted was a new hairdo and food. Her body felt shaky and weak from hunger. It was two o'clock, and she hadn't eaten a thing all day. After the pictures were over, she attempted to sneak away. She could practically smell freedom when Leslie intervened. "No one can leave. The wedding starts in an hour, and I can't afford to have something happen to any of you."

She heard the horse neigh outside the hotel.

"I'm really hungry."

"Snacks will be provided after the wedding."

Leslie's grandmother, a small woman wearing a snowy white wig and mink stole overheard the conversation. "Well here, honey," she said. "If you girls are hungry, I've got some peanuts in my purse." She pulled out a bag of nuts that looked too large to fit in her bag.

Cate wanted to kiss her on each cheek and hail her a hero. "Oh! I'd love some!"

Cate anticipated the crunch of the nuts and the taste of salt on her lips. Her hand was within a millimeter of the bag when Leslie snapped. "No!" she barked. "They can't have those. I don't want the bridesmaids ruining their clothes before all the pictures have been taken. Besides it's on the itinerary; no eating until after photos."

Leslie's grandmother looked startled. Obediently she sealed the bag and stuffed it back in her purse. Cate felt the moment fade as if she had turned on her radio and listened to the last five seconds of her favorite song.

For the love of God, Cate felt like she was going to faint. She felt like shaking Leslie's shoulders and asking who she was and what had happened to her *friend,* Leslie. She could rent an Arabian horse and order four hundred table linens from China, but she couldn't feed her friends.

Watching Leslie get heaved on top of the horse was worth sticking around for. She needed three grown men to hoist her on top, and it took five tries before they finally got her up there, sidesaddle. Apparently the horse wasn't comfortable either, because he reared, lifting his two front legs, just like in a Western. Leslie hung on for dear life as the beast attempted to lunge forward after bucking. Luckily, the trainer grabbed the lead line before any real damage was done. But she had to readjust her whole veil, which required her mother standing on a stool so she could reach her.

Ms. Van der Berke was just about finished pinning Leslie's veil when the horse parted its back legs and lifted its tail.

Cate heard someone behind her whisper, "Oh no," right before the horse dumped a giant heap of shit onto the lawn. The bridal party retreated as if a sprinkler had unexpectedly begun watering the lawn, barely missing grainy pellets of horse crap.

"The horse shit?" Leslie glared at the trainer. "Is he going to do that when I'm at the altar?"

"No. He just went to the bathroom. He probably won't have to go again for a couple of hours."

Cate felt sorry for the man. He was just a skinny horseman, probably used to lifting small children onto his pet at birthday parties—not a high-strung bride, using his horse to emulate a love scene from *Legends of the Fall.*

She was so curious to see how the horse would do when it came time to walk down the aisle that she forgot about Paul, her hairdo, and her gnawing hunger pains. She strode down the aisle at a comfortable pace, the idea of Paul as distant as the South Pole. She didn't even notice if he was there as she stood at the chuppah.

Excited gasps came from the guests when Leslie approached on horseback. A little girl stood on her father's knees and clapped her hands together when she saw the fairytale-like scene unfolding.

From her mount Leslie's gaze locked on Russ. Cate thought she saw tears glistening in his eyes. Mr. Lyons led the horse with a gold rope. The guests were mesmerized. Some dabbed away their tears with tissues. As instructed by the coordinator, Russ headed to the horse just as it reached the second row. Leslie's face was a spread of joy as she lovingly looked at her groom. This was her moment.

Russ lifted his arms, pulling the back of his coat up and revealing part of his tucked-in shirt. And for a moment it was like a scene from a gold medal Olympic pairs skating performance. *For a moment.* When Russ's hands locked onto her armpits, the horse shifted its weight. Instead of gracefully slipping into her groom's arms, Leslie was shoved forward, the layers of her satin skirt cascading over Russ's head and arms like a sheet settling over a mattress. The tent over his face made him disoriented. He lost his footing and accidentally toppled into the side of the animal. The horse, clearly agitated, began to jerk its head from side to side.

"Help!" Leslie screamed as she tried to pull at her skirts, revealing her stocking-covered calves. "Heeelp!"

Russ tried to maintain his balance, blindfolded and still suspending Leslie in midair. "Oh my God!" someone screamed as Leslie and Russ fell to the ground, tangled inside her gown.

The horse released a disgruntled neigh and shook his head, flaring his nostrils as strands of his long mane swung over his face.

"Ahhhhhhhh!" Leslie screamed as the horse backed up. *"My foooot!"*

Mr. Lyons yanked on the rope. The trainer sped down the aisle like a cop after a thief. Immediately, he grabbed the rope and led the horse away.

The little girl who had been clapping earlier held her hand over her mouth, and those who had been dabbing at tears now sat wide-eyed. Cate sensed that everyone was wondering the same thing: *What next?* Would they continue with the wedding? Was Leslie's ankle broken? Would they sue the horse trainer?

Leslie popped up, smoothed over her dress, and announced, "I'm fine! I'm fine! I swear! I meant to do that!" She grabbed Russ's arm, tossed her chin up, and proceeded to the altar. A few lime-colored grass stains were smeared across the bottom of her dress.

The rabbi and the minister stood next to one another, waiting for the bride and groom to approach the altar. When Leslie and Russ arrived, the minister took a moment to clear his throat. He lifted his arms to either side as he looked out at Leslie and Russ. "All right then," he said. "We are gathered here to—" He stopped, clenched his teeth, closed his eyes, and put a fist to his mouth. For each second that passed, his eyes squeezed tighter. Cate thought he was praying until he turned his back to the audience. His shoulders and chest shook with uncontrollable laughter, tears streaming down his cheeks. He shook his head. "I'm sorry. I'm so sorry," he said as the entire wedding party surrendered to their own battle, laughing like children caught in the most inappropriate fit of hysteria.

Meanwhile, the horse grazed on the Marriott lawn, his tail swishing back and forth.

After the ceremony, Cate was still dying for a snack and a moment of privacy in the bathroom to fix her hair. Drastic as it may seem, she was ready to submerge her head in the bathroom sink. Something had to be done. She was heading to the bathroom at the Marriott when two of the other bridesmaids stopped her.

"Where are you going?" Bethany asked. "We have to go to the receiving line."

"Receiving line?"

"Yeah."

What was this? A fund-raiser for a senate election? She needed to eat. It was nearing five o'clock, and she still hadn't eaten a thing. How could she be the only hungry one? Where was the rest of the wedding party getting their fuel from?

She ended up sandwiched in between George and Sarah. She was starting to feel hostile as she introduced herself to each and every guest at the wedding. After nearly two hundred handshakes, Cate looked to her left. The line of guests was still wrapped around the tent, the end nowhere in sight. She wondered where Paul was and could hardly fathom the thought of coming face-to-face with him under such harsh lighting, the glow highlighting her bad hair and outfit. As she waited for Paul, she shook hands with the freaky relative and the wedding drunk.

The wedding drunk was a toss-up between Mr. Lyons, whose voice had grown louder with each drink, and the uninvited girlfriend of one of Russ's friends. She had frosted hair with teased and sprayed bangs that should've been outlawed after the eighties. In her early thirties, she wasn't fat but also not designed for her black leather miniskirt and backless sequined top. She wore the same kind of stiletto platform shoes that strippers fancied. The heels had long, skinny straps that wrapped up her calves. They looked brand spanking new, the red paten shiny and tight. Cate could also tell the shoes were new by the way Mia walked in them. Each step she took was the equivalent of walking on stilts. She could hardly move in them. Or maybe it was just because she'd had too much to drink. She draped herself over Russ and the groomsmen, making neighing noises as she proceeded down the receiving line. Neither Leslie nor Russ found her impression of the horse to be as funny as she did.

Freaky relative: Leslie's skinhead cousin from Arkansas, who actually wore red knee-high combat boots to the wedding.

Sarah turned to her at one point. "Two-second rule for each guest. Limit conversation and keep 'em going. I'm sick of this," she said between gritted teeth.

"Me, too." Cate kept the guests moving, barely giving them a *"How are you."* She felt light-headed and weak from food deprivation. Even worse, the guests smelled of garlic and wore crumbs on their clothes. They had been enjoying a cocktail and hors d'oeuvre reception while Leslie had kept the wedding party at her mercy for a series of hellish postwedding photos.

Although no one had mentioned the mayhem with the horse, the incident hung in the air like an embarrassing secret that everyone knew. It would almost be better if Leslie and Russ would crack a few jokes about the mishap, lighten things up a bit. Leslie still limped, and after the ceremony she had instructed all of her bridesmaids to let the incident pass and proceed with the evening as planned. She was clearly in denial.

After an hour of hell, the receiving line ended. Cate turned to Sarah. "I guess Paul didn't come to the wedding."

"No. He's definitely here. I saw him."

She wondered why he hadn't gone through the receiving line.

She entered the reception hall as a pair with George. He held Cate's hand and would not let go, even after the DJ had introduced them. Apparently he had fallen under the impression that escorting a bridesmaid down the aisle meant he was dating her. Sure, it was sweet when he pulled out her chair and stood when she needed to use the rest room, but he was not her date.

The sight of a bread basket on their table was the best thing she had seen all day. She shoved a roll into her mouth, taking huge bites and chewing like Cujo. She didn't care if George thought she was a pig. She slathered enough butter to grease a car with on her second roll.

Then she noticed the custom-made table linens. She had to admit, they were definitely exquisite with beadwork and hand stitching. But come tomorrow, who the hell was going to remember the table linens? Leslie could've covered the tables with newspaper, and the only thing people were going to remember from this wedding was Russ stumbling around with her gown over his head.

"Your hair is so curly," George said while she stuffed her face. "It's just so curly."

Couldn't he see she was eating? "Thanks for pointing that out, George. I really needed you to remind me."

"Sure." He did not sense her sarcasm.

She needed an escape from George and remembered her cell phone in her handbag. She'd turned it off for the ceremony, but now she wondered if she had any messages. She pulled the phone from her purse.

"I don't mean to be rude," she said to George. "But I really need to check my messages."

She honestly didn't expect to have any messages and was pleasantly surprised to find one. Ethan chuckled before he spoke. "Hey, drunk one. I got your message last night. Thank you for all the kind words. You're not such a shabby friend, either. Anyway, I hope you're having fun. Throw a few cocktails back for me, will ya? I have to cater a wedding tonight, so I won't be drinking. I can't wait to hear all about your night. Gimme a call when you get a chance."

Hearing his voice made her feel homesick. It was like getting a message from her mother the first week of college. She felt as if she were surrounded by strangers. She had George to her left. Sarah and Miles were seated somewhere in the vicinity, but they were in Newlywed Land and couldn't be bothered with Cate. Leslie had become the Antichrist and had taken the meaning of demanding to a new level. Cate hardly knew her anymore.

Her eyes found Paul seated at a table with some friends they both knew from college. Relief settled over her when she realized that he was dateless. Seeing him with another woman would've been brutal when the wounds from their breakup were still fresh. He looked sharp in his gray suit and crisp blue tie. She felt a flicker of longing to nestle her head against his chest, to feel his arms around her shoulders. For a moment she debated going to him, saying hello. But her nerves ached at the thought of facing him for the first time since their breakup. Furthermore, she wasn't going anywhere near him until she did something with her hair. Instead, she called Ethan back. He didn't answer, so she left a brief message.

After dinner, a great number of the guests formed a ring around Leslie and Russ and began to dance in a circle around them. Cate skipped around with the ring of guests, watching as several of the groomsmen hoisted the newlyweds up over their heads on chairs. It was obvious that Leslie wasn't comfortable with this Jewish dance custom, as she clung for dear life to the corners of her seat, the ridges of her knuckles turning white. The upbeat, traditional Jewish music actually put Cate in a good mood, and she didn't care that she was holding hands with George on one side and the skinhead cousin on the other as they skipped around in circles. Then she remembered her hair and outfit and hoped to God Paul wasn't watching. Maybe he wouldn't recognize her with an afro.

She returned to her seat to avoid making a spectacle of herself. The people-watching at this wedding was much better than dancing any-way. The swing classic "In the Mood" played. Except for one couple who had obviously taken swing dancing lessons, no one else knew how to do it.

Mia stood on her stiltlike shoes, legs positioned like tree trunks against the dance floor. She could barely dance in her stripper sandals. She held her feet in place as her knees bent back and forth to the burst of trumpets. Her arms, the only part of her body that could safely move without causing her to fall, gyrated to the beat of the music. Occasionally she completed a safe and steady rotation on her feet. She reminded Cate of the plastic hula dancers that people sometimes stuck on their dashboards.

Cate noticed the skinhead dipping Russ's Jewish cousin. Maybe he'd been reformed tonight. Something good had to come out of this wedding.

And then there was Leslie with her wounded foot, limping to the music, acting as if she knew swing moves. "I paid for this band! I'm not going to let it go to waste!"

"Single ladies! Calling all you lovely single ladies!" the band leader announced over the microphone. He sounded like the man who did voice-overs for movie previews. "Single ladies, make your way to the dance floor. It's time for the bouquet toss!"

Sarah squeezed her arm. "Get out there. This is your bouquet, Cate. I can feel it."

Cate joined approximately fifty other single girls on the dance floor, half of them under the age of eighteen. She felt a twinge of humiliation when she noticed Leslie's seven-year-old niece joining the fray. At the rate Cate was going, Leslie's niece would beat her to the altar.

Leslie winked at Cate before she turned her back and hurled the bouquet over her left shoulder. Women screamed. Arms flew in the air. A herd of females darted toward the flowers like vampires after fresh blood. It moved fast, rushing over their heads like a missile. Cate wanted to beat the kid. But the bouquet had gone too far.

It came down, the pointed plastic handle facing toward its destination, like a spear targeting a buffalo for the kill. She froze, her mouth dropping, as she saw Paul lift his hand to block it, his face contorted in horror. He released a throaty, agonizing scream right before it pegged him square in the left eye.

The single women tore through one another, tackling the bouquet at his feet, knocking him to the ground as if he were merely an orange cone marking an out-of-bounds perimeter on a football field. Once they finally peeled themselves off one another, a teenager emerged the victor. She held the now practically ruined flowers over her head.

Except for a few guests who had been standing nearby, no one seemed to care about Paul as they applauded the girl. A cocktail had spilled down the front of his tie and jacket. An elderly woman dabbed napkins on his chest. Cate ran to him.

"Are you all right?" she asked.

"Yeah, I'm fine. I'm just kind of shocked. That's all." She noticed that his eye had started to swell, forming a goose egg.

"You should put some ice on your eye."

Miles slapped him on the back. "Here's some ice," he said as he pressed a cocktail to Paul's face.

A waiter approached with a bag of ice and a few other concerned guests offered their help. Cate returned to her table once she realized he was going to be okay.

She spent the rest of the reception fighting off George, who clearly could not handle more than three drinks. She wished he'd leave her alone so she could watch the wedding drunk and Leslie limping in peace.

She was on her way to the bathroom to hide from him when she ran into Ms. Van der Berke. Her gentleman friend stood off to the side. Cate found it strange that they never touched or came within a couple feet of each other. "I can't believe that tramp had the nerve to bring her little bastard to the wedding. Who brings an infant to a wedding? And did you see what she was wearing, Cate?"

Cate had noticed that Kim was wearing a stylish cocktail dress. She knew it had to be hard enough that Mr. Lyons had left her for another woman. It was even worse that the other woman was younger and prettier. Her pain must be torturous. But couldn't she handle it with grace and dignity? Eventually Mr. Lyons might get bored with his trophy bride and suffer with regret over losing his gracious, kind wife.

"Can you believe how inappropriate that outfit is for a wedding?" Ms. Van der Berke went on.

"I don't really remember," she said, avoiding further drama.

"The nerve of that bitch. For months she was sending me death threats, and she has the nerve to show up at my baby's wedding. They put dog poop in my mailbox and even smeared it all over the handle, too." Cate thought that sounded more like the work of bored teenagers than a gold-digging aerobics teacher, but she let Ms. Van der Berke continue to lament over her misfortune.

Tears welled in her eyes. "You know I had to get a restraining order? Don't you? Didn't Leslie tell you that they wanted to kill me?"

Actually, Leslie had not shared this with Cate. "Uh . . . no, I wasn't really aware."

"That bitch steals my husband and tries to take everything. When I put up a fight, she sends me death threats. For eight months I've been afraid to leave my house, and I have to make the cat sample all my food before I eat it, just to make sure it isn't poisoned." She glanced at her gentleman friend. "That's my bodyguard, Cate."

"Oh. Hi, nice to meet you." Cate waved.

The bodyguard nodded.

Then she looked over her shoulder, fearing that George was going to come rolling around the corner at any given second.

She began to inch away from them. "Well, I should get to the ladies' room."

"You go ahead, darling. We'll talk more later!"

No. Let's not.

She'd barely excused herself from the role of Ms. VDB's therapist when she was captured again.

"Cate, c'mere." She heard a slurred voice from behind her. Then he tugged on her arm. "I'm tired, Geor—" She turned to face him. "Paul."

With his good eye, he looked at her as if he were admiring a painting that he liked. The other eye was nearly swollen shut. For a moment she stared at him. She could tell he was drunk by the way his shoulders hung and the loose smile that was perched on his face. "It's good to see you," he said.

Then George interrupted. "There you are," he said. "I've been looking for you everywhere."

She didn't know whether she was grateful or irritated.

Paul gave him a once-over.

"George, can you give me a minute, please? I'm on my way to the bathroom."

"All right. Meet me on the dance floor."

"Is that the stockbroker?" Paul asked when George was out of earshot.

Stockbroker? What the hell is he talking about? Then she remembered that Beth had told him she was dating a stockbroker. "No. That is not the stockbroker."

"I want to talk to you. Come back to my room with me. I miss you, Cate."

This was the moment everyone dreamt about after being dumped. The begging. The regretting. The last word.

He touched her arm. "Please, can we talk?" He rubbed the side of her elbow. "I've been thinking about you a lot lately."

He was wearing beer goggles. How could he possibly be attracted to her when her hair looked worse than a high school science project? "Paul, c'mon. What is going to change now? You've been drinking. You made your feelings clear at the La Jolla cove. Let's not do this."

"Sometimes I think I made a mistake. I drive myself crazy thinking about you, Cate."

Gently, she pulled her arm away. "*Es desafortunado,* Paul." She left him watching her back as she walked away.

"What does that mean?" he called as she walked off.

Without turning around she said, "It's Spanish. You should know."

"What?"

"It's unfortunate," she said, having no idea if he had heard her or not.

Beth's Wedding •

"I can give youuu . . ." The cashier at PB Thrift and Resale surveyed each piece of the royal blue pantsuit, the silk falling in folds over his hands. "Well . . . hmmm . . ." He flicked his tongue ring in his mouth. "Two dollars."

"How 'bout three?" she shot back. All the hassle she'd been through with that ensemble. She was at least going to get a cocktail out of it.

He flicked his tongue ring again. Then he nodded. "Three? All right. We usually only take donations, but this . . . well. The eighties is huge for theme parties right now. I need stuff like this."

He pulled three dollars from the cash register. He leaned over the counter and counted out the bills, revealing more tattoos than Mötley Crüe and Blink 182 combined. She probably would've gotten more cash if she had brought the belt.

"Thank you," she said, before searching for Ethan.

PB Thrift was one of her favorite places to shop. Clothes from nearly every decade of the twentieth century were represented in the secondhand store. Sometimes she purchased things, even though she never planned on wearing them. She loved old clothes, the way they represented history.

She and Ethan—and about half of Pacific Beach—were all scouring the racks of the thrift store for Halloween costumes. Ethan had no plans to dress up, but he was helping Cate pick out a good Marilyn dress.

After they found the right dress, they planned to go back to Cate's for cocktails and then to The Casbah for another King Mother show. Beth and Jill were going to meet them there.

She found him standing next to a rack of dresses in a far corner of the store. "Here you go," he said, handing her a pile of gowns. "Why don't you get started in a room? And I'll pass more along as I find them."

"Thanks." She took the stack of clothes and caught a whiff of mothballs. Despite the crowd, she managed to snag a room.

After she yanked the curtain closed, she pulled a silver, fifties-style dress over her head. She faced her reflection in the mirror. The platinum dress sagged like a rag over her chest and knees. God no.

"Cate!" Ethan called as he approached the dressing rooms.

"Yeah! I'm in the second one."

"I think this one's a winner." He pushed a red halter-top dress over the curtain. She reached for the new find.

"Oh I like this one," she said. "It looks a little big, though."

"Well, try it on. Do you have one on right now?"

"Yeah."

"How does it look?"

"Awful."

"Lemme see."

"No." No way was she stepping out of that dressing room looking like a weathered Christmas tree ornament for Ethan or anyone else to see.

She slipped the red dress over her head. It felt a little loose, but nothing that her miracle seamstress couldn't fix. The ruby skirt was draped over a couple layers of tulle, so it had just the right amount of poof needed for the fifties look.

When she glanced in the mirror, she knew this was her dress. She could already picture the heels she had to go with it. She'd definitely need to purchase a water bra so she could have Marilyn cleavage for a low-cut chest.

Ethan was waiting outside with four garments slung over his left arm. "That's your dress, Cate," he said, as she pulled back the curtain.

Six dollars later, she had her bridesmaid's gown for Beth's wedding. Ethan also purchased an old, beat up suede jacket for eight dollars.

"I'll wear it sometime," he said.

On the way home from PB Thrift, they stopped at Chip's Liquor and bought a bottle of Tanqueray, a liter of tonic water, a bag of tortilla chips, and a jar of salsa.

When they returned to Cate's apartment, she checked her messages.

"Hi. It's me. Ummm . . . listen, I hate to do this, but Beth and I can't make it tonight. We're too busy getting ready for tomorrow. Anyway, have fun with Ethan and we'll see you tomorrow!"

Tomorrow was Beth's shower/beading party. She wasn't having a traditional shower. Instead, she had invited only her bridesmaids over for lunch, and they were going to make jewelry to go with their costumes.

"They're not coming?" Ethan asked as he mixed them each a gin and tonic.

"I guess not." She opened the chips and salsa. "I'm kind of hungry. I don't think this is going to be enough for dinner."

"I can whip something up for us," he said.

"Good luck finding anything in this house."

He handed her a cocktail. "Lemme have a look around. I'm sure I can find something."

"I'm telling you, the only thing I have is some salad stuff and wheat thins."

He rummaged through her fridge and cabinets while she sipped on her drink. "Why don't we order a pizza, and I'll make us a salad?" he said.

"Okay." She reached for the yellow pages. She ordered a cheese pizza while he pulled things like sugar and olive oil from her pantry. "We need some tunes," he said as he set a salad bowl and mixing cup on the counter.

"That's a good idea." Cate put on the King Mother CD she had purchased at the last show, then returned to the kitchen.

She sat on the countertop while he made a salad dressing from scratch. He mixed olive oil, vinegar, sugar, lime juice, salt, garlic, and a multitude of other spices he had managed to find in her cupboard. He chopped a head of lettuce and a bell pepper the same way someone on the Food Network would, rapidly creating neat little rows of precisely cubed vegetables.

She mixed more cocktails. "Oh hey! I forgot to tell you! I'm running an ad in *The Reader* as a freelance photographer. I'm offering to do brochures and candid photos for parties and stuff. Can I use you as reference?"

"Of course you can! That's awesome."

She handed him a cocktail. "Good God, girl!" he said after he took the first sip. "You make a strong drink."

She offered to water it down, but he wouldn't let her. They talked about work and school and Beth's wedding.

Grease played with his new favorite toy: the royal-blue satin belt that he had previously attempted to demolish. Cate had given it to him the day after Leslie's wedding. He had a routine of pouncing on it, dragging it across the floor from his mouth as if it were a fresh kill, then chewing on it. She continued to munch on chips and salsa until the pizza came.

They sat on pillows next to the coffee table. Cate ate more salad than pizza. The dressing was the best that she had ever tasted in her life. She made Ethan write down the ingredients, but knew that when she attempted to make the dressing, it would never taste as good.

She had a good time drinking gin and tonics and eating salad on her floor.

"So, have you talked to Paul?" he asked.

"At Leslie's wedding." She took a sip of her drink and was starting to feel the effects. She couldn't even taste the gin anymore. "He actually tried to get me to go to his hotel room with him. Can you believe that?"

"Yeah, I can. I knew he'd be back. I just didn't know when."

"Well, he can dream on if he thinks there is ever going to be another chance with me."

He laughed. "Good girl. That guy was an idiot."

"Ethan?"

"Yeah."

"What happened with your ex-girlfriend?" The alcohol had made her feel bold. She was curious.

He looked at the floor. "Oh c'mon now. You don't want to hear that story."

"Yeah, I do."

He took a long swig of his drink, practically draining the contents of his glass. After he swallowed, he looked at Cate. "We were together for three years, and she cheated on me with a friend of mine. She was the only girl I'd ever been with."

"I'm sorry. I shouldn't have brought this up."

He shook his head. "No. It's okay. I don't care anymore. I really don't."

"What a bitch." Cate said as she set her empty glass on the table. "I'm sorry. I shouldn't say that. I don't even know her. But what a bitch."

He shrugged. "Well, I was angry for a while, but now I know that things work out the way they're supposed to. I mean . . . think if I had married her. I would've married a bitch. I really felt like they both screwed me over. But they didn't. I was the lucky one."

He picked up her empty glass and went to the kitchen. He began to mix them another round of drinks. "Hey, I want to see those pictures of the bamboo forest that you took."

"Oh yeah. They turned out really good." She went to her room to look for the photos.

When she returned, he was sitting on the couch with two full drinks. Grease was perched on his knee, taking advantage of the opportunity for attention. She sat down next to him, and the cat trotted off.

His slender fingers flipped through each photo. He had good strong hands, with veins running from his sinewy fingers to his elbows. His eyes crinkled around the corners when he saw something he liked.

He always seemed so at ease with himself, so confident. His shoulders were always straight yet relaxed. His motions and mannerisms were always natural. He never tried too hard to impress anyone. He never tried to be anything but Ethan. He was cute.

He looked up, about to comment on one of the photos, but smiled instead. "What?"

She hadn't realized she'd been staring at him. "I don't want to go to King Mother." It was the liquor talking, and she could hear a little voice of reason telling her to get off the couch, go put her shoes on, and call a cab to take them to The Casbah. *Go to the damn Casbah! You won't think he's cute tomorrow. You'll only end up hurting him.*

"Okay." He set the pictures on the coffee table. Then he looked at her. His hands were pulling her closer. Her stomach felt warm. She had forgotten what it had felt like to feel waves of butterflies flocking through her middle, the nervous excitement of a first kiss, the shy yet excited feeling of becoming intimate. It shouldn't have surprised her that he was a good kisser, but it did.

A thought flashed into her mind. Beth and Jill—they had done it on purpose.

27 • Piecing It Together

There were arms around her, strong and heavy against her waist. She could feel his breath on the nape of her neck and her buttocks tucked above his thighs. She was spooning with someone. She knew this even before she opened her eyes. Then she remembered. Ethan. They had been drunk. He had seen her naked. She had seen him naked. Oh holy shit! This is why people shouldn't drink. They were friends. He wasn't supposed to fondle her boobs. She lay there frozen for a moment. Then she turned over and pulled out of his embrace.

He released a half-asleep groan and rubbed his hand over her shoulder. She needed a glass of water. As she sat up, she gave herself credit for at least having the sense to wear underwear to bed. She grabbed the first thing she saw from the floor and pulled it over her head. It was a T-shirt—*his* T-shirt.

She tried to recall exactly what had happened the night before as she pressed her thumb against the Sparkletts water tap. She had hooked up with Ethan. She had wanted it. No, she didn't. They were friends. She knew him when he was scrawny and running around playing "November Rain" on his brother's acoustic guitar. He washed his hair with bar soap! She was going to hurt him. She didn't want to go back into the bedroom. She couldn't look at him. But she was looking at him.

He entered the kitchen, bed-head and all, in his jeans.

"Good morning," he said, smiling. He seemed short.

"Hi." It came out sounding abrupt. "How are you?"

"Good." He nodded. "How are you?"

"Good." She backed into a far corner of the kitchen.

"Mind if I have a glass of water?" he asked.

"Oh no. Not at all. Help yourself. Go ahead."

He turned on the water tap.

Then she remembered Beth's. "I have to go to Beth's beading party today," she said, quickly scurrying past him.

"Oh yeah?"

"Yeah." She stood in the living room.

"I have to cater a bar mitzvah." He took a gulp of his water. "In fact, I should probably get going." He took a few chugs of water before he returned to the bedroom.

Cate sat down on the living room couch.

He returned to the living room wearing only his jeans and shoes. "I thought you had to go," Cate said, looking at his bare chest.

"I do." He lifted his hand in her direction. "You're wearing my shirt."

Her eyes darted toward her chest. "Oh, shit. I'm sorry."

"No. It's fine. You can keep wearing it. Really, it's fine. I don't mind going home like this."

She walked into the bedroom, closed the door behind her, and quickly switched shirts. Thinking of the good-bye process sent a surge of terror to her nerves. Should she hug him? What if he tried to kiss her?

When she returned to the living room, she handed him the T-shirt.

"I'll call you later," he said as they walked to the front door.

"Okay." She opened her arms and gave him a stiff, awkward hug. She felt a friendly, dry peck on her cheek and pulled away.

"Have a safe drive," she said. *Have a safe drive?* She was such an idiot. He lived two blocks away.

Cate was one of the first guests to arrive at the beading party at Beth's parents' house in La Jolla. Beth's mother answered the door wearing khaki pants, navy blue loafers, and a white blouse with a navy blue sweater tied over her shoulders. She had often hosted fund-raisers for local politicians. She reminded Cate of Elizabeth Dole. For years Cate had wondered how she could've produced Beth.

"Hello, Cate." Her coiffure was its usual crisp short cut, blow-dried just like Laura Bush's hair. "What can I get you to drink? We have lemonade, coffee, ginger ale—"

"She wants a Bloody Mary, Mom," Beth said as she entered the room.

"Would you like a Bloody Mary, Cate?" Mrs. Fitzpatrick asked.

"Um . . . er . . ."

"Yes. She does." Beth answered for her.

Cate had brought her a gift, even though it wasn't really a shower. It was a chip and dip platter she had registered for.

Beth gave her a big hug before she took the gift from Cate's hands. "Did you have fun last night?" she asked.

"You did that on purpose," Cate said.

Beth made a weak attempt at looking completely baffled. "What? Did what on purpose?"

"Flaked."

"Well, so what if we wanted you to be alone with him. Anyway, what happened?" She seemed more interested in Cate's story than the gift.

Cate's voice was nearly inaudible when she spoke. "Ethan slept over last night."

"Yes!" She clapped her hands together. "What happened? Did you have sex with him?"

"No!"

"All right. Well, tell me what happened."

"We ended up getting really drunk." She was whispering again. "I wanted to kiss him. I just . . . I don't know . . . he was sitting there, and it just seemed right."

"Oh! Finally!"

"Don't get too excited. I woke up this morning and regretted it. I was drunk."

"You like him. Your true feelings come out when you've been drinking."

"I'll just end up hurting him."

"Give him a chance. He's *so* great. I'm inviting him to the wedding."

"No!"

"Yes. He's an old friend. He's *my* friend, and I can invite whoever I want."

"Do not invite him. I am serious."

"I'm inviting Ethan." She sang the words. "I can't wait to tell Jill!"

Beth's mother returned with a Bloody Mary, complete with a celery stick. She was such the little Martha Stewart.

Two sips of the cocktail, and Cate's hangover was gone. It was amazing how that worked. She visited with Anthony and Beth's sister, Sharon, who took more after their mother. She was picking out some beads to make her necklace with when she felt a blast of hot air on her neck.

"I want details!" Jill whispered gruffly in her ear. "This is so great!"

"Beth told you already?"

"So, what happened?"

"We just kissed and fooled around."

"Did you see him naked?"

"Yes. I saw him naked."

"Did he have a big—"

"Jill. Please." He was nicely packaged, but Cate didn't feel like sharing that with her. "Seriously, Jill. I just don't see him that way. I don't know what to do now, because I am going to hurt him, and he is the last person that deserves it."

She was saved from discussing Ethan any further when Beth's mother called them to lunch. They sat down for a meal of homemade quiche and Chinese chicken salad. But for some reason, she could barely touch the food. She could still feel butterflies in her stomach and reasoned that it was because it had been such a long time since she had snuggled in the nude with someone other than Paul.

After lunch, Cate picked out clear, sparkling schwartzky crystals for her jewelry. The crystals gleamed and sent off beautiful rays when they were under light. They resembled diamonds, exactly what Cate wanted for her Marilyn look. She decided to make a complete set of earrings with a matching necklace and bracelet. While putting her jewelry together, she thought of her dilemma with Ethan. She wondered if God played cruel jokes on her. It was always the jerks that she liked, and then, here came Ethan—sweet, kind, sincere Ethan—and she was going to hurt him.

It didn't make sense. Finally, there was someone who really cared about her, who noticed her freaking freckle for crying out loud, who remembered things she said, who listened to her. Who appreciated her. She couldn't describe the weird feeling that crept up on her every time she thought of being his girlfriend. It wasn't that he was unattractive or annoying. He was great. There was just something strange about the notion of dating him.

How was she going to smooth things over with him? Then a horrible memory came to her. He had said, "It is so nice to hold you. You make me so happy, Cate." Then they had fallen asleep.

She was a bitch. A true bitch.

Beth interrupted her thoughts. "That looks good, Cate," she said as she looked at the necklace Cate was clasping.

"Thanks."

Cate looked at some of the things the other girls had made. She always thought she was creative until she looked at Jill's and Beth's jewelry. Their stuff turned out sophisticated yet edgy. They had such an artistic streak when it came to beading and decorating.

Jill was going as the bride of Frankenstein and had made a stunning, four-inch-wide choker using bone and black seed beads. The designs she had used with the seed beads were intricate and ancient. Beth had made herself matching bracelets for each wrist using opaque crystals.

Cate collected her jewelry and put it in a little Ziploc bag. Then she thanked Beth and Mrs. Fitzpatrick for the party.

Beth walked her to the car. "Now, go home and call Ethan," she said.

"I can't. And you and Jill are going to help me figure out a way to get myself out of this."

"Sorry, babe. You're on your own for that one." She closed Cate's car door for her.

When Cate returned home, she had one new message. "Hey, Cate. It's Ethan. I hope you had a good time making jewelry with Beth and Jill. I was just calling to say hi and . . . to tell you that I had a great time last night. I had a lot of fun, and I'd like to see you again soon. So gimme a call when you get a chance."

She hated herself. But she couldn't call him back. At least not now.

Cate and Jill were watching Dr. Phil. He was letting some married guy have it for flirting with coworkers. Cate was still in her clothes from school. Her bare feet rested on the coffee table, and she ate Ben & Jerry's Phish Food ice cream straight from the carton. Jill's hair was wrapped in Saran Wrap, undergoing a black transformation for Halloween.

"I wonder what Dr. Phil would say if he got a hold of me," Cate said. "How much do you think it costs for an hour of his time?" She imagined him in his suit, bald head glistening, veins bulging from his neck as he yelled at her in his Southern drawl: "*When are you going to wake up, girl? You have a perfectly decent man pursuing you, and you're passing him up! What in the hell is the matter with you? It's time for you to get real.*"

"You don't need Dr. Phil. You need Dr. Jill!" Jill sat up. "Just tell me anything, Cate. I'll be real with you."

"Tell me what to do about Ethan."

"You have to call him back," Jill said.

"I did call him back. I left a message."

"No. You called him when you knew he would be at work. That is not acceptable. Then you screened your phone calls when he called you back. That doesn't count."

"Yes it does."

Jill sighed. "Why are you so afraid to talk to him?"

"Because I don't want to hurt him. Don't you see? Everything has changed now. We hooked up. He has expectations. He wants more than friendship, and I am now in a situation where I have to tell him that I don't want the same thing. I'm going to hurt him, and I just haven't figured out how to do it yet."

"Well, totally blowing him off is probably the best route," Jill said sarcastically.

"I'm not blowing him off!" Cate was defensive. "I guess I'm just trying to lay the foundation—send him hints—so it's easier when I do have to break it to him."

"What you're doing is acting like a man."

"No, I'm not. Look, part of me doesn't know what to think about Ethan. Sometimes when I think about him, I get butterflies, but then something changes inside me, and I become afraid. I can't torment him while I try to figure myself out. It's not fair. I honestly don't know what to do."

"Why can't you just see where it goes with him? I don't understand why you have to make such a bold decision about him all at once. It's called dating, Cate. You don't have to marry the guy. You spend time with him to see if he is the one for you."

Before Cate had a chance to answer, the phone rang. She glanced at the Caller ID. "It's him!"

"Answer it."

"I can't! Not yet! Not now!"

In a flash, Jill grabbed the phone. Cate tried to rip it from her hand, but Jill was stronger. "Don't! Don't you dare answer that," Cate said between gritted teeth.

Jill looked at her the same way Timothy Sickle did the day she told him not to put glue in his mouth and he proceeded to shove the entire glue stick between his lips like a lollipop right in front of her.

"Hello," Jill said coolly into the receiver. "Ethan! How are you? Good. That's great. I've been good, too." She eyeballed Cate, who was making a dash for the front door. Jill raced to the door, barricading the only exit with her body. "What? Oh no. Everything is fine. The cat was just, um . . . doing something he shouldn't have been doing. Cate? Yes. She's right here."

She passed the phone to Cate. "You are going to pay for this," Cate whispered before she took the phone. "Hello." She walked into her bedroom and closed the door behind her. She didn't want Jill eavesdropping.

"Hey!" he said. "Finally, I got a hold of you."

God, she knew how he felt. She was treating him the same way Paul had treated her.

"I know. I guess we've been playing a little game of phone tag. I've just been so busy with school and other stuff."

"Yeah." There was an awkward silence. "Well, I'd like to see you again soon."

She wanted to blink three times and disappear into the Twilight Zone. "All right." She said it cautiously.

"What are you doing Thursday?" he asked.

Think of something—fast! "Thursday . . ." Her mind was blank, completely devoid of excuses. "Thursday's um . . . okay."

They planned to meet at six.

"What are you gonna do?" Jill asked after Cate told her about the Thursday plans.

"I don't know, Dr. Jill. Thanks for putting me on the spot."

"Well, just go out with him and see what happens."

"I can't! That would be fine if he was some average Joe that I met last weekend at some average bar. But he's not. He's Ethan. He is my friend, and I can't just play with his feelings. You can't experiment with people you care about. You can't just see where it goes."

"Well, it's a little late for that, sweetie. You've already crossed the line."

Cate spent the following two days dreaming up excuses to cancel. Parent-teacher conferences. A wedding-related event. A mandatory family function that she couldn't refuse. She knew it was terrible, but she could not go out with him. She tossed and turned all night. She became even more conflicted when she was struck with unexpected flashes of desire to see him. She liked the way he never beat around the bush and the way his eyes stayed round even when he smiled. But she knew she couldn't lead him on. He didn't sweep her off her feet. She'd never become giddy or nervous when he called. There had never been an immediate spark like she'd had with the rest of her boyfriends. The chemistry wasn't there, and she couldn't toy with his emotions.

She even asked her mother for a good excuse.

"You can't cancel!" Connie yelled into the phone. "That isn't nice. It's bad manners, Catherine. You can't do that to him, unless you are bent over sick in the bathroom."

Sick. That was it. She'd be sick on Thursday. "I'm just going to tell him I'm sick. These things happen."

"Ethan is a nice boy who wants to take you out. You will hurt his feelings if you cancel."

Even her mother was campaigning for him. And he wasn't even Catholic! They all loved him.

Thursday morning, she made the call. She wanted to catch him before he left for work. He answered after the second ring.

"Hey, what's up, Cate? Are we still on for tonight?"

"Well, actually, that's why I was calling. I'm sick. I don't know what's wrong with me. I've been throwing up all morning."

"Oh no." He was disappointed. "Do you think you have food poisoning?"

"Maybe. It could be bad sushi or something. I had sushi last night." That wasn't a lie. She did eat sushi.

"Geez. I hope you're okay."

"I'm sure I'll be fine by the weekend."

"All right. Well, give me a call. We'll have to get together this weekend."

She felt sick with guilt after she hung up.

The following night, Cate went over to Sarah and Miles's house for dinner. She didn't return until three A.M. because they had made caramel apples, then watched their wedding video. She even caught glimpses of Ethan in the background wearing his catering uniform. Each time she saw him, she was tormented with stabs of guilt and a surprise punch of confusion.

She felt fleeting flickers of warmth in her stomach, like on the night they kissed, or how she felt each time Paul called in the beginning of their relationship. But the heated feeling in her tummy was always followed with an unexplainable, strange feeling that made her want to run and hide from him. The thought of kissing him or letting him touch her seemed exciting yet embarrassing and peculiar.

When she returned home, she had one new message. The Sprint lady indicated that it had been sent at two-thirty-three A.M. Who would call at that hour?

Ethan's voice came crackling to life. Blasting music and the sound of lively blended voices filled the background. "Hey, Cate! It's Ethan." His voice sounded chipper, his words a tad slurred. "I was just calling to say hi. I just wanted to see how you were doing and if there was any-thing you needed. I hope you are feeling better, Cate. I really want to see you soon. Okay? I miss ya."

They played phone tag all weekend. This was mostly because of Cate, who deliberately called when she figured he wouldn't be home. They were on round three of phone tag when she called on her lunch break on Monday. She knew he wouldn't be home in the middle of the day. She was all set to leave a message when he answered.

"Ethan! Hi." She felt ambushed. "How are you?"

"I'm good. How are you? Are you feeling better?"

"Yes. I am."

"Good. What are you up to tonight?"

"Uh . . . I don't know. Nothing."

"Well, do you want to grab a drink or something?"

No. She didn't, but again was at a loss of excuses. "All right."

They made plans for him to pick her up at eight.

After she hung up, she realized that this was probably for the best. She couldn't go on avoiding him for the rest of her life. Besides, it was cruel to string him along. She was confusing him even more. Ethan was a very mature, understanding person. He deserved the honest truth. She wanted to explain that while she loved and adored him as a friend, she didn't see a romantic future for them. Just thinking about it made her ache with nervousness.

Again, she wanted to blink her eyes three times and escape to another galaxy.

He wore a hooded sweatshirt with stripes up the sleeves and baggy jeans when he arrived. His hair was still wet from the shower he had apparently taken before he came to pick her up. She inhaled a whiff of a clean-smelling bar soap. Irish Spring perhaps. He gave her a hug.

"It's good to see you finally."

"You, too." She meant it. It *was* good to see him.

"I was beginning to feel like you were avoiding me."

She released a nervous laugh.

"Cate, you're not weird about the other night, are you?"

She sat down on the couch. "Actually, I'm glad you brought this up."

He took a seat next to her.

She took a deep breath before she spoke, and she could feel her hands shaking. "Ethan. It's not that I'm weird about it. I'm just . . . look, I love our friendship. I'm so glad that we started hanging out again and I just . . . I don't know if I want to be romantically involved." She found it hard to make eye contact with him, especially since his round eyes were focused on her. "I just don't want to ruin what we have."

She babbled, filling the awkward silence with insignificant words. "I don't know . . . I wish it could work. It's just that—"

"It's okay, Cate."

"It is?"

He nodded. "I understand."

"You do?"

He feigned a weak smile, but his eyes were more telling. He looked hurt. "Yeah. It's just not there for you, and that's okay. You can't force something that isn't there."

"Please promise me that we can still go to China Inn and World Famous for happy hour." God, she sounded like Paul.

"Yeah, of course. Always." He was taking it well. "Maybe it's best if tonight we just . . . do our own thing."

"Yeah. Maybe that's a good idea."

Grease jumped between them on the coffee table, and Ethan rubbed his ears. The cat nudged his nose against Ethan's palms the same way he did when he was rubbing against furniture.

"Well, I should probably go then." He stood up. His eyes had a far-away gaze in them and his lips were a thin, straight line.

She walked him to the door. She opened her arms. "Let's do lunch this week," she said as she hugged him.

"Yeah. I'll give you a call."

She watched him walk down the hall. His shoulders looked relaxed, but his every move seemed determined to get out of the building quickly. For a second she wondered if she had just made the biggest mistake of her life.

New Faces and Names

The lunch date didn't happen. He failed to call, and she was struck with a vicious case of the flu that kept her out of school, and in bed, for a week. Jill was tentative about spending too much time at the apartment because she couldn't afford to have any sick days at beauty school. But she occasionally dropped off magazines and videos to keep Cate entertained.

By the middle of the week depression had snuck up on Cate, and she felt not only physically ill but emotionally drained as well. A continuous dull ache inhabited her heart, and she cried over episodes of *It's a Miracle* and reruns of *Terms of Endearment*.

It was worse than when Paul had dumped her. This time she wasn't sure why she was sad. Everything seemed empty. She was alone. She had Jill and her mother, who called every day. She had Grease. But she didn't have a partner, someone to share everything with. It seemed like everyone—with the exception of Jill—was getting married. They all had someone to pick out movies with at Blockbuster, someone to keep them company at the laundromat, someone to make boring errands seem like a blast when they ran them together.

She hadn't realized how much she would miss Ethan. She missed hearing his voice say hello when he answered the phone. She missed listening to his stories about all the crazy parties he catered. She missed watching him pet Grease, and picking out appetizers they were going to order whenever they ate at restaurants.

She realized what an important part of her life he had become. She'd always looked forward to spending time with him. The thought of him had always put a smile on her face. Now it all seemed to be over. She should've abided by a three-drink limit rule. She wanted to call him but couldn't. It wasn't fair. She'd just be confusing him.

She received one business phone call from an aspiring fashion designer who wanted Cate to shoot a fashion show she was having in November.

"So you must've seen the ad?" Cate said after they set the date.

"Ad? Oh no. I'm a friend of Ethan's. He referred me to you. He's *so* helpful."

After she hung up, her heart sank. After all that she'd done to him, he still wanted to help her. For a moment she felt happy. She could call him. And thank him for the referral. She dialed his number, eager to hear his voice, but was only greeted with the familiar sound of his answering machine.

On Thursday night, Jill came over, dressed to the nines, and looking for a partner in crime.

"Are you feeling better?" she asked. "Nick was asking about you. I'm meeting up with him and some other friends tonight. Do you want to come?"

Cate shook her head before she released a sneeze that made her brain shake. She felt a headache coming on.

"Bless you," Jill said as she offered her a Kleenex. "Well, rest up, because I want you to go out with me tomorrow night."

"We'll see."

She made Cate a cup of chamomile tea before leaving.

After the door closed behind Jill, the apartment seemed deathly quiet. Was this how it was going to be the rest of her life? Nights spent alone in front of the television.

The phone rang, and for a moment she hoped it was Ethan. It was her mother. "Have you been taking the vitamin C I gave you?" she asked.

"Yes," Cate lied.

"Why don't you come over for dinner tomorrow night? I'll make soup and cornbread."

"All right."

She said good-bye, then took two aspirin and a cough drop and tried to ignore the stinging sensation around her nostrils from blowing her nose so often.

Then she checked her E-mails. Her in box was full of lame advertisements that she deleted without opening. She thought it was odd that she had not heard a single peep from Leslie since the wedding. She was kind of curious to know what Bora Bora was like, so she sent her an E-mail.

> Hey Les. I haven't heard from you in a while and was wondering how married life was treating you. I'm dying to hear all about the fabulous honeymoon in Bora Bora!
> Love,
> Cate

The following day, Cate felt somewhat better. Instead of blowing her nose twenty times an hour, it was down to twice an hour. The mountain of used Kleenex next her bed had ceased to grow, and she had an appetite for more than chicken broth. At around three, Jill showed up.

"How are you today?" she asked.

Cate could smell her strong scent of perfume. That must mean she was getting better. "I'm feeling okay. How was your night last night?"

"It was all right. Oh! I saw Ethan."

"You did?" Curious, she sat up. "Where did you see him? At the Fox?"

"No. It was actually at the end of the night at Ramone's. He was with some girl."

"Who?"

"I don't know."

"Did it seem like they were dating?"

"I couldn't tell. I think he paid for her food."

"He paid for her food? Was she pretty?"

Jill thought before she answered. "Yeah. She was pretty. She was really petite, long blonde hair, blue eyes."

Cate pictured Sarah Michelle Gellar. "Who was she?"

"I forget her name. He introduced us, but I can't remember." Jill smirked. "You're jealous."

She was but didn't want to admit it. "No, I'm not. So what are you doing tonight?"

"Well, that's why I stopped by. I'm going out with Ted and Nick again and I thought I'd see how you were doing. It doesn't look like you're going out though."

"No. I'm going to go over to my parents' for dinner."

After Jill left, Cate checked her E-mail. One new message:

FROM: Leslie Lyons
The Subject box was empty.

Hi Cate.
Sorry it took me so long to respond. I've just been getting settled and getting used to married life. Bora Bora was nice.

I've been meaning to cal you. I had a minor breakdown the first two days of the honeymoon.

What? Breakdown? Cate read on.

When the ticket lady at American airlines called us Mr. And Mrs. Rose I broke down crying. I guess I wasn't prepared to lose my identity. I'm fine now and the rest of our honeymoon was good. Well, how is everything going? I'd love to catch up. I'll call you next week.

    Love,
    Leslie

That was the most bizarre thing Cate had ever read. *"Lose my identity"?* She had wanted the party, the dress, the horse, not the name change. Maybe she should've hyphenated her name. Cate couldn't help but wonder if all of Leslie's fantasies about getting married had been geared toward the wedding, not the marriage. Or had it been winning that Leslie wanted? Was getting the ring a prize rather than a lifelong commitment of love to another person? Now that Leslie had one, marriage didn't seem all that fun.

She wondered what Russ was doing during the two days that Leslie had a breakdown in Bora Bora.

When she arrived, the house smelled like a home-cooked meal.

"Hi!" her mother called.

"Well hello! How's my trooper?" her dad asked as she entered the kitchen.

"All right. I guess."

Her mother threw her arm over her shoulder. "Why don't you go lie down?"

"There's a bull riding championship on in five minutes," her dad said.

Bull riding. It was a guilty pleasure. Her father, a legal prosecutor and graduate of Harvard Law School, was the last person anyone would've ever expected to watch bull riding. Cate and her father both loved it. The excitement. The clowns. The funny announcer with the silly-sounding drawl.

"I bought you some cat food and groceries," her mother said. "I know you've been too sick to run errands."

"Thanks, Mom."

"You're welcome. Now go lie down."

Cate made herself comfortable on the couch. She threw a quilt over her body and curled up on the cream-colored cushions. She wondered if Ethan liked bull riding. Probably. She'd been doing this a lot lately, thinking about his opinions. What he would think about the clothes she chose to wear every day or the scent of her new lotion.

They ate their soup and cornbread on TV trays.

"Why don't you just sleep here tonight?" her mother suggested as she cleared the dishes.

"Okay."

It had been a long time since Cate had slept in her old bedroom.

"I found some old pictures of yours when I was cleaning out the closet in your room last week," her mother said. "I put them on your bed."

Her mother had spent the past three months weeding out all of Cate's old possessions and redecorating the room into a guest bedroom.

Cate found the pictures on her pillow. She flipped through them. There were prom pictures of her and Beth with their dates. She couldn't believe that they actually thought they looked good back then. Cate wore a teal-green gown made from spongy, elastic material that clung to her like a gigantic scrunchy. Beth sported a magenta silk dress with black faux fur trim around the hem and sleeves.

She found a candid picture of her and Ethan at graduation. Who had taken the picture? It must've been Beth. In the picture Cate was talking to someone. Ethan's gaze was settled on her. He looked content. His skin appeared softer, but he still had the same round, sincere eyes. They'd kissed for the first time that night in Beth's Jacuzzi. She studied the photo for a while. Again, her stomach felt warm. She shoved it back into the stack and placed the whole pile on the nightstand. She wondered what he was doing. Probably kicking up his heels in Pacific Beach with the petite blonde who undoubtedly appreciated him. The chilly October air had seeped into her room. She slept with socks and an extra blanket, but no matter how hard she tried to warm up, she still felt cold. She woke up once every hour for eight hours to tighten the blankets around her body.

When she returned to her apartment the following morning, she was not only tired but disappointed to find that she had no messages. She scanned through the Caller ID just to see if she had any friends left. Ethan Blakely, three-forty A.M. He had left no message.

Rain dumped over San Diego on Halloween. Despite the early fall storm, trick-or-treaters were still in full force throughout the neighborhood. It seemed as if they had all resorted to apartment complexes as their primary resource for candy.

Jill and Cate had turned Jill's place into their prewedding headquarters. This was because Jill had all the hair and makeup supplies they needed to get ready.

Earlier that morning, Jill had talked Cate into adding some platinum highlights to her hair, *"just to make it look a little more Marilyn."* Cate had been feeling careless lately, and she didn't care what the hell Jill did to her hair. She could've shaved lightning bolts on either side of her scalp and it wouldn't have mattered.

When Jill finished, Cate was glad she had agreed to proceed with the highlights. Marilyn or not, they looked good.

They took turns answering the doorbell every time a trick-or-treater visited, trying not to eat all the Snickers and Milky Ways they had bought for the kids while they helped each other with their makeup. Jill was going as the bride of Frankenstein, so she put their hair in rollers. While they waited for the rollers to set, they watched *Halloween* on television and drank a bottle of Pinot Grigio.

Cate absentmindedly munched on her fifth mini–candy bar while staring blankly at the screen.

"What's wrong with you?" Jill asked.

Cate snapped out of her daze. She knew she'd been zoning out a lot. It was partly because of the wine and partly because she had a lot on her mind. "What do you mean?"

"I mean . . . you've seemed out of it all day. Like something is wrong."

She waited before answering. "I miss Ethan. There. I said it. I really, really miss him. I can't help it." She looked at her dress, hanging on Jill's bedroom door. "We picked out that dress together, and now he won't see what I look like. I think about him all the time."

"Call him. Call him now."

"No." She shook her head. "I can't. He'll think I'm crazy. I hurt his feelings, and now I can't just call him out of the blue."

"I bet he'd love to hear from you." Jill handed her the phone. "Just tell him you want him to see the costume." She pushed the phone at Cate. "Call him, Catherine Agnes Padgett."

"He'll think I'm a bitch."

"Call him."

Cate stood up to answer the doorbell, taking the bowl of candy with her. She gave Harry Potter and Pocahontas a good portion of chocolate before she returned to the couch.

"You know what?" she said as she sat down. "I've been thinking anyway. They're all nice in the beginning. *All men.* And then they change. Once they get comfortable, they start wanting guys' night five nights a week, and they take calling for granted, and they don't want to cook dinner for you anymore. They forget to compliment you, and they never really ask how you're doing. They all change." She poured more wine in their glasses. "Why should Ethan be different from the others? Eventually he'll change, too. He likes me now because I am the mysterious, intangible Cate Padgett. But as soon as I'm the girlfriend, and he sees me without makeup and he knows that I wake up at least once a night to pee, the mystery will be over. He'll take me for granted and freak out whenever the 'M' word comes up. He'll call whenever he *feels* like it, and he won't care about how my day went. He'll lose interest in my candid photos, and getting him to hang out with my friends will be like asking him to spend time with imprisoned murderers on visitors' day. And then . . . I will be madly in love with him. Obsessed. It's human nature."

"I hear what you're saying, Cate. Yeah, a lot of guys change. And a lot of people love the chase. It is human nature. It's human nature to weed out the ones you're not supposed to be with. There is no chase when it's meant to be." She stood up. It was her turn to answer the door. She looked at Cate, candy bowl in hand. Then she shook her head. "All this time." She continued to shake her head. "All your excuses. I thought you were really afraid of ruining a friendship. You're just afraid of getting hurt." She headed for the door.

When she returned, she plucked her wineglass from the table. "C'mon, we have to go finish our hair."

"What should I do, Jill?" Cate asked as she followed her to the bathroom.

She shook her head. "I don't know. You're the only one who can stop being afraid. You're on your own with this one."

Their costumes turned out amazing. Cate had purchased a water bra and had done some additional stuffing with socks in the chest department. Her hair had turned out exactly like Marilyn's. Jill had applied her black eye makeup and glossy lipstick exactly the way Marilyn would've worn it. She felt sexy, and she knew she looked good.

Jill's jet-black hair was bigger and frizzier than Cate's had been at Leslie's wedding. She wore a draping white gown and had shaded her eyes with kohl-colored shadow. She drove them to the Hotel Del Coronado.

The hotel was a nineteenth-century castle on the beach. It was an old hotel, built when women still wore bustles and carried parasols. While beautiful, it had a touch of gothic appeal to it. There were stories of ghosts and hauntings in at least two of the rooms.

The sky was dark, and gloomy clouds passed over the yellow moon above. The rain had ceased, but she could still hear the sound of dripping water falling from the eaves and pillars around the hotel.

Beth wouldn't get the outdoor wedding that she had hoped for. Yesterday at the rehearsal, everything had been planned for an outdoor candlelit wedding, complete with the sound of the waves crashing behind them. The hotel wedding coordinator had warned them of rain, and as a backup plan they were going to hold the ceremony in the ballroom. Beth had to be disappointed with Plan B.

As instructed, they headed to Beth's room in the older building. As they approached, Cate could hear Beth's father ranting from the opposite side of the door. "I still can't believe we're dressing up for my daughter's wedding." He said it as if complaining about the price of gasoline.

"Oh, Daddy," Beth said. "It's fun. You look great, and you're going to love looking at the pictures later."

With the mention of pictures, Cate realized she'd left her camera in the car. She decided to say hi to Beth and the others first, then return to the car for her camera. She was eager to see their costumes.

"I feel like we're the white trash family," her father grumbled.

Cate could hear the other bridesmaids as well as Beth laughing.

"Stop it, Frank," Beth's mother said with a chuckle in her voice. "We haven't dressed up in years. It's fun."

"Vavavoom!" Anthony yelled when Jill and Cate entered. "Cate, you could stop a train! You look stunning."

He was dressed as a gangster, even wearing tinted shades like Al Capone.

"Wow! You guys look great," Beth said.

Beth was dressed as a Shakespearean type of bride in an ivory dress with flaring sleeves. Her hair was left down, and she wore a flowered crown. She looked like a princess from medieval times.

Cate could understand why Beth's father might be uncomfortable dressed as a giant yellow dinosaur. His chubby cheeks were smooshed between the small face opening in the felt costume, and he probably wouldn't be able to sit down with the massive spiked tail that trailed behind him. He belonged in a theme park. Five-year-olds would've been enamored of him.

Beth's sister was dressed as a roller-blading waitress, and her mother was dressed as a Southern belle, wearing a giant hoop skirt and straw hat.

They all exchanged compliments on one another's costumes. Beth didn't seem to be the least bit nervous. She sat calmly in the corner, admiring everyone's outfits. Cate put her arm around her friend's shoulders. "How are you? You seem so calm."

"I'm great. I am getting *married*." She practically glowed.

"So I guess we're going to be in the ballroom," Cate said.

Beth nodded. "Yeah. I don't care though. Ike sent me two dozen roses this morning with a note attached saying, 'I can't wait to start our life together.'" She released a pleasant sigh and squeezed Cate's hand. "I'm so happy, Cate."

Cate wanted pictures of everyone. "Do I have time to run to the car for my camera?"

"Yeah. We still have half an hour before we have to be down in the ballroom."

"All right. I'll be right back."

The air was freezing on her bare shoulders when she left the hotel. She stepped over a few puddles as she headed to the car. As she crossed the main driveway to the hotel, she circled a giant puddle of mud, careful not to let any part of her shoes become soiled. She could feel tiny droplets of drizzle dotting her nose and shoulders and hurried to the car. She found her camera and made sure she locked the doors before heading back to the hotel. She tried to run in her heels, afraid that it would start to pour rain at any moment.

She was two steps from circling around the puddle and crossing the driveway when the headlights of a giant van blinded her. She paused, allowing the van to go first. It was dark, and the driver might not be able to see her. The airport shuttle circled around the bend so fast that its front tire dove into the puddle. A giant spray of muddy water splashed over the side of the curb, as if a whale had landed in a swimming pool. Cate tried to jump back, but it had all happened too quickly. Dirty, frigid water covered her from head to toe. It slithered down her face, dripping down her neck, saturating her dress and sliding down her arms like cold goop. A horrified scream roared from her throat. Over the wind, no one heard.

She could see the shuttle driver helping clean people with their luggage. In their dry clothes they all tipped him.

Salty tears began to mix with the grimy water. She hated this, all of it. She was tired of her worn-out life, of mud puddles, of being disappointed, of having to clean it all up on her own. She had no partner to help her. She was solo, arrived alone, left alone, and cried alone. This was her world.

And the worst thing of all was that she felt consumed with regret. She had let him go. It was no freaking wonder she was lonely. She couldn't even appreciate a good thing when it came along. She'd been too busy worrying about Paul, or waiting for a fantasy man to emerge from the darkness and fill her world with light to notice that Ethan was right in front of her face. Not only was she going to be alone, but she was also going to have to live with her mistakes.

She was starting to freeze to death and decided that hypothermia combined with self-pity was a bad mix.

The most embarrassing moment of her life: walking through the most elegant hotel in San Diego looking as if she'd just been to Woodstock.

She tried to hold back her tears as she headed to the ladies' room. A crying frenzy was on the verge of erupting. She wanted to walk to the front desk, check into a hotel room, scrub herself from head to toe in scalding hot water, wrap herself in warm blankets, and fall asleep forever. However, hotel security would probably mistake her for a bag lady and phone the police. She was sobbing now. She wanted to go upstairs and tell Beth, "No more. I need to go home. I need to curl up and not exist."

People had begun to stare. She could hear the whispers: *"The crying girl covered in mud."*

Go to hell, she wanted to growl.

She couldn't go upstairs like this. Beth had been so relaxed. Cate entering and looking as if she'd just been hosed with shit might put a damper on things. She stumbled into the ladies' room.

Get a grip. Get a freaking grip, Cate. Pull it together. It's your best friend's wedding. It starts in fifteen minutes, and you are a disaster. You have been in worse situations. Now put your bad bitch cap on, and get it together!

One glimpse in the mirror, and she felt on the verge of the kind of breakdown that could take her away from the hotel in a straitjacket. She honestly didn't know whether to laugh or cry. The dress was ruined. There was no way she could walk down the aisle looking like Marilyn Monroe who had just fallen down a mountain. Luckily, her hair hadn't gotten wet. If she really improvised, she could clean herself in the ladies' room, using towels and hand soap.

Then she began to laugh. The absurdity of it all. The wedding on Halloween, her luck of ruining her costume before it even started. It was kind of funny.

She cleaned her face first, washing it thoroughly with hand soap and warm water. It killed her to wipe away all the makeup that Jill had worked so hard to apply. When she lifted her head, a little river of black mascara washed down the drain. She scrubbed her body from neck to toe with hand towels and soap. She could still feel damp water beneath the bodice of her dress, but there wasn't a thing she could do about her wet chest until she changed clothes. And what exactly was she going to change into?

Her eyes darted around the bathroom, searching for nothing in particular—only ideas. She looked at the pile of towels she had used, so many that they couldn't even fit in the trash can. She decided to head back up to the room. Maybe someone would have an extra something that she could borrow. She felt guilty leaving all the towels on the counter, but she was in a hurry. On the way out, she noticed a cleaning cart outside the men's room. A maid was pulling a bucket from it.

"Excuse me," Cate said. "Do you have any extra trash bags?"

She nodded as she pulled a roll of thick white trash bags from the cart. "How many you need?"

"One, please."

Then she thought of something. It was a stretch, but she was desperate. It was the kind of thing that people would either find terribly tasteless or absolutely clever.

"Actually, could you please make that two?" Cate said.

She realized that time was getting short. Upstairs, they were probably beginning to worry about her. She walked to a hotel courtesy phone and dialed Beth's room.

"Cate!" Beth answered the phone "Where are you? We've been

wondering what happened to you. In fact, Jill just went down to look for you."

"Well, it's kind of crazy, but my whole costume was ruined."

"What? What happened? Are you all right?"

"I'm fine." She told Beth what happened.

"Oh my God. You are kidding?"

"I'm not. But I'm fine, and I'll be up in a minute. I have a new costume. It's a scrounge, but I think it will do."

She locked herself in a bathroom stall, removed her dress, and washed her chest with a damp soapy towel. Then she pulled open a small hole in the bottom of the extra trash bag. She carefully tore two small holes on either side of the bag for her arms. She slipped it over her head. Her new costume: a trash bag and heels. It wasn't something Marilyn would wear, but it would suffice. She threw her dress in the other white plastic bag with the towels.

As she approached the room, she thought it felt nice not to have her chest stuffed with socks. There was a light, airy feeling beneath the bag, and she wished trash bags were in style. She could hear Beth's father's voice booming from the hall again.

"I should go stand in front of a mud puddle, so I can put my other clothes back on again. How the hell did she get so lucky?"

The door had been propped open with a tennis shoe. They all waited for Cate. Beth's father saw her first. His eyes quickly darted over her new costume. "Well, what are you?" he asked.

A moment of silence followed as they all waited for her to reply. She looked at Beth's father. "White trash. I'm white trash."

Hysterical laughter filled the room. Beth and Anthony applauded. Her father slapped Cate on the back and laughed so hard that Cate thought blood vessels would break on his face. "Now that's the way to make the best of it!" he said.

* * *

Cate's costume turned out to be a hit, probably even better than Marilyn. She was bombarded with a million varieties of "What are you supposed to be?" But once she told them, they loved it. Being covered in a gallon of muck was almost worth watching the different reactions and listening to the peals of laughter she had provoked. At least three people told her they were stealing the idea and going as white trash the following year.

Overall, it turned out to be a fun wedding. It was like an extravagant Halloween party with a romantic twist. There were gigantic bags filled with candy for all the children who'd been invited, and there was an apple bobbing station. Live music. Food. Cocktails. Poor Mr. Fitzpatrick had knocked over at least five drinks and a small child with the back of his dinosaur costume.

The wedding drunk was Ike's seventeen-year-old nephew, who was dressed as a girl scout. His bowed, hairy legs looked like they belonged to an ape beneath the green skirt he wore. He stumbled around the room, hitting on all of Beth's friends who had been going to the prom when he was still in diapers. It was hard to pinpoint the freaky relative, because so many people were dressed as freaks.

There was a Marilyn Manson lookalike, a couple in their seventies who came as a pimp and a ho, and a Santa Claus with fangs and blood dripping down his beard. Instead of bearing gifts he held on to a fake headless chicken. His wife was dressed as an elf with an alien face. The statement they were trying to make was unclear.

A whole crew of Ike's friends came dressed as the monsterlike orc creatures from *The Lord of the Rings*. Their costumes were frighteningly real, and they went around grunting and moaning all night. Cate was kind of afraid of them.

By eleven, Cate was ready to retire. She wanted to go home. She wanted to call Ethan. She didn't care if he was dating Buffy the Vampire Slayer. She didn't care if she looked like a fool by calling him after all she'd done. She just needed to hear his voice. And if he'd forgotten her and moved on, she didn't care.

It didn't matter anymore, none of it. There were only a few things that came along in life that were worth holding on to. Ethan was one of them.

Jill was dancing with an orc and having a blast. She tried to convince Cate to stay for another hour, but Cate just couldn't. The thirty-dollar cab ride back to Pacific Beach was worth it. She managed to steal Beth and Ike.

"I know it's a little early, but I'm exhausted," she said. "And I'm kind of ready to get out of this trash bag."

"No! You can't leave!" Beth said. "Stay for another hour."

"Really, I'm exhausted."

"Let's get you another drink," Ike said. He had dressed as a handsome wizard.

"I think if I have another drink, I'll fall asleep on one of these tables."

"Please stay for at least—" Beth was interrupted by a distant relative dressed as a cowboy.

"I haven't had a chance to congratulate the bride and groom yet," he said.

Cate took this as her opportunity to slip away. She went back to her table for her camera and wallet. Then she made a stealthy exit. The bustling lobby of the hotel had quieted since her arrival. Near the exit, she stopped dead in her tracks. Warmth filled her stomach, and she suddenly felt charged with a mix of fear and joy. At first she wasn't sure if her mind was being overly wishful. But then she was positive it was Ethan taking a ticket from the valet parker.

He wasn't in costume. Instead, he was dressed in a turtleneck sweater and jeans. She could see his round eyes, unassuming, unaware that she was watching. God, he was adorable. She was nervous and excited and thought she might have to run to the bathroom to puke.

As he headed up the stairs, he still didn't notice her.

"Ethan," she said, practically whispering.

He turned. "Cate." He looked at her costume. "What . . . what are you wearing?"

"My whole costume was ruined. It's a long story. I was forced to dress as white trash."

They took a step toward each other. "You were . . . what? Your Marilyn costume was ruined?"

She quickly shared the shuttle puddle story with him. A smile lifted the corner of his lips. "Only you. Only Cate Padgett. You poor thing."

"What are you doing here?" she asked.

"Beth and Jill invited me—this evening, actually. I had to cater a company Halloween party, but I promised I'd stop in for a drink."

"I'm so glad you came." She practically blurted it out.

"You are?"

God, she didn't want to start crying. It had been such a rough day, and she thought that any words coming out of her mouth at this point would trigger tears. She nodded. "I've . . . really missed you."

He was quiet, as if he were unsure of what she meant.

"A lot," she said. "I've missed you a lot."

He reached for one of her hands. "I've missed you, too." Then he pulled her against his chest. "Come here."

She put her arms around his waist and inhaled the scent of his soap as they hugged.

"Ethan, I'm so sorry for everything. I really messed up." She didn't care if she sounded stupid, if her words were too late. She had to explain herself. "When I told you that I didn't want to be more than friends, I didn't mean it."

She felt his body stiffen. He moved his hands up to her shoulders, and his arms made a space between the two of them. He looked at her for a moment. She'd never seen his blue eyes look so expressionless. She couldn't tell what he was thinking, and it nearly drove her crazy. It felt like eternity had passed before he spoke. "Cate, what took you . . .?" For a moment he seemed puzzled. "I mean why . . .?"

He couldn't finish his question, but Cate knew what he meant. Why, after all this time, had she only now decided she wanted him? His crush had spanned a good portion of a decade, and Cate had finally decided it was time to take their relationship a step further. She was afraid that whatever words she offered wouldn't satisfy him. There wasn't a good explanation for what had taken her so long. She'd been stupid, then afraid, and worst of all, she hadn't appreciated him. She was just going to have to tell him the truth and hope that it would be enough for him. "Ethan, I don't blame you for asking—"

Then he shook his head. He took each of her palms into his own and squeezed them. "No. Please stop. Never mind. You don't have to explain. It doesn't matter."

Then he pulled her back to his chest. His lips brushed over her forehead, kissed her nose, then settled on her lips. He tasted subtly sweet and mild, like warm tea that had steeped for only a few seconds.

For a moment she was tempted to pull away and fill the air with her explanations. He deserved more. He needed to know that she'd been foolish and afraid. But then she realized what she loved best about Ethan. He knew when to recognize a good thing. He had appreciated that the moment was right. Instead of dragging out an awkward conversation, he had saved their special time. Explanations and excuses didn't matter. They were together, warm and close.

She never wanted to leave his arms. She felt as if she had known him forever, but she also felt as if she had just met him. They still had so much to explore with each other. She couldn't wait to learn new things about him, to wake up to his blue eyes in the morning, to feel his feet next to hers at night.

"I want to get out of here," he said. "I want to be with only you tonight—nobody else. But I told Beth I was coming. I have to go congratulate her."

Cate nodded. She imagined her friends' faces, the way they would react when she walked in with Ethan. They would be happy for her. "All right," she said. "But then you're mine," she said playfully.

They held hands as they entered the reception.

At first no one noticed them. Beth was talking to a group of guests. She'd removed her shoes and the flowered crown that she had worn on her head. She looked comfortable. Jill was still dancing with her new friend and probably wouldn't have noticed if Brad Pitt had walked past her. But then Beth's eyes caught them. At first she nodded toward them in recognition, but then she noticed their fingers curled around each other's palms, and her mouth dropped.

"Excuse me," she said to her guests and hustled toward them. Apparently, Jill had noticed them, too. She sprinted across the dance floor, directly toward Cate and Ethan, leaving the orc in a state of confusion.

Beth kissed Ethan on each cheek, then turned to Cate and did the same thing.

"You're holding hands!" Jill said, out of breath.

Cate's face turned red, and Ethan smiled. For a moment Cate wished she had waited outside. It seemed as if everyone was grinning like fools, searching for words. She could tell that her friends wanted a formal update on the new developments with Ethan.

Beth was considerate but still curious. "I'm so glad you came, Ethan, and I'm glad to see that everything is going well." She glanced at their hands.

"I just noticed something," Jill said. "Well, no. Never mind. I won't embarrass you guys any further. It's just that . . . well." She shook her head and chuckled to herself. "No. I can't. It's really interesting though. But never mind. I can tell I'm embarrassing the hell out of Cate."

"Tell us," Beth said.

"Yeah. Go ahead," Ethan added.

Cate knew she didn't need to encourage her friend to speak whatever was on her mind. Jill would spill it eventually.

"Well, all right. I'll tell you." She grinned. "I just noticed that Cate looks pretty damn good wearing white."

Cate and Ethan exchanged a startled glance. Then their faces burst into smiles, and they laughed the kind of laughter that made them feel high from adrenaline. She felt Ethan's hand leave her own. Then his arm slipped around her shoulders. He pulled her tight and planted a warm kiss on her forehead. She could hear the white trash bag crinkling beneath his arms as they pulled each other closer.

Whitney Lyles knows whereof she speaks. Her inspiration for *Always the Bridesmaid* was her own experiences as a bridesmaid. She has stood up as a bridesmaid five times. She is twenty-six years old and this is her first novel.

Please visit the author's website at www.whitneylyles.com.